THE METAMORPHOSIS . . .

"All right, come on out of there," the farmer says, and the intense beam of his light sweeps above me, solid and blinding in the dusty air. I close my eyes, keeping him fixed in my spatial sense. His body is chest-deep in the hole. His voice is strained with fear overtones, but he is determined.

"You come out of there now," he says. "Or I'll shut you in and call the sheriff. So now you take your pick."

My nose wrinkles at his fear scent, although he must be twenty feet away. Now I shall use what I have been taught. Listening to the old farmer breathe, I feel for the appropriate form and concentrate myself to a tiny, isolated point like the sun focused through a magnifying glass. My fur erects, and I see the sparkling point into which I fall, saying the name that comes to me: Robert Lee Burney. I shift. . . .

"Vivid, earthy  ous coming-togeth⟨ ⟩oul in us all. The ⟨ ⟩ve and violence, o⟨ ⟩

—Fritz Leiber

THE ORPHAN

ROBERT STALLMAN

A TIMESCAPE BOOK
PUBLISHED BY POCKET BOOKS NEW YORK

This book is dedicated to Patricia,
who introduced us.

Another *Original* publication of TIMESCAPE BOOKS

A Timescape Book published by
POCKET BOOKS, a division of Simon & Schuster, Inc.
1230 Avenue of the Americas, New York, N.Y. 10020

ISBN: 0-671-46758-1

First Timescape Books printing March, 1980

10 9 8 7 6 5 4 3 2

POCKET and colophon are registered trademarks
of Simon & Schuster, Inc.

Use of the trademark TIMESCAPE is by exclusive license
from Gregory Benford, the trademark owner.

Printed in the U.S.A.

That I may reduce the monster to
Myself, and then may be myself

In face of the monster, be more than part
Of it, more than the monstrous player of

One of its monstrous lutes, not be
Alone, but reduce the monster and be,

Two things, the two together as one. . . .

—Wallace Stevens, from
    "The Man with the Blue Guitar"

PART I

FIRST PERSON

(From the *Grand Rapids Register*, May 6, 1935)

In Mount Clemens yesterday, the wild dog problem was relieved by a local farmer, Gustave Hohenrikt, who cornered a pack of stray dogs in his barn and killed four of them with a shotgun. Mr. Hohenrikt reported the dogs had been raiding his chicken and sheep pens, and he decided to take action. Reports from Bay City also indicate wild dogs are becoming more of a nuisance there. Police Chief R. B. Matthews of that city issued a shoot on sight order for all stray dogs in rural areas. The order came after several farmers in the area reported night attacks on their livestock.

SHEEP SLAYER TO DIE

(From the *Cassius Daily Post and Examiner*, May 6, 1935)

Judge John Feldman of Circuit Court today condemned to death a sheep stealer who has been raiding local pens and has a record of several previous convictions on the same charge. The indictment charges him with slaying at least eight sheep. The condemned is a large yellow hound named Rufus, formerly owned by Mr. and Mrs. J. C. Mooresby of this city. Rufus sat in the courtroom and appeared contrite as Judge Feldman passed sentence on him. The dog will be gassed to death at the County Pound, an object lesson to other canine malefactors.

(1)

I am and will be. There is no time when I am not.
  This is the first lesson.
My need creates my self.
  This is the second lesson.
Alone is safe.
  This is the third lesson.

Eyes would see nothing in the blackness of the hayloft. The dove whose nest I have just plundered cannot
see me, but I perceive her panting and succulent form
clearly as she sits on the steel trip bar of the hayrake
that hangs from the center of the ceiling. I cannot leap
that high. I want her now that my appetite is strong,
and although I could easily slip through the hole in
the floor and find a chicken or two, I want the dove.
I wait, curled beneath the ledge where the nest is scattered. A rope hangs from the hayfork. It is fixed to the
wall above my head. If I twitch it, she will fly toward
her only exit, the break beneath the eaves near her
nest. She will not fly downward to the hole in the floor
as a sparrow might. In the blackness she might even
blunder against a wall and stun herself. I slip over to
the tied rope and give it a flip. The dove flutters from
the steel bar.

Each beat of her wings produces a ripple of pressure
that widens to the walls of the huge loft. Blind in the
darkness, she is the center of a quite beautiful arrange-
ment of concentric waves of pressure that I sense di-

rectly. She appears transfixed, the living center of the whirlpool of her own wingbeats, bright with life in the center of a rippling web. She swerves as her mind catches hold. She heads for the break under the eaves. I could knock her down first, but it is sport to leap up and snag her in one claw. I snap her from the center of her web and bite swiftly. She is hot and good. The taste is distracting enough that the farmer traps me while I am lying back flicking feathers out of my teeth. Suddenly I sense him at the hole in the center of the floor. He carries a four-pronged steel pitchfork. He raises his flashlight as I roll behind the mound of hay I am lying on. There is not much hay left up here this time of year.

"All right, come on out of there," the farmer says, and the intense beam of his light sweeps above me, solid and blinding in the dusty air. I close my eyes, keeping him fixed in my spatial sense. His body is chest deep in the hole. His voice is strained with fear overtones, but he is determined.

"You come out of there now," he says, "or I'll shut you in and call the sheriff. So now you take your pick."

My nose wrinkles at his fear scent, although he must be twenty feet away. Now I shall use what I have been taught. Listening to the old farmer breathe, I feel for the appropriate form and concentrate my self to a tiny, isolated point like the sun focussed through a magnifying glass. My fur erects, and I see the sparkling point into which I fall, saying the name that comes to me: Robert Lee Burney. I shift.

And then the farmer sounded different, larger and menacing. I felt prisoned in heavy coverings, my spatial sense blanked out, my ears deadened, my sight depending on the beam of light that searched the walls. Fear overwhelmed me in that form. I retreated to allow the person to emerge, and Robert let out a cry that sounded strange, a helpless sobbing. The farmer stopped talking and pointed the light at the mound of hay behind which Robert Burney crouched and wept.

"Is that a kid up there?" He kept the light steady

12

and came another step up the ladder. "Come on out and let's see you."

Robert got to his feet, dizzy with birth, and stepped from behind the hay. The light crashed in his eyes. He was crying and shivering, naked.

The farmer carried the little boy to the house while the two dogs wagged their tails and nosed the old horse blanket he was wrapped in. Robert shivered with cold and fear although the night was almost warm. He felt new and helpless, holding the rough liniment-smelling blanket around his skinny shoulders. The farmer's wife stood in the open back porch door, the light behind her casting a long monolithic shadow onto the wet grass.

"What did you find, Martin? It's a little child? A boy?"

The farmer put the little boy down, pushing him gently into the kitchen that was warm and yellow with lamp light. The long black wood-burning range was still hot. The tall woman took the blanket, turned Robert around and around, looking at him. He looked down at his own white body, hairless, funny looking feet like toad feet, skinny legs, tiny point of penis, litle bulge of belly. He was about five or six years old and scrawny as a spring possum.

"What's happened to your clothes, child?" She seemed enormously tall, bony and rectangular, and when she asked Robert questions, she put her face close to his and opened her eyes wide so that she looked astonished. Her face was long and freckled and not at all pretty. Her nose had a hump in the middle and her lips were too wide, but her smile made Robert feel safe. The farmer was not as tall as his wife, red faced with squinted-up eyes and a heavy mass of gray hair that stood up in tufts in back. He looked so thick and solid he reminded Robert of a walnut burl. The woman kept asking questions. Where was the boy from? Who was he? What was he doing up in the barn? And at the same time the farmer was telling how he had thought it was another tramp in the hay like they'd found last winter.

Robert began to cry again. He couldn't think about the questions. He was tired and his stomach felt strange. He began to shudder and hugged the woman's legs for warmth. She got very motherly at that, brought blankets, made oatmeal on the stove that was still hot from supper, and there was creamy milk and brown sugar. Robert ate until he could hardly breathe. Then the farmer carried him upstairs to a bed warmed with hot water bottles. He felt secure and curled up and wondered with his last thought before sleep if the dove was in there with all the oatmeal.

I wake in the new shape and almost bolt out through the bedroom window from the shock of unfamiliar senses and feelings. It is the gray dark before dawn. My spatial sense will not work in Robert's body, and I feel trapped with nothing but his very imperfect eyes and ears to depend on. The farmer and his wife are not in the room. They are some distance away, one of them making gurgling sleep noises. I crawl from beneath the bedclothes. There is a cloth thing around my body, a shirt. I scramble out of it and the chilly air hits me so I feel my fur go erect. No fur. I shiver. With the discomfort I shudder and I shift back suddenly and comfortably into my own form.

The room springs into being around me. The sounds of the sleeping farmer and his wife are loud and distinct, a ragged symphony of noise two rooms away. My room is small with the bed, some sort of stand with a basin and pitcher of water, an open closet with two wooden hangers in it. The bed smells of little boy flesh and mildew and house dust. The two windows are curtained with gauzy stuff pulled back and tied on each side so I can see the last stars going away into the lightening sky. I want very much to slip out and grab a late rabbit. Then I will come back and be a little boy. I creep to the door, sniff the cold porcelain knob shaped like a solid egg, turn it carelessly with a claw. Locked. I peer into the crack between the door and the frame. A short piece of iron connects the two. My irritation at being balked builds, and in a moment I will go through a window or smash through the flimsy

14

door. Wait. Wait! But my body is not in a waiting mood. I have to shift now or lose this opportunity. Even as I concentrate my self to a point and say the name, I see a fading image of myself lunging through the door panels in a burst of broken wood, leaping down the stairs, skidding around the corner to gallop through the dining room and kitchen and sail grinning right through the back screen door, leaving a great hole whose edges point ballistically to my path of flight into the cool gray dawn. I shift.

The cold hits Robert's skin. Nothing to do but get back in bed and sleep until the farmer and his wife get up. The windows are gray with dawn. The chickens in their house beside the back garden were shuffling on their roosts. He heard one fall to the floor like a soft bag and squawk. A cockerel rooster tried a creaking sort of cry and was cut off by the older rooster who gave a long, perfect cheer for the morning. Then it began to seem far away, and Robert fell asleep.

When he woke again, sunlight stood against the wall over his head, radiating heat from a golden rectangle, and the door stood open. He lay a minute in the covers, hearing the murmur of the farmer and his wife talking in the kitchen. He got up quietly and used the chamber pot he found under the bed. Then he slipped to the top of the stairs and waited. They were talking about him.

"What else? An orphanage, I guess," the farmer said.

"Well we can't just keep him. Now you know that," the woman said. "It's not like he was a stray puppy."

"No." There was a long pause. The farmer made a funny sound, a snort. "We always wanted a boy."

"Martin!" The woman sounded amused and shocked at the same time. "Your daughters have brought you two fine sons-in-law now, and you're proud enough of them." The woman was laughing "And two grand-daughters—too many girls, Martin?"

"I love our girls, big and little. And they've done well in their marriages, but it's true." He paused again. "You know what I mean."

"But we don't know what sort of folks he has. Maybe

15

he's wandered off from some hobo jungle or a gypsy camp."

"Nope. I think he's been dumped. Least I figure he's been on his own a couple days and he don't know much about it."

"You're guessing now. You don't know the first thing about the poor little naked thing." She seemed thoughtful. "Crept up in our hayloft to keep warm. Lucky this is a warm May we're having. Last May would've froze the little tyke."

"There's no camps around here. Somebody dumped him like a dog. He was hungry enough, I believe, to eat a set of dove eggs and maybe the dove too."

"For Lord's sake, Martin. Et a dove?"

"I found that dove's nest up in the hayloft all scattered and pieces of the bird back in the corner where the boy was hiding. That takes a pretty hungry kid."

"Martin Nordmeyer! That little child kill and eat a dove? Some weasel snuck up there and got that bird. Why, of all the silly things you've ever said." Robert could hear the woman laughing, and now the farmer too was chuckling.

"Ain't that crazy though, Cat. Can you beat that? I forgot for a while how little the boy is. I imagine it was a weasel all right. Why he'd a had blood all over his face if . . ." But then they were both laughing again, and the woman asked if he wanted some more coffee.

Robert walked on down the stairs. He was hungry.

"Martin, go get one of your clean shirts and put it on this boy. My goodness, little lad, you can't walk all around naked like that. What'd you do with that big old nightshirt I put on you?" The woman fussed around him, got him seated at the big oak table that seemed much too large for two people, and began melting grease in a pan to fry him some eggs. The farmer brought a huge blue shirt and draped it over Robert's back.

"Put your arms in," the farmer said, his blunt fingers strangely delicate in touching the boy. He rolled up the sleeves neatly and buttoned it up the front so that

Robert looked like the top half of some little wizened guest come to breakfast.

"There you are, son," the farmer said, standing back. "Don't he look better this morning, Cat?"

"He looks rested and a little less sick than he did last night. How are you, boy?" The woman bent over to look directly into his face, raising her eyebrows as if astonished. "Do you talk?"

Robert did not know how to answer this. Should he say yes? And then what? What sort of question was that?

"You can understand us, can't you, son?" said the farmer, squatting down beside Robert's chair. Robert looked into the old man's eyes set deep in the walnut burl wrinkles. They were light blue with broken red veins, and the lids looked tired. He wondered how old a person had to be for his eyes to get tired like that.

"Maybe he's foreign," said the woman, returning to the stove and breaking eggs in a pan. "But he'll eat, I suppose."

"Come on now, boy, tell us your name," said the farmer, very lightly stroking Robert's hair.

There was a question he could answer, at least. "Robert Lee Burney," he said in a surprisingly clear, high voice.

"There now," said the farmer, smiling. "You just didn't have anything else to say, hey?"

"Well, if he's got a name, he's got a place in the world," said the woman. "And it won't likely be ours."

The farmer stood up, his hand still lightly resting on Robert's head. "He's welcome here until he finds that place."

The woman turned halfway from the stove, looked straight into the farmer's tired eyes. She had to look down slightly. Robert watched the look and the subtle change he saw in the woman's expression puzzled him, a softening, something *less difficult* was the only thing he could think of as he watched the tall, homely woman in the cotton print dress and apron looking down the slight incline of her gaze into the blue eyes of her husband. The hand on Robert's head touched lightly but

17

did not shake or waver. He watched the woman's face change, and something beyond his understanding passed between her and the man. He suddenly wanted to know what that was, more than I had wanted the dove last night, more than he wanted the bacon and eggs he smelled frying in the pan. She turned back to the stove, pushing up some hair wisps that had come down out of the mass of gray-streaked black hair she had tied up in a bandana.

"You're so soft hearted, Martin, you'd take in a hurt Indian and make him a new tomahawk." But she said it in a different voice, as if it were an aside, and now the matter of whether Robert would stay or not had been settled.

"I'll call the sheriff's office after a bit, Cat," the farmer said. He too acted differently. Somehow the question had been resolved. Robert was mystified.

"Well you can tell him we got lots of room here," the wife said. "And he's not going to be a bit of trouble. Except for a couple pair of overalls and some dove eggs for breakfast now and then."

They both laughed.

To the many questions from the farmer and his wife, and later from the sheriff, Robert could honestly answer that he did not remember.

"But you do recall your right name?" Sheriff Kendall asked for the third time.

"Yes sir," Robert said, and repeated it.

The sheriff was tall and bent over with hardly any hair and a little round stomach that made Robert think he must have swallowed something big like a snake does. The sheriff had written a few things down in his notebook with a yellow pencil. But now he had put the notebook away and was, as he said, saucering and blowing the coffee Aunt Cat had poured him. He put the cup down and swung around to Robert suddenly.

"*¿Habla usted Español?*"

Robert jumped, but looked blank.

"Well, Mrs. Nordmeyer, I just don't know what to

say." The sheriff tipped up his saucer to pour the cooled coffee back into the cup. "This little feller seems bright enough and well mannered, and he's not from the migrant camp, probably, or he'd know Spanish."

"Martin and I have agreed that he can stay with us, if it's not against the law or anything," Aunt Cat said. She put a protective hand on Robert's shoulder.

"Oh, it ain't against the law, I guess." The sheriff smiled. "It ain't if I don't file the missing person report right away."

Martin came stomping back into the porch, scraped his feet and walked on into the dining room and sat at the table. He was sweating through his blue shirt.

"Got the bales in your pickup, Len," he said, wiping his forehead with his bandana.

"You'd oughta waited, Martin. I was going to give you a hand with them."

"No trouble." Martin squinted his face up, concerned. "What do you think about this young man now? Is he legal?"

"Oh, I think we can let it ride for a bit." The sheriff got up from the table, tucking in his khaki shirt. He picked up his ranger hat from the chair. "The township's got enough expense right now. And it don't make good sense to ship the boy away until we know more about where he came from. I'll get the judge to appoint you foster parents in the case until some more evidence comes in." He jammed the hat down square on his bald head as if he were a floor lamp putting on its shade. Robert thought he looked better with his hat on, more like a Texas Ranger, maybe.

"And who knows when that'll be?" he said, smiling.

After the sheriff had driven down the lane, Robert felt more at ease. He had not known certainly how entangled he might become with the law.

"You're not going to give me away?" he asked, looking up at Aunt Cat and Martin in turn.

"Little Robert," the woman said, smiling, "Martin and I are *not* going to give you away."

"It would be nice to know where you dropped from,"

Martin said. "But if you've got a touch of amnesia, well, it's not your fault."

"Does the . . . does that word mean I don't remember?"

"That's right, but you'll probably have it all come back to you one of these days," Martin said. There was something like a frown on his face, Robert thought, but it was hard to tell. His brown face was so seamed and creased. You could always tell when he smiled though.

"If I remember, and I don't have umnesia, then I have to go away with the sheriff?"

The two adults looked at each other. "Well," Aunt Cat said, "if you do remember, won't you want to go home to where your own folks are?"

"I guess I'll keep the umnesia for awhile," Robert said, sliding off the chair. "Can I go out and play with Biff?"

Martin would carry Robert around the farm, showing him the barns, the corncribs, the chicken and brooder houses, the milk house and the tool shed, talking in a low toned, expressive murmur as if it were all a secret between Robert and him, as if one day all this would belong to the little boy. Robert loved riding on the solid arm that held him as if he were a hawk being trained for flight. He shouted over the tractor noise as they disked the new cornfield, asking even more questions, for his mind was empty and waiting for the whole world. And the farmer would squint up his eyes so they almost disappeared in the walnut burl wrinkles and laugh quietly at all the questions, and answer them all. In the early morning, Robert would go to the barns for milking, carrying a tiny galvanized pail the farmer had found somewhere, and he would have a try at the milking, working on the "stripper" teats at the back while the old farmer sat tilted forward on his one-legged stool, his gray head against the Guernsey flank, making the front teats squirt in rhythm and fill the big buckets with sudsy warm milk that the cats cried after. And sometimes a cat would sit patiently beyond the cow's swinging, lion tail and Martin would bend the teat and squirt a long stream of foamy milk right into the cat's mouth, the cat sitting up, taking it in the eyes, ears, whiskers, chest, everywhere just to get some in her mouth, and Robert leaping around and laughing until he cried to see the cats all happily bedraggled with milk and Martin murmuring a low laugh against the cow's red flank that dented just right for his head to fit in while he milked her. Robert thought it all seemed to fit together perfectly, the nests fit the chickens, the chicks just filled the warm brooder hood, the cows fit their stanchions and walked along the lane to the pasture in a line that just fit the path they had worn. All of it seemed right and perfect, even the smells of manure and sheep dip and fly spray, all the pungencies of the farm, seemed to fit in their places in the whitewashed barn and the animals' houses laid out so neatly around the big, hard-packed barnyard.

One morning coming downstairs late in his nightshirt, Robert's hair bristled and I almost shifted, hearing new voices coming from the living room. There was also a strange, rhythmic train of sounds that accompanied the voices. I had never heard music before, nor had Robert, but then I had not attended to the doings of humans much until now. A group of voices was going up in pitch, then down, seeming to smile and shout at the same time, their words slurred and drawn out in unison. Shrill scrapings and whistling noises accompanied the voices, keeping pace with them. "We're glad to see ya!" they screamed, and then the music broke off and someone said as if suddenly finding it was spring, "It's the Breakfast Club!" And there was a lot of garbled laughter and hooraying. Robert was appalled that this was taking place in the living room and presented an obviously frightened face to Aunt Cat who was calmly preparing some bread dough in the kitchen.

"Good morning, Little Robert," she said, her arms floured to the elbow. "Oh my, what's wrong, little fella?" she said, suddenly catching his expression.

21

"Somebody's in there," Robert said, looking toward the living room where the voices were proclaiming their intention to "march around the breakfast table." The voices sounded flat, as if they were speaking through a narrow crack.

Aunt Cat looked down at him for a long minute, absently rubbing flour off her arms. Then she began to laugh and picked him up, making long flour marks on his nightshirt, and carried him into the living room.

"Look here, Little Robert. Look at that. There's not a soul in here. See?"

Robert looked around. The living room was deserted except for the old upright piano, the upholstered sofa and chair, and the usual bric-a-brac. The voices were coming out of an arch-shaped thing that at first looked like a chair back.

"That's the radio, Robert," Aunt Cat said, jiggling him on her arm as if that motion would help to settle the knowledge in his head. "Didn't you ever hear a radio before? My goodness, child, *where* have you been? I thought all little boys nowadays listened to Jack Armstrong and Dick Tracy."

Robert did indeed become so enthralled with the radio that he had to be pulled away for meals for a few days. I was equally taken with the music, and often was dissatisfied with Robert's choice of program, his taste running to Buck Rogers, while I would have searched the dial for Benay Venuto or the Merry Macs. In the sitting around time after supper, Martin would listen to the deep voiced Boak Carter and the news, and Aunt Cat would turn to One Man's Family or the Easy Aces. The conflict generated between Robert's need for adventure tales and my own intense curiosity about music led finally to a standoff on the radio question, one of the few times I found myself interfering in his life. We had to take turns listening. To the Nordmeyers, it must have seemed the little boy simultaneously possessed an obvious love of mystery and adventure and a peculiar need to listen to almost any kind of music. He would be pressed to the gothic speaker of the Philco for the serials and even some daytime shows like Helen Trent; and later he would sit glumly, almost angrily in a chair at some distance from the set listening to Guy Lombardo, but would protest violently if anyone offered to change the station.

The kind of music Robert liked best was Martin's harmonica playing. The farmer would take the old Hohner from his shirt pocket and play "Go Tell Aunt Rhody," or "Peanut Sat on a Railroad Track," or "Pop Goes the Weasel," with a real pop in it, and Robert would smile until his jaws hurt. He even got so he could play a few notes predictably, so that Martin made up a simple tune consisting of in and out notes in a, descending scale. They made up lyrics together (to the tune of "Put Another Nickle In, In the Nickelodeon") and the first one they made went like this:

> In a little cubbyhole
> Sits a tiny mousie-O
> Playing on her piccolo
> To make her whiskers shiver.

There came to be a dozen or so verses eventually, some of which made no sense at all, but Robert would play the in and out tune until Aunt Cat was driven from the room. It seemed to be something only Martin and Robert could stand for very long.

One evening after supper, Martin and Aunt Cat sat in the dining room listening to the radio, each drinking beer from a tall brown bottle, a thing they did so seldom that both Robert and I were interested in it. Robert expressed a desire for some beer. Aunt Cat said it was not for children, but Martin thought that a little beer wouldn't hurt a fly.

"Just a little bit now," said Aunt Cat. "You don't know what influences . . ." Her sentence trailed off into a significant look, to which her husband raised his eyebrows and nodded while he poured Robert half a glass.

The light golden fluid sparkled as Robert drank off a big mouthful and choked it down, his throat trying to close it out while his little boy honor made sure it went down. As it hit Robert's stomach, I felt it as strongly as if I had swallowed a piece of green rhubarb. It is a rare thing for me to be involved when I have shifted. For the most part I am a detached observer, partially because my usual senses are in abeyance and I find the scene rather boring, and partly because the physical nature of the shift seemed to be such that I could not really interfere very much without forcing a transformation back into my natural form. But the beer had something in it wholly new and exciting to me, something that ran instantly through Robert's veins and my own with such a meaningful, tingling pleasure that I almost flickered into my natural form standing directly in front of the farm couple. As it was I must have wavered a bit, for I heard Aunt Cat laugh and say, "Look at the poor little thing shudder. Now Martin, you take that away from him."

I clutched the glass tighter and tossed off the remainder before the farmer could take the glass from me.

"He's bound to have it," Martin said, laughing and taking the empty glass.

I heard their words from a distance as the alcohol spread instantly through my nerves, giving me an acute tickle of pleasure. I wanted more. But Robert's eyes were watering and his mouth was spurting saliva. His face grew white, and a ripple of muscular spasm ran up his body. It reached his stomach just as Martin got his big blue handerchief over the boy's mouth. The second spasm, Robert, and Martin made it to the kitchen sink at about the same time, whereupon Robert ridded himself of that which had been such a pleasure to me. Even though he detested the idea of drinking another drop of beer, Robert did notice later, at my prompting, that Martin kept the brown bottles stored in the milk house tank behind the big ten-gallon milk cans.

(2)

The rind of the old moon slips down the wide sky. It is warm and pleasant to sit in the grass behind the milk house sipping at my third bottle of beer. They are all mine, all mine, the nest of brown, elongated egg-like bottles of beer I am holding between my furry thighs. Fortunately I am a slow drinker, for it takes only two bottles to disable my judgment and make me the silliest creature in all nature. I laugh and roll on the wet grass for the pleasure of feeling the blood rush tingling from one side of my drunken body to the other. I roll over and it rushes back, numb to tingly, tingly to numb. I roll and scratch up the grass and laugh until I am foaming at the mouth.

The Nordmeyers have two yard dogs, one a large female Springer Spaniel named Josie, the other a witless German Shepherd named Biff. Josie leaves me alone, crawling under the brooder house whenever I appear. Biff has never learned anything in his life. He is so stupid that he swallows the cockleburrs he pulls out of his fur, unable to think of anything else to do with something that is in his mouth. He hears something (me!) behind the milk house, and while Josie is retiring to her hiding place, I hear him tiptoeing up to surprise me. I lie flat in the grass, my body spread-eagled like a bear rug, my jaws yawned open. Biff springs from behind the milk house, stiff legged and masculine, expecting to find a neighbor dog. He has no nose, really. I look up at him from behind my gaping muzzle, trying not to laugh.

Biff stands there, astonished at the bear rug in the grass. He approaches inch by inch, stretches his neck out, jerking back at an imaginary sound, stretching again to sniff my outstretched paw. Suddenly I snap my jaws shut loudly and grab him by the throat. He cannot make a sound and coils up like a salamander trying to get away.

"Nice Biff," I say, holding him by the neck, not choking him much. "Wanna play, Biff?" I roll over on my back and hold him with all four paws, just tight enough so he can't get away. The minute I let go of his throat he begins to squeal. I have never heard a dog squeal before. It is an interesting sound. I set him on his feet with his back to the milk house wall. He stands hunched up, a dog hunchback. Very funny. I reach out to pat his head, and he crumples as if I had hit him. I get down, butt in the air in dog play position. He stares at me from his crumpled shape. I get up and hop about him like a big demented bunny. His eyes roll, and he looks as if he wants to become part of the cement wall.

Then it seeps through my foggy brain. I really do want to play with him, roll on the ground with another creature and bite in fun and rough each other up. Could I shift into a dog shape? The thought unsettles me. I giggle. Biff groans. The two dogs are always playing, running in circles, rolling on the grass, chasing the bull Humphrey out in the back pasture, going halves on a rabbit.

I get down on all fours. "Now watch this, Biff," I say playfully. I concentrate as much as the beer will allow, on Josie. JOSIE, I think, trying to pull my mind into a doggy point. JOSIE! Something happens. Biff jerks back, bumping his head against the wall. I am *almost* Josie, but my head and shoulders remain me. Must look awful. I try again. I concentrate. Shift. This time I've got it. I look back over my shoulder: dog from ears to black spotted tail. I wag the tail. Biff is terrified, looking at my legs. Oh cripe. I am a large edition of Josie but I have four of Little Robert's legs, pink toes and all. As I close my eyes to concentrate again,

Biff makes a break for the corncrib where he has a hidey hole. I follow him slowly, shift back to my own form and peer under the building at the drooling, quivering dog.

"Just a minute, dammit," I say to Biff. "I'm doing this so we can have some fun."

It is becoming difficult to hold an image. All this concentration with my weakened mind is tough to do. I manage another shift. No. Wrong again. I hear Biff scrabbling back further under the crib, banging his head and elbows on the floor joists. I am dog on one end, nothing on the other. I look like a horrible, dog faced caterpillar. Biff begins to howl a deathly, hollow sound from under the crib. Maybe I can't be a dog. It is like squeezing a balloon. One part gets squeezed into the right shape, but another part pooches out wrong, so to speak. I let it go and shift back to my natural form.

"Ooooeet?"

Damned smartass owl. I catch his vibrations from the first branch of the walnut tree next to the garden fence. I slip into the shadow of the fence, drift across and under him while he swivels his head around and asks again, "Oooooeet?" I leap.

"Gotcha!" I bite into him so fast he doesn't have time to blink. I do not notice the porch door opening a crack. The owl tastes of mouse, and I drop to the ground to rub my muzzle in the grass. Thunder crashes from the back porch, and the tree splatters bark just over my head.

Shotgun!

Running low and fast, sober as a weasel in a henhouse, I zip along the fence and over the creek embankment. Damn! Whenever I eat a bird that farmer sneaks up on me. Raising my head slightly in the weeds I feel about for the man with the gun. Still behind the back door, he is shielded by the screen. I can barely detect him. The door slides open, and Martin edges out into the shadow by the rain barrel. He walks into the faint moonlight as far as the garden gate calling Biff and Josie, neither of whom appear. He disappears

27

back onto the porch, and I hear the click of the hook on the screen. He fades from my perception.

What has he seen? I mentally lay out his line of sight from the back door to where I stood to eat the owl. He couldn't have seen much in this light, a shadow standing on its hind legs against a tree, running along a grassy fence row. But I am forgetting Robert. Martin might easily check his room before returning to bed. I take a step up the bank when another sound comes from the porch. Crafty hunter! He is still there, invisible and undetectable behind the screen. I freeze, turning up my hearing to the limit, seeking through the metal screen with my spatial sense. There he is, lowering the gun, walking back into the kitchen. Gone. No lamps are lighted. Maybe that means he will not check Robert's room, but I do not take the chance.

I slip out of the weeds, follow every shadow over to the peach tree beneath Robert's window, carefully inch my way up through the thick branches until I can reach up and grab his windowsill. With one claw I flip the sash up hard so it jams sideways near the top. In the next instant I hear Martin's footsteps coming along the hallway, hear him swing up through the window and drop to the floor of the room. The instant I hit the floor, I shift, so that Little Robert seemed to have just turned from the open window as Martin's stocky shadow appeared in his doorway.

"What was it, Daddy?" I congratulate Robert on the "Daddy." Every distraction helps, for I do not know yet what the farmer has seen.

"Sorry to wake you up, Robert," the farmer said, walking softly to the naked boy who stood by the open window. "My goodness, you always take your nightshirt off. You'll catch your death. Must have been a stray dog out there rummaging around. I had to take a shot at him. They're a bad lot, you know." He carried Robert back to bed.

"Now you stay under the covers. I'll shut your window."

From the bed, Robert could dimly see Martin's

heavy shadow struggling with the window. It was jammed tight.

"How'd you get your window in this kind of fix?"

He grunted and strained and finally with a heave pulled the sash out of the frame altogether with a ripping, splintering sound that brought Aunt Cat striding into the room, a tall, flat shadow, angry and holding her robe tightly around her.

"I swear, Martin. What *are* you doing? First it's shoot 'em up at midnight, and now what've you done? Look at that. My Lord! Ripped his window right out. What in the world?"

The ensuing explanations and arguments were more than enough to take Martin's mind off of what he might have seen, and Robert dropped into sleep as suddenly and softly as an owl would take a mouse.

Now that Robert is no longer locked in at night, it is no trouble for me to slip away for a good rabbit chase in the open fields or some sneaking around creek and hedge rows for more sporting game like foxes, mink, or even wild dogs. One moonless night near the end of May when the seedlings are just beginning to give the fields a tamed and ordered look, I slip out as usual, leave Robert's nightshirt in the barn, and relax. It is always a relief to shift back after a long time in changed form. The world springs back into its real shape, night sounds take on their old meanings, my spatial sense fills me with confidence as I perceive each living shape and movement around me, and I feel my eyes dilating with predatory efficiency. My claws are sound in their sheaths, and my hide prickles with joy under the fur. I am fast and gleeful, and nothing can stand in my way or escape my grasp. I feel like singing, or killing something, or running a fox to ground and telling her my secrets while I hold her neck tightly, staring into her bulging red eyes, then setting her back on her feet and tweaking her tail to make her run. How complete is the freedom of the natural body and its perceptions, its beautiful muscles that coil and spring, leap and bunch, and hold the bones in their trance of motion and speed.

I am trailing a female fox, sneaking through the hedges, crossing the creek twice, until I am almost to the railroad bridge south of the town. The fox scent crosses the creek again and seems to head toward the darkness under the bridge. But then it is blotted out by the odor of people, very dirty people. I crouch in the weeds along the creek to scan the area under the arch of the bridge. The smell comes from there. Human excrement, old and new, alcohol, canned food spoiled and fresh, dirty skin and clothing. The mounds are human forms rolled up in rags to keep warm. People asleep under the bridge. Tramps. They walk the highways and railroad tracks, have no place to stay, no way to dig burrows for themselves, and they sleep in places like this. There is a camp for these people in the town. I have heard the farmer and his wife talking about it. It is called a "Roosevelt Roost," a name I do not understand. I wonder why these people are here in the dirt when they could be roosting with Roosevelt in a dry building? Perhaps they are outcasts.

I step warily through the weeds, keeping low, wondering at such filth. How can they stand to sleep so near their own excrement? Even dogs . . . but suddenly, not able to sense much because of the powerful smell that is blocking out part of my mind, I step down on a human hand.

"Sonuvabitch!"

I leap sideways and drop into the weeds where I land, startled half out of my skin. It is always humans who remind me of my limitations. They are always surprising me in surprising ways. I flatten, hoping the person will go back to sleep, but the man has gotten up on his hands and knees and is feeling around in the grass near me. I will have to get away without hurting him, and I cannot shift into Robert's form, for it would be too dangerous to him. His hand blunders into my fur.

"What the goddamhell?"

I sense his every movement, the direction of his gaze in the darkness. I know he cannot see much, and I wait

30

for the moment when he is off guard for an instant. It comes.

"Hey you guys. There's something like a . . ."

At the moment his head turns slightly to look in the direction of the sleeping forms under the bridge, I throw my weight up and against his belly, digging in my back claws, and push him over backwards into the creek. I leap the creek as his form hits the water under me, and I am a hundred yards up the railroad ditch in the tall weeds before he can get out of the water. I lie quiet, controlling my panting, listening to the man's curses and screams as he wakes the others under the bridge.

I creep back along the opposite side of the railroad tracks to the other side of the bridge opening. The shapes are sitting up now, three, no, four of them. They are passing cigarettes around, the glowing ends momentarily lighting up the faces, bearded and stubbly, one old man, three younger ones, but all with a common haggard look, as if they might be from the same sickly litter.

"Dumb shit," the oldest one says, coughing heavily. "Had you a dream about guys in fur suits and fell in the crick. Too much wine."

"It wasn't no dream. It 'uz a big dog, maybe."

"You was dreamin' about that little gal that give us the bakery bread," says the skinny younger one.

"I wasn't never dreamin' and I ain't drunk. It was somebody, maybe a bear," the one they call Gus says. He is wrapped in an old overcoat, shivering.

They all laugh.

"Gus got pushed in the crick by a bear."

The hilarity does not last. Their bodies have a rank, sick smell. They are not healthy like the farmer and his wife. The oldest one is sick with something that wastes his body. I smell it, but have no experience of what it might be. After a bit the oldest one lies down again and the short, silent man leans back in the dirt and pulls a wide brimmed hat over his eyes. Gus and the skinny one sit up finishing a cigarette, staring blindly out into the dark weeds where I am crouched looking back at them.

31

"Rusty says we ought to get on down to Chi tomorrow," the skinny one says.

"Yeah, I reckon," says the other one. "And workin' the stem in this town ain't bad. I made forty cents off one old lady yesterday." He draws on the cigarette so that his face emerges from its silhouette. He is narrow faced, like a chicken, hardly any forehead, eyes set back almost to the side of his face. He looks pinched.

"Tommy!" says the voice of the one called Rusty who has his hat over his face. "Getcher ass over here. I'm cold."

Tommy says nothing, gets up and goes over to lie close beside Rusty.

Gus stands up, holding the overcoat around him. His hair almost touches the arched concrete ceiling. He is a big, wide shouldered man with a large head, but when he walks back to his nest in the weeds, his shoulders fall into a stoop and he seems smaller.

Being close to them, listening to their words, smelling their rancid odors has a strange effect. I have the feeling that if I shifted, I would not be Robert, but someone different. It is an unsettling feeling, and I turn away finally from the little camp under the railway bridge and lope back to the farm without hunting further.

The next day, Aunt Cat's older daughter came out to the farm with her little girl, Anne, who was a bit older than Robert. The mother was called Vaire, but that was not her real name. Anne was half a head taller than Robert, with her mother's golden hair and blue eyes, but her hair was long and curled into ringlets that hung around her face like golden springs. Having been introduced and told to go outside and play, they found themselves at the sandbox beside the garden fence. Anne took a position in the middle of the sand with her hands on her hips. She wore a flouncy pink dress with a white apron over it.

"Grandpa Nordmeyer made this sandbox for me," she said.

"He said I could play in it," Robert said, standing just outside the box.

"Well you can't use my pans," Anne said, picking up a half-dozen miniature kitchen utensils Robert had found in the sand.

"I didn't know they were yours," Robert said, watching her stuff the pans and dishes in the pockets of her apron. They made her rattle when she walked. "Are these cars yours too?" he asked. He watched her try to fit the little cars into her pockets too. She settled at last for stacking the cars against one wall of the sandbox and drawing a line in the sand around them.

"Now," she said. "Those are mine, and you mustn't touch them."

When Robert did not object to any of these proprietary measures, Anne began to soften somewhat.

"How old are you?" she asked, taking the pans and dishes and stacking them behind the line with the cars.

"I don't know," Robert said, and then he thought he'd better say about how old Aunt Cat said he was. "Five, I think."

"You're just a little baby," she said. "I'm going to be six in June, and I'm going to be in the first grade when school starts." She stepped out of the sandbox and swaggered over to the garden gate, climbing up and swinging on it so that the iron weight on the spring creaked up and down. "And I can already read," she said.

"How do you read?" Robert wondered. That was something he wanted to know. Then he could read in the bedtime story books about adventures.

"It's pretty hard," she said, jumping off the gate and letting it bang. "But I'll show you." She walked away primly toward her mother's car. Robert followed, expecting to learn in the next few moments how to read. He tensed his muscles, clenching his fists. If it was hard, he would do it anyway. Anne opened the car door and got a thin book from the door pocket.

"Here," she said, putting the book down on the grass under the lilac bush. "See this story?" She opened to the first pages where there was pictured a black Scottie dog and a couple of children, a boy and girl who looked unnaturally clean and hysterically happy.

33

There were some black marks under each picture. Anne put her finger on the first line of marks. "This is the dog's name. It's Happy."

"His *name* is happy?" Robert said in wonder. "How can a name be happy?"

Anne looked blank. She looked to see if Robert was smiling. "That's silly. I said the dog's name is Happy!"

"I know, but . . . Oh, like Martin's big dog's name is Biff." Robert relaxed somewhat, thinking it wasn't all that hard yet.

"Now this says," Anne screwed up her face until one eye was shut. "This says, ah, 'See Happy run.'" Her face came unscrewed into a smile.

Robert looked at the marks. He felt baffled. "Which marks say that?"

Anne pointed to the first line.

Robert looked harder, trying to force his face into a grimace and squinting his eyes. Nothing happened in his mind. "Read some more, please?"

"All right. Here on this page it says," and her face went into the spasm again, "'Run, Happy, run.'"

"That's a funny thing to say," Robert said. "Is something going to get the dog?"

Anne looked blank again. "Nothing's going to get the dog. What do you mean? The boy is telling the dog to run."

"But you don't have to tell a dog to run just for nothing," Robert said, trying to understand this strange, pointless story.

Anne decided to ignore his comments. "Here it says, 'Look, look, Jane.'"

Robert looked at Anne with respect. "Who is Jane?"

"She's the girl. My goodness, I bet you're never going to school."

"I will sometime," Robert said. He looked at the marks and then at the pictures. He could have told a story from looking at the pictures, but he wouldn't have known the right names. It wouldn't be reading. He got up from the grass and walked around the car. It *was* hard, and not in the way he had thought it would be.

"What's this writing on the front of your car, Anne?"

34

Robert said, pointing to some writing on a metal plate fixed to a bar between the headlights.

She walked around the car. "That's, ah, let's see. That's a B, a Buh sound, and that's a U, a oo sound." She brightened. "Oh, it just says Buick, because our car's a Buick."

Robert was incensed. He wanted to read, and I was listening too, intrigued by the marks that made sounds in the mind.

After they had eaten a bacon sandwich and had some chicken soup for lunch, Anne and Aunt Cat went out to weed the strawberries. Robert sat at the table watching Anne's mother. He had not seen much of the world, but he recognized that Vaire was beautiful. It was all he could think of. He watched her lips when she spoke, her eyes when she was quiet, and her every move as she walked back and forth from the dining room to the kitchen.

Her face was more round than Aunt Cat's was, but she had the same comforting smile. Her body was slender with more flare at the hips than was fashionable. She wore her skirts tight and in bright colors, and Robert thought he had never seen so marvelous a thing as the suppleness of her waist when she did such a simple thing as put a dish in the sink, or the grace of her shoulders as she went down on one knee to wipe off Anne's milk mustache. Her lips were full like her daughter's with sharp uptilted corners that made a dimple when she smiled. She did seem happier than anyone Robert had met, singing little bits of songs like "Dream Train" and "The Isle of Capri" in odd moments as she helped her mother in the house.

Each time she reached to pick up a plate or the silverware, he saw her marvelous, slender fingers, moving as if they played invisible strings, producing harmonies inaudible to all but the thin faced little boy. Once she looked up and accidentally met his gaze, her wide blue eyes caught by his direct stare. He could not look away. His stomach felt as though a drawstring were pulling it tight as he looked for a long moment

35

before she crinkled her eyes as her father did and laughed.

"Little Robert, why are you watching me? Afraid I'll fly away?"

Robert was not able to say why he watched her, but he knew he did not like to stop looking at her. He seemed to be memorizing each golden wave of her bobbed blonde hair, each angle of cheekbone, curve of chin, red of lip, and every tone of her voice. She came over to his chair.

"Walter and Anne and I are coming to take you to church in the morning, Robert. Did you know that?"

"No. I've never been to church," he said faintly, inhaling the odor of her hair and skin.

"Didn't your mother or father ever take you to hear about God?" she asked, sitting down at the table.

"I don't know what God is," Robert said, his mind still out of focus. Now he was watching her breasts move as she breathed, how the button at the neck of her blouse drew tight and eased slightly each time she breathed. It was a warm day, and a fine bloom of perspiration made the woman's skin glow as if it emitted light of its own.

Vaire became aware of the little boy's absorption in her breathing. She flushed slightly, feeling both amused and guilty, as if she had been caught listening to an off-color joke. She laughed again.

"Come on, Little Robert. Let's see what Anne and your Aunt Cat are up to out in the strawberry patch."

That evening Aunt Cat and Martin and Robert took baths in the kitchen. The water was heated in the copper boiler on the stove for hours until it was steaming, and then Martin hefted it by its handle with his husking gloves on because even the handles were hot, and poured a bright steaming fall of water into the wash tub set on the big braided rug in the middle of the linoleum. The hot was tempered with cold water from the pump, and Aunt Cat scrubbed Robert top to bottom with a bar of perfectly transparent soap that smelled like crushed apple blossoms.

"Are you and Martin going to go and hear about

God tomorrow?" Robert asked as Aunt Cat scrubbed each foot with a little brush.

"No, Robert. We don't go to church often anymore. Your girlfriend Vaire and her husband and Anne will take you to the Baptist church."

Robert did not know what "girlfriend" meant in connection with Vaire, and he felt the emphasis on "Baptist" church was unusual, as if there were a preferable church, but this one had to be gone to instead.

"Do you only go to hear about God once?"

"No. People go all the time because they like hearing about God, and because it makes them feel good."

Robert was not really concerned about God but with the fact that he would be with Vaire. It was to that he looked forward as he fell asleep, feeling clean and warm between the sheets.

There had been a noise. I shift to hear it. The house takes form in the night sounds and in the feeling of spaces and blocks that being inside a house always gives me. The sounds are strange, coming from the room where the farmer and his wife sleep. I slip out of bed and down the hall to their door. It is closed, locked to my soft, tentative paw. Sounds of clothing pulling across skin, happy noises from two people, grunts and soft smiling noises that are not laughter, but are the happy animal sounds and squeaks two creatures make being happy together. Some more rubbing sounds, faint as a hand on the hair, on the breast, on the skin of the back. I try to peer through the cracks around the door, through the hole where the iron key is. My spatial sense will not work through the door. The bed is creaking now with rhythmic movement. I sit on my haunches and cock my head in the dark hallway, figuring what the two people must be doing. They are naked in the dark room, rubbing each others' skin, pressing together parts of their bodies, murmuring words and little sighing sounds to each other. They are rolling? bouncing? on the bed to make it creak and creak. They are breathing as if they are running hard. Their breaths interlock, move apart, interlock, panting, faster. Words: "Oh, Martin!" "Cat, I love you, I love you." They are saying the words over and over, a magic chant. They stop.

I wait. Their breathing becomes slower, but they do not move. I begin to feel prickles of irritation along my back. Robert wants to be here. I feel thwarted, sitting in the dark hallway of a house listening to two humans making themselves happy in some way. Robert wants to be here, but I feel irritable, as if I were chained to a post while a strange dog eats my kill. I move along the bannister to the stairway, silent as smoke in the dark hallway. It is a bemusing thing.

The porcelain nude stands in the center of the oak table, the moon flooding her with a liquid light so that she seems soft, although I know from Robert's having secretly touched her that she is cold and hard. The farm wife has removed the flowers from the bowl the figure stood in and placed her there on the table as if for me to see when I sneak out at night. Robert calls her the wash-lady. He asked Martin one day what the lady was doing standing on one foot and holding that cloth in a great arc from under her raised foot to over her head. Martin had said she was doing her washing, and that made Aunt Cat laugh. The figure is heavily glazed, her breasts mere humps under the gleaming finish, but there is grace in the curve of her waist, the slender legs like those of some womanly centaur, a woman-gazelle perhaps.

I lean over the table to sniff the figure. Robert wants to touch her, wants to think about the two people upstairs and their happiness sounds in the dark bedroom. It smells strongly of cold solid, like the doorknob, but without the sweaty hand smells that the doorknob always has. The lingering scent of dying flowers, sweet decay, is around the base of the figure. I touch it with the side of my muzzle, gently, caressing the coolness. That is all it is. But Robert is interested in it because it is a woman figure. It holds power for the little boy. I am curious, but I cannot touch it properly. I shift.

Robert crawled up on a chair and carefully onto the table until he was sitting in the strong white moonlight in the center of the polished oak beside the wash-lady in her flower bowl. He enclosed her with finger and thumb, smoothing her down from her Dutch bob haircut which was like Vaire's, down across the glassy mounds of her breasts, into the S-curve of her back and the faint bulge of her belly, unmarred by navel, felt on down the double hook shape of buttocks, the disappearing vee of pubis, the long gazelle legs. He ran a finger along the thin white arm holding out the cloth that rose from her feet like a frozen white wave in an arc over her head. It was almost like the crescent moon he saw last week. He was very delicate, very careful, for she would smash if tipped, and Aunt Cat had warned him never to touch. And here he was sitting on the table, naked, caressing the porcelain nude full in the moonlight that fell through the south window in a tall rectangular beam like a chute from the moon down the clear white lighted night, through all the air above the world, right through the glass of the tall window, to light the naked boy sitting on the dark polished oak table, holding in his thin hands the white porcelain figure of a nude woman who held an arc like the crescent moon from her feet to above her head as if she were standing in the dark space of the new moon, as if she were the phantom of the moon, the woman in the moon. Robert sat holding the figure now next to his cheek, smoothing the cool porcelain against his lips, across his eyelids, touching the tender places next to his eyes with her cold porcelain hand. He looked up through the window directly at the moon's off center face. His eye looked between the figure's arm and the arc of moon she held, into the marred face of the moon, the disfigured and leering face of the man in moon. He shivered, and a terror of dropping the figure came over him so that his hands shook as he placed her back in her bowl, set carefully on her round base. As he removed his hand, she rocked forward precariously—and his heart split in his chest—but his hands sprang away in horror rather than trying to leap forward to catch her. It is well they did, as his nervous hands would surely have knocked over the figure in trying to catch it. It rocked once and shivered to a stop, upright, whole, cool and white under the flood of the moonlight.

Later, in a sharp triangle of shadow I trap two rats behind the manure pile, and bite their heads off, although I do not like to eat rats. It is an irritable, moping sort of night, full of strange sounds along the creek bank that I cannot understand, muskrats I do not care to chase, weasels I cannot find, a stupid pheasant hen that eludes me. In the wet dew of dawn I slink back to the house. Robert sleeps until they wake him for church.

Anne and Robert were allowed to stand up in the pew so they could see when everybody stood up to sing. Anne knew one of the songs, but of course Robert knew none of the words, so he just made "ah-ing" sounds while everybody else sang. Walter, Vaire's husband, thought that was fine and smiled down at him. Walter was a red-faced young man with wavy blond hair and a hearty manner with boys. He had talked to Robert all the way to the church, as the two of them sat in the front seat of the Buick while Vaire and Anne sat in the back. He talked about school next year and selling insurance, things Robert was not interested in because he could smell Vaire sitting behind him and constantly wanted to turn around and look at her.

The telling about God turned out to be a different thing altogether.

"Is there a hell?" the preacher began. "My friends, I know you may wonder at a question like that. But I have heard people today ask that question, young people, followers of the false gods of science and the almighty dollar, followers of their own pleasure."

The preacher appeared to be very old, the oldest man Robert had seen yet. He had almost no hair, and many large freckles on his head and face, and a wrinkly wattle under his chin like the turkeys on Martin's farm. He seemed very unhappy all through the telling about God, and did not actually tell about God at all.

"They ask me as a man of the Holy Word if I *think* there is such a thing as HELL!" His voice broke, rising to the pitch of that last word. "If I THINK there is a Hell. My friends, as if I ever had the right to think such a thing when I KNOW there is a HELL because the Bible says so!" Having leaned increasingly forward over the podium toward his listeners, he now stepped back until Robert could only see the top of his head like an overripe canteloupe resting on the top rim of the podium. Then his face appeared again.

"They ask me if I can believe in Hell when God is Love. Whether I can think about God sending anyone to burn in everlasting fire. Whether there can be a God who would let his children be in pain forever? And I say to them, YES! YES! For God is a God of Love. He is a God of infinite mercy, and He will not allow his wayward children to become the innocent victims of Satan, of EVIL! He has told us all there is a Hell. He has told us we must obey Him, must worship Him as the fountain of everlasting life, and that if we do not, if we insist on going against His commandments, if we do not believe the sacrifice His Son Jesus Christ made for us on the Cross—then surely we *shall* find out there is a Hell. Surely we shall find that there is a place reserved there for US! And yet they will ask me: Preacher, is there a Hell? Can this thing be? And I say to them, and I say to you this fine morning when all of God's creation is singing and bursting with the glory of spring, I say to you, Yes, there is a Hell. Yes, there is damnation. And it is eternal. It is the fire that never stops, the pain that nothing can wash away, the loss of heaven compounded with the torments of bodily and spiritual pain that will NEVER end."

Robert felt sick and a bit dizzy. He wished a breeze would come in through the tilted windows, or that he had one of the yellow straw fans.

"It is an unrelenting and never ending pain. It is the pain you have never felt on this earth. It is the pain sent by God Himself for those who will not believe in Him. It is the just punishment for Evil, for following false gods, the evil and false gods of selfishness and Mammon, the false gods of pleasure and of the forget-fulness of Heaven and Salvation. EVIL, my friends,

EVIL is your enemy. EVIL is the Satan in our midst who never rests, who wants you to forget God, forget Jesus looking down from His Cross and asking you for your heart, the Satan who is always at your side tempting you with the bounty and pleasures of the flesh. And that very Satan who will tempt you to Hell if you let him, will tempt you to the fiery pit where tortures await you, where the rending of that same flesh is Satan's pleasure, where his devils all clawed and fanged will drag you down bodily into the pit where they may tear your flesh, where they may burn your miserable body forever, FOREVER!"

Robert was aware of my anger underneath it all. The old man felt rotten inside. I shift momentarily out of pure rage, and one extended claw scores the oak pew deeply under my angry grip. Then I recover, thinking of Vaire, of her beauty. I shift back. Had anyone seen the flickering shift?

Robert felt fear as he looked at the deep gash in the oak pew, a fresh white cut as if a whirling saw blade had nicked the wood. He put one small hand over it and looked up at Walter's face, then at Anne sitting beside him. Walter seemed absorbed in the sermon, which continued as a sort of ugly chant; Anne was slumped awkwardly into herself, her chin down on the lace collar of her pinafore. She was asleep sitting up. Robert could feel the cut beneath his hand, but he knew it had been a simple accident. He looked past Anne at Vaire and met her wide blue eyes staring down at him. Her mouth had compressed into a scarlet line. He looked directly at her with all his innocence, holding the gaze but not smiling. She held the stare a moment, then released her held breath with a gasp as if she would take the next breath and scream. Robert held her eyes with his, looking at her with all the love of her beauty that he felt, with all his innocence. Vaire shook her head slightly, breaking the eye contact, looked about her as if about to appeal to the church full of people, caught the sound of the preacher now winding up his sermon with a series of rhetorical periods, looked down at her hands in her lap. She rummaged in her blue cloth purse, found a hanky and began dabbing at her face. Robert looked away.

Aunt Cat had gotten a box down from the top of her closet. She set it on the dining room table, carefully pulled its top off and drew out a long, thick book of black pages bound with metal rings and with many pictures attached to each page. She and Robert looked through the last pages in the book where there were pictures of Vaire and Anne and Walter, and some pictures of a pretty, black haired woman standing with a tall, heavy looking man in a suit. They looked bright and happy. The man had a white flower in his lapel.

"That's Renee and her husband, Billy, when they were married," Aunt Cat said. "Here's their little girl, Wilhelmina, and here they are when Mina was a year old."

"Is this book all about your family?" Robert wondered. There seemed to be thousands of pictures earlier in the book. He thought Martin and Aunt Cat must have hundreds of children.

"Yes, it's pictures that go back to the first Kodak we had in my mother's family. See here, toward the front. That's me in the long dress and the funny hat." She laughed and motioned for Martin to come over. "Look at this one of Claire, Martin. I don't recall this one. Look at her in that suit. Wouldn't she just have a fit?" Aunt Cat and Martin both began to laugh at a faded picture of a frowning young girl in a funny black suit that covered her whole body. She was standing in ankle deep water with an out-of-focus lake behind her.

"Is she your daughter too?" Robert asked.

"Oh my, Little Robert," Aunt Cat said, widening her eyes. "That's my very own Claire, my sister, when we were just girls, oh thirty years ago and more."

Robert tried to think about that, but time in such quantities was a blank.

"Do you love all your families?" he asked seriously.

Aunt Cat caught his tone. "Yes we do, Little Robert. And we love you too, for now you are part of our family." And she gave him a hug and kissed his cheek.

"Is love when you're in a family?"

"That's how you *get* a family," Martin said, winking at Aunt Cat.

She turned and looked at the man, smiling in a certain way again. Robert watched with a hungry look. What was it that they were doing? That invisible thing that went between them sometimes? He watched and listened, but he couldn't understand it.

"Do I love you?" he asked Aunt Cat.

"Well, I think you might, sometime."

"Don't I now?"

"Robert, you are so funny. Only you can know if you love someone. We can't know before you do."

He thought about that for a minute. I begin to listen from far back, for this conversation is having strange effects. Emotional waves are originating from somewhere within Robert.

"Do I love you like this?" he asked, suddenly putting his arms around her neck and crawling into her lap.

She caught him in her arms and hugged him.

"Yes, Little Robert," she said. "That's the way."

(3)

The tall one named Gus carries the jug. When the others want a drink they have to ask Gus, and he keeps one finger crooked through the eye of the handle while they drink. They crunch along the right of way in the cinders, stumbling over the ends of ties now and again. I keep up with them in the weedy ditch with my head just touched by the moonlight coming across the high rails. If they look they might see my head listening to them, floating along silently in the white moonlight.

"Yer fullashit, Tommy," says the old man, the one who is sick inside. "You ever gonta make a buck again, it gonta be selling quarts of your blood fer antifreeze." He coughs and spits.

"That's better'n you, you old fart. You ain't got any to sell." Tommy's shoulders hump as if against the cold, although it is a hot night. His legs are so thin his pants seem to be walking by themselves.

"We can make some dough picking strawberries soon," Gus says, swinging his big head from side to side. He holds the jug up so even I can see there is only about a fourth of it left. "Pick a couple, eat a couple. . . ." His words trail off as he takes a sip delicately from the mouth of the jug as if receiving a kiss.

"Yah," the old sick one jeers. "Workin' fer the fat farmer. You know the farmers making money outta this depression. They the ones doing all right. Nobody makin' any money but the farmers and the pol'ticians now."

"That's the god's truth," says the short man in the ragged suit coat, the one who is usually silent. "Groceries comin' up outta the ground."

"Farmers ain't so rich," Tommy says. "I got an uncle's a farmer, and he . . ."

"Tenant farmer," the short man says.

Tommy whines his voice when speaking to the short man. "He ain't. He's got forty acres of muckland, and he ain't rich. He works his ass off."

"Well, that muss be what happened to you, punk," says Gus, taking a long stride and kicking at Tommy's rear. "No more ass than a sandhill crane."

"Lay off a him, Gus," the short man named Rusty says very low and menacing.

"Punk," Gus says, but he stumbles across the rails to the other side of the track.

"Gimme a drink of that dregs you got there, Gus," Rusty says.

"I'm savin' the rest for my nightcap," Gus says. "My money bought it, and I've give it most away already to you thirsty bastards."

"You tight assed jack roller," Rusty says, and he leaps over the tracks at Gus, knocking the bigger man sideways before he can get ready.

They scratch around clumsily in the cinders like two boys in a schoolyard, and I think they must have had another jug, for both are nearly falling down drunk. Then the short man gets an advantage and brings his knee up between Gus's legs. Gus howls and drops the jug, going down in the weeds at the edge of the embankment.

"Gimme some too, Rusty," the old man wails.

Rusty tips up the jug, pouring much of the wine over his panting mouth instead of into it.

"Shit, Rusty, yer wasting it all," the old man is sobbing.

Rusty holds the jug up until the moon shines clear through it, and then he tosses the jug away in my direction. I almost catch it. After Gus has gotten up silently and is limping on after the others, I pick up the jug and smell it. The fumes make my head widen suddenly.

I stick my tongue into the jug and by tipping it up get a few drops. It is like golden fire, burning, beautiful to the tongue. I want it, and shake my head with baffled desire.

I slip through the tall weeds to the concrete wing of the bridge footing and listen. The old one is coughing and coughing down by the creek. The others are sitting up close to the concrete arch.

"You guys had any guts, we'd make a lot more than two bucks off a sack of soap." The voice is the low, raspy one, Rusty's.

"I ain't goin' to get tossed in the cooler," Tommy says. "None of my family ever been in jail."

"Yeah, I know," Rusty says. "There's about enough guts between the three of you to pull a dead cat off a manure pile."

"Whatta you gonta do, big mouth," says the old man, trying to catch his breath. "You gonta walk up to one of these rich farmers with their big dogs and shotguns and sheriff's bulls on every highway, and you gonta say, gimme some money?"

Rusty staggers out from under the shadow of the bridge and stands half in the moonlight urinating out into the weeds. His body wavers slowly back and forth as if he were under water, moving with a slow current.

"Here's your wine, Gus," he says, his chin down in his coat. He tries to get the buttons on his pants closed, cannot make them work and finally gives it up. He staggers back into the shadow of the bridge.

"How would you do it, yer so smart," Gus says to him.

"Same way you go for a handout," Rusty says. "Only it's a bigger handout, see?" I listen to his body lying back in the dirt. They are all settling down, curling up like homeless dogs to sleep.

"Come along the lane, you know? The lady's maybe out hanging clothes, the old man's in the field with the hands. You make a pitch to do some odd jobs while the rest of us wait somewheres." His voice is getting smaller, almost a whisper. He is falling asleep.

"And then what?" Gus is still sitting up.

"And then you get the old lady for bait," Rusty whispers.

"How d'ye mean?"

There is no answer. Rusty is asleep.

"You really thinking about robbing a farm?" Tommy whispers from his place beside Rusty.

"Nah, nah. Go to sleep," Gus says. He shakes his big shaggy head. "I'm gettin' tired of sleeping in the dirt is all."

I listen for a time, but the only other sound is the old man coughing and coughing.

In the world of animals, reflexes are the ticket to each night's life. The mouse must move at great speed to escape the owl, the ferret, the cat; and they in turn are operating far above anything a human set of reflexes could match. The human must be excited by adrenalin to nearly a mindless state before his responses can even come within range of those of most animals. The snake also, much admired for the speed of his strike, is relatively slow in comparison with the rapid reflexes of some mammals. The morning Robert was collecting eggs and heard the rattler as he reached into a nest box, we could have sustained a painful and poisonous injury. But my reflexes responded before Robert even fully heard the rattle, and when the snake struck it was at my fast disappearing paw, not Robert's slow little hand. The snake, extended almost out of the nest box by its awkward strike, is easy to pluck out of the air with my other claw, even as the basket of eggs is smashing on the floor. One quick bite behind the flat head finishes it off. I do not like snakes, to eat or to look at, but they are no danger to me unless I am completely off guard, say if I were to lie down on one. It occurs to me as I dispose of the rattler that there might be more of them about, but before I can look or sniff around, I hear the farmer coming and must shift.

"What is that, boy?" Martin said, staring at the snake Robert was dragging. Carrying a full pail of milk in

48

each hand, he set them down so quickly that the foamy milk slopped out onto the ground.

"I found it by the chicken house," Robert said, holding it up as it continued to coil and uncoil. "I think it's dead, but it's still winding up."

"That's a rattlesnake," Martin said, picking the mottled snake from Robert's hand. "Don't see them very often around here. Hey!" He looked at the head which hung by a few shreds of muscle where I had neatly bitten through the spine. "Looks like a dog did a job on this fella." He held the snake up admiringly. "Must have been Biff. Look at the size of those tooth marks."

Listening, I feel disgust. As if that stupid old Shepherd could have even caught the snake, much less have done such a neat job on it. Robert was aware, of course, of the truth, and aware too that there were probably more snakes in the area. "I thought I saw another one in that pile of straw in the corner of the chicken house, but I'm not real sure."

The farmer knotted his brows together so that his eyes almost disappeared. He tossed the snake away into the weeds. "Well, we'd better see about that. Part of that old chicken house floor's just dirt. Could have a bunch of them living in there for the eggs." He smiled down at Robert. These snakes are dangerous, you know. So I want you to keep out of the chicken house until we find out if there's any more in there."

"I broke a bunch of eggs," Robert said, holding up the pail.

Martin took the pail from him and set it down. He picked Robert up and swung him high in the air, grinning the whole time. "We can throw the eggs to the hogs, but we want you without a bunch of tooth marks in you, son."

Later, Robert watched from the doorway of the chicken house, for Martin would not allow the little boy to come in while he lifted old planks out of the hard-packed dirt that formed the uneven floor. All the chickens had been herded outside into the run and the little wood panel dropped over their entryway. The old planks came up each one with a groan and a cloud

49

of choking dust, ancient manure, feathers, and chicken-feed. When he lifted the one that had the snakes under it, Martin hollered out in a tight voice Robert had never heard him use.

"Hey! Hey! Look out there, boy. This'n is it!" He flung the plank aside like a twig and grabbed the shovel he had brought and began stabbing at the writhing mass of snakes. They were mostly about a quarter grown, one very large one and a half dozen small ones, but in the nest they looked like hundreds, roiling and twisting in and out of each other. Then they seemed to explode in all directions, and Martin stabbed and leaped like a man with hornets in his pants.

"Hi! Hi! Look out! Yi!" Martin was stepping high, sometimes on the snakes, sometimes trying apparently to stand up in the air without touching the ground at all, and never ceasing to stab down with the point of the shovel. Robert thought it funny and began to laugh and dance around. Martin's leaping was so comical, the heavy brown farmer in his overalls dancing like St. Vitus and singing out in that high, excited voice made him sound like a young man again.

When the snakes were all chopped to pieces and looked like an old pile of garden hose or bicycle inner-tubes all cut in sections, Martin came over to the door with his gray hair in his eyes and sweat and dirt all over the wrinkles in his face.

"I guess that was kinda funny, hey, Robert?" He leaned the shovel against one side of the doorway and himself against the other side and just panted for a few minutes. "I don't think I got bit any," he said, breathing more slowly.

"I didn't mean it was funny," Robert said. "I mean it was funny to watch you dance, but I know it wasn't *really* funny."

"That's all right, son. I haven't danced like that since your Aunt Cat and me went to Renee's wedding up in Grand Rapids and just about did ourselves out doing the polka."

But I am thinking how slow it seemed to watch the old farmer try to hit the snakes, who were surprised and

50

befuddled by the light and completely panic stricken. It would be so easy to pick them up and kill each one while they are twisting around like that. It bemused me for a time to think about how slow humans are. But then they are clever and treacherous too.

Little Robert had got used to being played with by the farmer and Aunt Cat, played with as human children are, thrown around on a bed, swung by the arms, ridden horsey on the foot. And it is my necessary habit to avoid any hint of shifting while these physically surprising things are going on. It is for this reason, the safety of the home environment, that Tommy was able to grab Robert when he came downstairs that last morning, and I did not respond immediately. When Robert had heard soft voices that were different from usual as he came down for breakfast, he had simply assumed they were part of a radio program.

"C'mere, kid," the narrow faced young man said, holding Robert very hard by his arms. "Now you sit in that chair and don't you move or I'll knock yer head off."

Robert sat in the chair at the dining room table taking in the scene slowly because it was so strange. Tommy seemed frightened. His feet were in constant movement as if he were a little boy and had to go to the toilet, and his narrow chicken face was white. Aunt Cat was sitting in a chair at the same table with her hands unnaturally still on the dark wood. Her long, homely face looked fearful, but her lips were held in a tight line, and her eyes followed the short, red haired man with more hatred than Robert had imagined was in her. Rusty seemed larger in the house than he had seemed under the railway bridge, but then I had seen him in different circumstances. While Robert sits in the chair, I wonder if Gus and the old sick man have come along, and where Martin is. I think of shifting suddenly, but it is not clear to me how serious the situation is, and Robert was reluctant to leave his new family, as certainly he would have to do if I were seen in so direct a way.

Rusty walked up and down between dining room

51

table and the back porch screen door where he would peer out across the garden, tossing the butcher knife from hand to hand easily as if it had been his for a long time. He walked back, easy on his feet, smiling a little. He had a red bandana around his neck and wore an old sleeveless undershirt under the black suit coat that he must have picked off some dump, for the pockets were ripped off and padding stuck out of the shoulders. On a stage, he would have made a comic tramp. But he walked like one in command of the situation, and the knife seemed to be his friend.

"Goddammit, Tommy, stand still or go piss," he said, sliding into a chair at the table so he was sitting between Aunt Cat and Robert.

"What if they don't get him?" Tommy said, shuffling his feet back and forth as if he had something on the bottom of his shoes. "What if he gets away and goes for the sheriff?"

"They got his shotgun," Rusty said. "And that farmer ain't goin' anywheres with his old lady sittin' in the trap." He put the knife down on the table in front of Aunt Cat and clasped his hands behind his head, teasing her to grab for it. She did not move or speak. Robert looked at the two men, trying to think what they wanted, wondering if things might still be all right. I began to be closer to events now, my attention aroused by the fear scent that filled the room. I begin noticing things now: the light from the windows getting darker instead of being bright with sun. It has sprinkled rain earlier this morning. Now it feels like a thundershower coming on. It has rained every day the past two weeks with great displays of lightning and thunder rolling in long reverberations across the farmlands like combers on a long, flat shore.

"I see 'em. I see 'em," Tommy said, peering out the kitchen window through the lace curtains. "Old Hackett's bringing him right in. He told him a good story, I bet."

Rusty picked up the knife but did not otherwise move. "Shit yes. I knew they'd get him in here." He began sticking the butcher knife into the table top in a pattern of deep cuts.

"Do you have to ruin our table?" Aunt Cat said suddenly.

"Oh, you can talk, huh, old lady?" Rusty said, sticking the point in again. "Yeah, old lady, I got to do this. It keeps my nerves down."

"Now Gus has got the gun on him," Tommy said in a strange whisper from the window. "They got him! Here they come, and he ain't makin' any trouble."

Robert sat very still. He obvviously did not want to precipitate me into the middle of this situation. There was Martin in front of his own shotgun, and Aunt Cat with a butcher knife too close to her neck. For my own part, I am content to wait. When three more people have been added to the dining room and kitchen, the whole house begins to look smaller. Gus is much bigger than Martin, his huge shaggy head almost touching the top of the door frame. The old farmer seems to have shrunk in the presence of these ragged, filthy men. The coughing old one they call Hackett seems most concerned with money, while Gus and Tommy are frightened at what they are doing and would like to get quickly out. Only Rusty is cool, and so it is him I watch with most attention.

"So you boys going to be criminals," Martin said. "I've seen you around town, but I thought you were just good folks down on your luck."

"We ain't criminals," Tommy began.

"Just get the money now, you rich bastard. That's all we want," Hackett said.

"We ain't aiming to hurt anybody," Gus said, holding the shotgun in the crook of his arm like a duck hunter would. "We need the money and you folks can spare it." He kept jerking his head for no reason, as if he had a fly on his neck.

"You think we got money here," Martin said, smiling at them. "We're not rich people here. We have to work for everything, just like you do, I mean when you can get work. I know it's not easy now, but . . ."

"Will you shut yore mouth?" said Old Hackett, his

53

voice rising to a scream and then vanishing in a coughing fit.

"What he means," Rusty said, stabbing the table again, "is you *better* have some money." He suddenly held the knife level with Aunt Cat's chin, pointed at one of the blue veins in her neck. She flinched and looked at Martin.

"Now don't get mean," said Martin, holding up his hand. "You've got no reason to get mean. We'll give you whatever you want, whatever we got to give. I don't carry money with me. There's the money I was going to buy some pigs with up on the dresser in our bedroom."

"Go see, Tommy," Rusty said, taking the knife away from Aunt Cat's neck and sticking it into the table again.

While we all waited, it was like a different group of people, as if we were just strangers waiting for a stoplight to change or for a movie theater to open. The kitchen was getting darker.

Tommy's nervous feet came down the stairs again. "It's here," he shouted. "Look at that, look at that, forty, fifty, sixty dollars!" He did a little shuffling dance in front of Rusty. "Wowee, we gon have a time."

"That's nice, old man," said Rusty. "Now where's the rest of it?"

"You got any grocery money, Cat?" Martin said, his eyes looking very tired.

"In the cupboard there behind that sick old man's head," Aunt Cat said without moving her hands from the table.

Old Hackett gave her a vicious look and turned to pull open the cupboard door. In a blue pitcher that had a lid on it, he found fourteen dollars and some odd cents.

"There's a car comin' up the lane," Gus said in a high, changed voice. He shifted the shotgun to a ready position.

"Let's lam out," Tommy said. "We got plenty."

"You know that car, old man?" Rusty pointed out the window and motioned for Martin to look.

As Martin bent to look out the kitchen window, a bright flare lit up the room and the stunning crack-boom of close thunder made the whole group of people jump at the same time. Watching them with increasing awareness, I see each person leap in his own way, Martin hunching his shoulders, Gus jerking the shotgun up and blinking, Tommy flinching sideways as if he were about to be hit, Aunt Cat rising slightly from the chair, the old sick Hackett shuddering as if with a chill; only Rusty does not move, like a stone figure in an underwater world, he is the only one who does not respond with the current, and in his perfect immobility the others sense an unnatural control.

Martin pushed the curtains back. "It's our daughter Vaire, with her little girl most likely." His voice was low and sad.

Vaire came running from the car as the first large drops of rain began splashing into the dust of the garden and hitting like hail on the back porch roof. Anne was not with her. She was wearing a smooth green skirt and a white frilly blouse, looking happy and full of summer with her hair golden and bouncy in the mounting wind coming under the rain cloud. She dashed into the back porch, saw the big shaggy man with the shotgun and stopped, her face frozen in a smile.

"Get on in here," Gus said almost in a whisper, motioning with the gun. The thunder hit again, farther away, and the rain began to come down heavily.

Vaire had stopped near the sink, touching her father's arm, looking at him as if he would suddenly explain it all.

"For an ugly couple of farmers," Rusty said, holding the butcher knife between opposed fingertips, "you two got a real peach for a daughter. Come on over here, doll." He indicated the chair between Aunt Cat and Robert. Vaire walked on into the dining area and around the table, touching Little Robert's head as she passed.

The whole time she sat at the table, she looked at her father, with whom she seemed in full sympathy. She did not once look at Rusty, and it was as if he and his comments did not exist. Robert felt her as a source of strength, for she seemed to banish evil by ignoring its existence.

"There's no more money here," Martin said. "We got a small bank account, but they wouldn't let you fellas cash a check."

"Let's look around, farmer," Old Hackett said. "Cause I just don' believe you. Gimme that gun," he said, pawing at Gus. "I'll get the money outta this damned liar."

"Get away," Gus said in a low voice. "I'll take care of the gun." He pushed the old man back and swung the shotgun to cover the room again.

"Tommy, you and the old man take the farmer around and see if you can help him recall where he's got his savings hid at," Rusty said. "Gus and me will stay here and talk with the ladies."

"I swear," said Martin, his face pale in the dusky kitchen, "there isn't any more money. It's not . . ." Thunder crashed in a long rolling roar, drowning the rest of his words, and continued as Old Hackett said something fiercely, pantomiming silently in the crashing sound with his arms raised, a funny little Punch figure on a puppet stage, weak and ridiculous.

Tommy and Hackett each took one of Martin's arms and led him out the back door. "Let's look down the cellar," Tommy said. They all ducked out the door into the gray downpour of rain, becoming hazy figures at once, humped against the fall of water, moving past the screened porch out of sight.

"Bunch of fools," Aunt Cat said so suddenly that Gus jumped and swore. "We haven't got any more money. That pig money was just about the whole savings we had. We had to borrow this year to put the soybeans in the ground."

"Well, we're going to find out," said Rusty. "Happen I don't believe you. I seen all that farm machinery, and that car ain't but two years old." But the whole time he was talking, his hands were touching Vaire, her hair, her bare arm, the side of her neck, her cheek.

56

And his eyes looked at her with the bright blank stare a cat gets watching a hurt mouse that can't run.

Robert's stomach felt like a fist squeezing. Above the pounding rain now they could hear splintering and crashing sounds from the cellar.

Rusty was touching Vaire's bare arm with the point of the knife now, making the flesh dimple. "You gotta be that farmer's daughter in all the jokes," he was whispering in her ear. "You're pretty enough for a whole train load of salesmen, baby."

Vaire shook her head as if a fly had buzzed too close. Robert's eyes were fixed on Rusty's face, following each movement of his head as he sniffed the young woman's hair and whispered in one ear and then the other.

"It's all right, Little Robert," Vaire said, reaching over to take his hand. "It's going to be all over with soon. These bad men will be gone. It'll be all right again."

"Quit messin' around, you goddam fool," said Gus. He was more tense than before, holding the shotgun at the ready, his finger inside the trigger guard.

"Fuck off," said Rusty. "This's my party." He allowed the hand not holding the knife to slide down Vaire's shoulder until it rested on her left breast. He was saying something in her ear, and this time she could not ignore it as a flush rose in her neck and face. Robert could hear the spit working in Rusty's mouth.

The noises in the cellar had stopped, and the rain was pounding steadily like huge drums beating in different rhythms, making no rhythm at all but just a heavy sound that made you feel deaf and stupid.

"You watch 'em for a minute or two, Gus," Rusty said, his hand sliding over to take Vaire's wrist. He twisted her arm behind her with a sudden move, bending her body forward over the table, and then pulled her up off the chair. She let out a tight little gasp, but otherwise did not indicate she knew such a person as Rusty existed.

"The farmer's daughter and me goin' to explore upstairs and see if we can find something."

Vaire looked across at her mother whose hands were

now gripping hard on the table edge. "Just be quiet now, Ma," she said, her body bent over to one side as if she were crippled. "I'm going to be all right." Her voice shouted unnaturally over the pounding of the rain.

When she had to drop Little Robert's hand, I knew he couldn't hold on much longer. The blood seemed to be filling his body tight, burning in his face and hands. His mind was blanking out as Rusty shuffled past his chair, pushing Vaire ahead of him toward the stairs. The little boy's hands leaped out to grab the man at hip level, pulled himself, chair and all, to the man's leg and bit as hard as he could.

That is what Little Robert intended, but as the adrenalin rushed into his veins, he could not hold his shape, and as he bit down the shift came suddenly.

I find myself biting Rusty's hip. My teeth grate across his pelvic bone as my claws spring into his groin and buttocks to hold him still. His screams are very shrill, and he jabs at me with the knife. I flip it out of his hand and try to disengage from him, but his fists are tight in my pelt. I hear noises at the back door over the heavy throbbing of the rain, and I bite the screaming man again quickly and knock him away with a back-handed blow as the table came crashing over, pinning my feet to the floor. The farm woman has tipped it over either in surprise or in an attempt to help. A woman is screaming. I am most concerned for the shotgun, and I kick at the table and spit out the man's flesh as I crouch to avoid the blast.

The crash of the shotgun going off is different from the thunder, but splits the ears in the close room. It is not directed at me. Martin had evidently seen the struggle going on and made his own move at the same time as Robert grabbed Rusty. Gus is facing the back door, the shotgun at waist level. In the doorway three men are down in a struggling pile. I smell more blood and see the shotgun swinging around. Gus's eyes are points of light beneath his shaggy hair, his face white as pond ice. I note the old farm woman crawling around the table toward the young woman who is lying on the

58

floor partly beneath the floundering and bloody Rusty whose inarticulate screams continue without stopping. The gun is swinging as I get out from under the bodies, the chair, the table edge. The linoleum on the floor of the kitchen is slippery as my claws spring out for a grip, not like wood, and the gun swings farther, almost on me as I see its twin black holes searching like eyes for me in the dim kitchen. I can almost look into those deadly sockets, but I make a long leap and swing my arm far out so that one extended claw hits the barrels.

The shotgun blasts into the ceiling, bringing down a shower of plaster and wood. Gus is staggering as I come out of my roll and leap for his throat. I miss and bite high into his shoulder, feel the collarbone snap and a rush of hot blood as I rip away, digging my hind claws into the linoleum, twisting the shotgun away as his screaming begins. I break my hold and twist the stock off the shotgun and hurl it hard at a window. It smashes and goes on through out into the gray pounding rain. Gus is falling now, on his hands and knees in the dimness while the hot blood pumps out of his neck in long jets. I leap for the back door and find Tommy rising in front of me, wavering, holding his arms around his chest. I take a swipe at him and knock him like a bundle of sticks into the corner of the porch where he lies silent.

In the back doorway where the rain blows in upon him in great wet sheets lies the old farmer, his chest punctured with purple holes, and blood washing from the wounds with the rain. The old sick Hackett sits against the wall of the porch, his eyes wide, his hands lying palms up. He seems to be looking at me and not believing what he sees, holding his breath.

I turn for a last look into the dim farmhouse while the rain pounds down on my back. Gus is lying in his blood on the linoleum, moving vaguely as more blood spurts out of his neck very fast. He will die, I think. Back farther in the dining room I see the two women standing over Rusty who is convulsing on the floor like a spine-shot rabbit. The older woman has a long knife in her hand, and the young, blonde woman's green and

59

white clothes are smeared with blood. The two women are looking directly at me with frightened eyes. I sniff the old farmer again. His faded blue eyes with all the wrinkles around them are looking at me. There is no fear in them, but I see that they are glazing over. He is dying. His gray hair is plastered down in streaks around his face by the rain. The harmonica is sticking out of his shirt pocket. For no reason I can imagine, I grab it in my teeth and run out into the gray fall of the rain.

(4)

The Grand Rapids Examiner, Tuesday July 2, 1935

TWO PERSONS DEAD
IN ROBBERY ATTEMPT

Local Farmer Shot to
Death, Waif Missing

Mr. and Mrs. Martin Nordmeyer, their daughter and a foster child were the victims of a robbery attempt at their farm south of here Monday. Dead are Martin Nordmeyer, 61, and his alleged assailant, Aldo (Gus) Hamner, vagrant. Robert Lee Burney, foster child of the Nordmeyers, is missing and is believed to have run away in terror during the fracas. He is described as five years old, brown hair, brown eyes, slender build, and wearing only a white nightshirt.

The three surviving robbery suspects are under police guard at the Sisters of Mercy Hospital with varying injuries received when they were attacked by a "wild dog or bear" that mysteriously came to the aid of the family. Hamner died at the scene from loss of blood, his jugular vein severed by a bite from the animal that Mrs. Nordmeyer described as a "cross between a bear and a gorilla."

Sheriff Leonard Kendall reported the farm family's kitchen "looked like a slaughter house" when he arrived late in the morning to answer a call from Mrs.

Victoria Woodson, daughter of the Nordmeyers. "There was blood everywhere, splattered on the ceiling even. Mr. Nordmeyer dead from a shotgun charge in his chest, one suspect bleeding to death, two others in bad shape with the worst claw and teeth marks I ever seen." Suspect Roger Rustum was hospitalized with deep hip lacerations and internal injuries; Thomas Prokoff, the third suspect, is reported in fair condition with two broken ribs and a concussion. Sheriff Kendall reported the fourth suspect, Oliver Hackett, was not injured in the battle but is suffering from advanced tuberculosis and is in poor condition.

The search for the little boy, a waif the family had found in their barn about two months ago, is continuing today.

The mystery animal that broke up the robbery attempt has not been positively identified or seen since it ran out of the Nordmeyers' house after mortally wounding one suspect and severely injuring another. Upon his being asked if he thought it was a large wild dog, suspect Rustum said, "It wasn't no dog. It was a fiend out of hell." Comments from the Nordmeyer family indicated they too were mystified at the appearance of the animal.

Martin Nordmeyer is survived by his wife Catherine, two daughters, Victoria Woodson of Cassius and Renee Hegel of this city, and two granddaughters. Funeral arrangements are pending.

I foolishly allow my mind to think about this terrible morning, so that I stop too soon at the little railway hut that is less than a mile from the Nordmeyer farm. I do not think about the hut or what it is used for, only that I must hide, since I cannot shift form at the moment. I dig under a shallow foundation and emerge into the stuffy little tool house where I will wait for darkness. The torn, wet rag that was Little Robert's nightshirt hangs about me. I tear it away, knot up the harmonica in one strip of cloth and tie it around my waist. The hut contains shovels, rakes, pick axes, other tools leaning against the walls, and a platform with iron wheels and long levers on top. I am steaming wet and sticky with blood, and the smell of creosote in the hut is suffocating. I block it all out to sleep.

I wake full of fear at the sound of crunching cinders. The hut is without cover of trees behind, the nearest ones down the track half a mile or more on the side. How have I been so stupid? The crunching cinders get louder. Men's voices, many of them. I slip to the hole I have made under the back foundation, but there are already men outside settling against the shady side of the hut. Now they are all around the hut in the shade, talking, rattling metal pails. I smell bread, meat, stale fruit. They are eating their lunch. At the double doors in front of the hut the lock begins to rattle. They will come in. My head is foggy. I force my rage to form, clearing my mind, so that I can visualize the layout of the countryside. I have been here in the nights. Behind the hut it is open country at this point all the way to the river, but directly out front and across the track is first a small creek, then a thornapple hedge that extends a long way to the south. The end of the hedge is almost opposite the hut. I have to go out the front or be in sight for a long while to the men sitting in back of the hut. The lock springs open with a rusted sound and the doors are being lifted and pulled across the cinders. I wait behind the iron wheeled platform crouching low, wishing at that moment to shift, but unable to. I put it out of my mind.

"Let's wait till after we eat to get it out," a short round man in overalls is saying. "It's a heavy sucker."

As his companion who is partly behind the opened door is about to answer, I charge toward the half opened door, hitting it hard with my shoulder.

"Crise-a-mighty!" The fat man is screaming as I hit him with my shoulder and he spins away and down. The other man is larger and is carrying a shovel. I slam past the door, but the other man is swinging his shovel at me. In mid-leap I kick with one hind leg, striking him in the chest so the shovel just grazes my back. Then I am down the embankment, sliding in the cinders into the weeds, leaping the creek awkwardly as I hear a great commotion and crying out behind me, and around the hedge for what should be a long straight run that will put me out of sight and reach. I have forgotten the fences. Barbed wire, the first two of four strands, then another one of five tight strands, and in the distance I can see at least two more. They slow me down, and I can hear the men on the railway embankment running and crying out. I wait to pant a moment, lying up under the thorn hedge. It is very hot, the sun's heat wavering up from the dark soil of the cornfield where the stalks with their dark green leaves are standing about two feet high. The vivid green rows dwindle in perspective toward the far fences where I see clumps of trees, a barn roof, other buildings. That is behind the Nordmeyer's east field, the one where the Guernseys graze. My mind snaps, clearing my perceptions at once. I smell the dried blood in my fur. I am being foolish again. I wonder for a second if I am ill, then I hear the noises of iron wheels along the track and excited men's voices. They are catching up with me on some sort of car on the tracks. There is no cover beyond the end of the hedge, and now they will arrive there before me. I glance back along the hedge row, my eyes just above the weed tops. In the waves of heat rising from the dark soil I see the distorted figures of half a dozen men spread out in a line, carrying shovels, picks, iron bars. Their voices come to me now from two directions as the men on the handcar arrive at the far end of the hedge row. The hedge is too thick and thorny to get through. Not time to dig under it, so many roots in hedges. The cornfield with its endless ranks of low corn plants offers no cover at all. I am trapped, and it is because of my own foolishness. But there is no time now to wonder about the cause of such muddleheadedness. The men are at both ends of the hedge, advancing cautiously, sticking their shovels and bars into the weeds and into the hedge itself as they advance. I smell my own fear. I try to concentrate on Robert Lee Burney, but I cannot. There is some block there preventing him from emerging. In wonder I realize that *he* does not want to come out. To try another animal form would be worse. I am too inexperienced for that. I do not wish to hurt humans. The ones at the Nordmeyer farm threatened my own survival, but I do not wish to harm these men. Also, to show myself to so many witnesses is certain to bring on a hunt I would have great trouble escaping in my present state.

"I'll come out if you'll go back," says a high clear voice.

I jump, then flatten back in the weeds. The voice is Robert's, and it comes from inside my own mind. He is making a deal with me. I have the urge to laugh. I think the words, "If you don't come out now, we will both have great trouble, maybe be killed."

"Promise you'll go back."

"I can't. They have seen me. It would be a danger to you also."

"Promise!"

The men at both ends of the hedge are closer, coming slowly, spread out into the cornfields. It is too late to run now without having to fight with some of them. As Robert's voice screams inside me the one word again, I hear something, a metallic rumbling, then a far off whistle, slightly elevating in pitch. A train is coming, fast.

Now the men at the south end of the hedge hear it too. They are hollering and running back around the hedge. I begin to slip through the weeds in their direction.

"The Lakeshore. The Lakeshore!"

"Get that handcar off the right of way!"

"C'mon, get your ass in gear. That baby's gon splatter us all over the county."

The south end of the hedge is free of men now, and I begin running faster. I arrive at the end of the hedge to see half a dozen men in work overalls struggling with the iron-wheeled platform, trying to get it off the tracks as the train appears to swell in size down the track, trailing a flat plume of smoke back along its length. Its black, blunt form approaches at unbe-

65

lievable speed, the details of the iron engine face becoming clear so fast I have trouble seeing it all. The men on the track have the handcar derailed but sideways on the track. They will not make it. The train whistle begins a shattering scream, the pitch rising unbearable. Only two of them are still trying to get it off the track, the rest are running down the embankment as the train's wheels begin to grind on the iron rails, a thousand metallic notes higher than the ear can hear, couplings crashing like hammers on anvils back down the length of the train. I stand up to watch the sight as the last two men dive away, one on each side of the track and the towering black engine seems to gobble up the little handcar and blow out its wreckage in a giant blast. A terrific smashing of wood and clanging of iron, and one heavy iron wheel comes sailing over the hedge, spinning and flailing its torn-out axle like the stem of an iron flower cut by the mower. A shower of wood splinters bounces back along the length of the black engine as it rushes on past in spite of its squealing brakes. As the engine flashes past above me, I see the white round faces of two men ducking away from the cab window.

Behind me I hear again the men coming along the hedge. They are running now, shouting. I double back on the railroad side of the hedge in the shadow, and when I am half way back, I see the men gathered around the wreckage of their handcar. The train is on beyond me, just coming to a stop, its last car a hundred yards up the track. I slip down into the creek, up the embankment and across the tracks almost crawling on my belly. On the other side is a small stand of oaks and maples that leads into a woods. I have made it.

Now that I have been clearly seen by two groups of people, there will be much more difficulty getting out of this country. I must have the ability to shift so that I can pass unnoticed. And Robert is now a part of me. I promise him that we will go back to the farm for just a little bit. After two nights in an abandoned pump house, I return to spend a whole day in the Nordmeyer's hayloft in the dusty dry heat, peeking out of the cracks in the hay door as black automobiles drive in and out of the lane, people come in black clothes and go in and out the front door. I have never seen people use the front door of the farmhouse before. Many of them are weeping. I recognize Vaire, Anne, and Walter, and see another group that must be the other sister, her husband and child. At intervals in the long, hot day I sleep, trying to recuperate my senses that seem to have been deranged by the battle and flight. I wake to see the narrow sunbeams striking down from tiny cracks and holes in the roof, standing like wires and ribbons and slender pillars in the dusty air. It is quiet in the high, empty loft, like an aisle in the forest when the sun shines down through morning mist. I am thirsty, but cannot go down for a drink until dark. I push back the thirst and wonder at the numbness of my senses. The part of me that is Robert is clearly delineated by a sick sensation inside me. I push it all away and resolve to sleep until dark.

I wake to feel the need for Robert to appear. I have never felt this before. I concentrate and shift, easily.

Robert stepped carefully in the dark to avoid getting slivers from the old, rough plank floor. He carried a rag that had the harmonica tied up in it. The barn was quiet, the cows asleep, the dogs chained up outside the big sliding doors. Biff came over to Robert dragging his chain and wagging his heavy tail, his head down as if it was all his fault.

Robert stood outside the back screen. No one was awake inside, but there was a lamp burning in the living room. The screen was not hooked. Robert opened the door and walked carefully in across the scrubbed dark spots on the porch floor. The kitchen was very clean and empty looking, and the dining room table had been set up again and polished. In the living room, sitting across two sawhorses, was a gray, oblong box made of metal with rod-like handles along the sides. The top of the box was laid back so that it opened up like Aunt Cat's jewel box on her dresser. Inside, the

67

box gleamed with slick cloth that looked almost wet, it was so shiny. The lamp was sitting where the radio used to be, on the little side table with the spindly legs. It was turned low, the flame unmoving as if it were painted in a picture.

Robert could not see into the coffin, so he had to pull a chair from the dining room. Standing on the chair, his hands on the edge of the long box, Robert looked in at Martin, who appeared to be sleeping with his hands folded on his chest. Robert had never seen Martin asleep, had never seen him so still. He had always been working, walking about the farm, telling Robert things about the animals and about planting and caring for crops. Now his eyes had disappeared behind the walnut burl wrinkles, his mouth closed hard on something, as if he were gritting his teeth, and the corners turned down in disapproval. He wore a black suit that Robert had never seen either, and a white shirt that was starchy clean, and a blue necktie. It looked like Martin, Robert thought, but it certainly was not the happy old farmer Robert had known. He gazed for a long time, leaning closer as if to catch a breathed word or see the beginnings of a smile, as if Martin were only teasing him as he used to do, pretending to be angry. Then it seemed the face began to change indeed, and the wrinkles to move outward into a smile, the eyes to flutter and perhaps would have opened if Robert had been able to watch one more moment.

"Robert!"

The voice was a loud whisper, as if from off stage, calling back an actor who had entered at the wrong cue. Vaire stood in the dining room door in a long quilted robe, her face a white oval in the half light. Her eyes seemed unnaturally large, owl eyes looking into the darkness. Then she walked quickly over to Robert and was hugging him in her arms, against her warmth, kissing the top of his head and crying, putting his skinny little body inside her robe and closing him in.

Robert at that moment began to sob and shiver as he had on that first night. He suddenly felt so weak he could not stand, sick in his stomach, dizzy in his head. He hugged Vaire and cried against her shoulder as she cried against his hair.

Robert had to say something, of course, about the creature they thought had carried him out of the farmhouse that day. To his advantage was the fact that he actually did not remember much of what had happened, at least not very clearly. His own emotional turmoil and the sudden shift blurred his mind so that he retained only the terror and the blood and the sight of the old farmer with his glazing eyes and torn chest. He held to the harmonica as if it were the talisman of his safety and told his fragmented story to the family, the deputy coroner, and some state police officers who looked very large and efficient in their gray uniforms and Sam Browne belts with pistols holstered under leather flaps. The testimony of the section gang whose handcar ended up as a handful of decorations on the Lakeshore Limited helped confuse the issue, for their accounts were highly imaginative, only two of the gang having had a clear glimpse of what came out of the tool shed that morning. Roger Rustum and Thomas Prokoff gave conflicting accounts also: Rustum maintained the creature had jaws like a shark and bear-like arms, while Prokoff saw it more as a mountain lion sort of thing. Oliver Hackett gave no account of anything, as he remained heavily sedated to allay the pain of the tuberculosis which would shortly kill him.

The evidence would not have convicted a sheep-stealing dog, and the authorities wanted to believe it could have been an ape escaped from a circus that had been in Cassius the week before. Telegraphed inquiries to the circus, however, ruined that theory, as nothing had escaped, not even the geek.

Further evidence of the strange creature's existence began to arrive at police headquarters in half a dozen

Michigan towns as soon as the evening paper carrying the account of the incident hit the streets. In the next weeks people saw every sort of nightmare monster from King Kong and the Wolf Man to Frankenstein's creation, with King Kong running ahead by a margin of three reports to one of any other type.

Vaire and Walter had taken Robert to their house in Cassius and given him the room across the upstairs hall from Anne's room. There he slept in a vast, sagging double bed with springs that talked to him whenever he moved at night. The bed, like the house itself, belonged to Grandmother Stumway who was Vaire's grandmother and Aunt Cat's mother. Robert, trying to line up these adults in ascending generations, believed she must be nearly as old as the earth itself.

Robert is comfortable, but sometimes I feel like slipping away and heading for the woods, except that the wide publicity I have received would make traveling difficult. Vaire has seen my form on two occasions, although the one time in church was probably hallucinatory and perhaps not even consciously remembered. She would casually approach the subject of the strange animal at odd times, after breakfast when Anne and Robert were carrying dishes to the sink, when the three of them were picking tomatoes in the back garden, when dressing for bed. She would wonder aloud how the creature had got into the farmhouse so suddenly, and answer her own question by saying it might have come in during the night and been hiding somewhere, or that it had leaped in through the back door and been the cause of the fatal shot from Gus that killed her father. And what had become of the thing, she would wonder, while Anne and Robert waited for the direct question they knew was coming.

"Poor Little Robert. You were probably too frightened to even remember where the creature came from, weren't you?"

"I was really scared," Robert would say while Anne looked at him curiously. She had gained a new respect for him now that he had been carried off by a mad gorilla and barely escaped with his life—and Grandfather Nordmeyer's harmonica. That last always puzzled Anne, as it did some others in the family, for Robert had been holding the harmonica knotted up in the rags of his nightshirt when Vaire had surprised him that night at the coffin.

Walter was inclined to be stern with Vaire when she brought up the subject on an evening after the children had been put to bed. In his forthright and clear-sighted opinion, no such creature existed. The thing was a wild dog that had been hiding in the house overnight and been frightened out by the shotgun blast and started biting people. Little Robert had simply been mad with terror and run away. His ruddy, open face seemed almost to convince Vaire while he was talking. It seemed all quite correct and true to life as she knew it when Walter sat calmly in the long dim parlor of their house and looked directly into her face and said, "It's nothing but mass hysteria, Vaire. It's the same as people believing they've seen the Indian Rope Trick. Once they've been told something supernatural or horrible has happened, they begin embroidering on it, and soon it's all out of hand."

"But a dog couldn't have carried Little Robert away."

"Of course not, dear," Walter would say, certain on this point. "The poor tyke ran away. The dog probably knocked him around, and he ran and hid in the barn. That is where he was hiding, didn't he say?"

"Yes, but for three whole days while those people were searching all over the farm? I'm sure some of the men must have looked up in the hayloft, and that's where he said he was." Vaire honestly hated to contradict Walter in anything. He was such a good person. But it really was inconceivable to her that the little boy had hidden naked in the loft for two days and a half while the farm was swarming with deputies, detectives, tracking hounds, and newspaper reporters.

This always exasperated Walter, so he would refill his pipe, which he had recently taken up as an aid

71

to his public image. The refilling and lighting and adjusting took some time and gave him the look of someone with all the answers at hand, although at times when he spoke without taking the pipe out of his mouth it would swing wide as if on a hinge and he would have to be fast and ungraceful to catch it. And then when the process was completed, his answer was notably weak.

"Well, what else could it be?" he would ask finally, as if the lack of an answer were proof of the superiority of common sense in all matters.

I am in the habit of lying in bed for some time in the dark shifted into my natural form to relax. It is comforting, even in cramped places, to be oneself again, and additionally, I can then easily listen to any conversations taking place downstairs. In fact, Robert would have been able to hear most of it if he had gone to the register in the floor of his room and pushed it open slightly, as it was a square hole with a register grate on both sides that opened into the corner of the dining room ceiling nearest the sliding doors to the parlor. Sitting on the floor, looking into the warm darkness through my screen and listening like a prisoner to the orchestration of the summer night, I hear Aunt Cat, Walter, and Vaire who are sitting around the dining room table drinking some of the home-made wine from the farm. Aunt Cat has had more than enough of the wine already, and Walter keeps trying to slow her down, although he is powerless before the tall, older woman who brushes off his remarks as if he were a child.

"But you've said many times, Mother," Walter says, "that you couldn't recall clearly what the creature looked like. Now you're saying you can remember exactly." He begins filling his pipe again, scraping it out with the handle of a spoon.

"You can't say everything to strangers, newspaper people, detectives, and the like. You don't know what they're up to," the older woman says.

I listen to Vaire whispering to her mother about the

wine, that it is good, but too much is no help for grieving, and her mother saying back that nothing is any good, but wine is better than most. The conversation becomes more carefully noncommittal on Walter's part, more pointedly angry from the farm woman. Vaire comments that the children are sleeping right above them, but Aunt Cat is not to be put off. She has something to say, and it appears she is going to say it.

"Don't sit there, Vaire, Victoria, my very own and very first daughter, and tell me you did not see that thing."

"Now, Mother, if a big wild dog came leaping in . . ." Walter was saying, but he was being ignored.

"I saw it, Mother, but I can't remember it exactly. You know that man had my arm twisted up and then he was jumping around waving the knife and screaming, and I thought he was going to kill me."

"When that thing stood up in the back doorway over your father's body," her voice rising now, "and looked right at us." And she stopped for emphasis and to take another drink. "With Martin's harmonica in its teeth!"

I am listening so closely now that I am almost not breathing. Perhaps I have underestimated the human capacity to accept the strange.

I hear Walter's chair scraping back, Vaire getting up also. The older woman making sounds of moving around. They are all standing now.

"You saw it, Vaire!" She is almost screaming. "There was no little boy near that thing, no Little Robert near it, and it had poor Martin's harmonica in its mouth, that he played that very morning while I made breakfast." She stops and sobs, but angrily, and then says, still weeping, "Vaire, did you *see* it? Say. Did you see it standing in the back door? Those big unnatural eyes, those jaws?"

"Yes, Mother," Vaire says very softly.

"You've got good eyes, Victoria. You saw it." I can hear from her slurred words now she is drunk.

73

She keeps sobbing while she says again, louder, "You saw it." There is a pause and then suddenly she seems to turn on the two young people.

"What was it wearing?"

"What, Mother?" Vaire asks, her voice full of fright. Walter comes in with the same question. "Wearing?" he says.

"It was wearing Little Robert's nightshirt!" she screams, and the words make my fur erect suddenly in that hot August night as if a blast of snow from the north woods had engulfed me.

"Oh my heavens. Oh, Mother," Vaire is saying.

"I'm going to get Doctor Fleishman," Walter says. "Mother, sit down." Walter is being stern.

"Are you afraid to say it, Victoria?" Mrs. Nordmeyer asks. "Are you afraid to say what that Rustum person said, that it was a fiend from hell?" She is screaming loudly now. "Well it was. It was. A fiend from hell, and it killed my husband."

I am standing near the window now, listening to everything: Walter is starting the car in the driveway; Mrs. Nordmeyer has apparently fallen to the floor, and Vaire is getting something in the kitchen. I extend my unused senses: Anne is asleep. There is no one on the street where Walter's car is swinging its headlights away toward the corner where the streetlight is hidden by maple trees. No one is approaching.

"Mother, Walter's gone to get the doctor. Put this under your head, and here's a cold cloth for your face."

The older woman's voice is so soft her daughter must have trouble hearing it: "What can it be, Vaire?" she is whispering. "What can it be?" She rolls her head on the pillow. I can almost feel her eyes burning holes in the floor where I crouch. She is whispering again.

"It's up there, you know. Up there with Anne, up there in your house, living with you, the devil, the fiend from hell."

"Mother, please. You've got me so upset." Vaire is

74

crying too now. "But you can't say that about a little child no older than Anne. It can't be such a thing, Mother." And she is weeping openly now.

"What does it want?" the older woman goes on whispering in so eerie a way that my fur prickles again. She is frightening *me.*

"Mother, please stop," Vaire is wailing now. "You're scaring me."

I wait for Vaire to come up the stairs, but she does not come. She is apparently torn between her mother and her child, and the fear is overbalancing her to stay downstairs until her husband returns. I hear no more words from the older woman, only mumbling as her mind fades out. In a few more minutes the car returns with the doctor, and there is a roomful of masculine solidity and heartiness to replace the wavering fear that had infected us all. By the time anyone comes to check Robert, he is in his bed asleep, sweat on his head from the hot August night, his nightshirt rucked up around his stomach.

Little Robert is an enigma to me now. He knows of the superstitious feeling of dread he evokes from Aunt Cat, and the often poorly concealed nervousness shown by his beloved Vaire. He is really only comfortable with Anne and other children who have no unconscious fears to make of him a sort of freak. But he does not want to leave the family, and I am reluctant to force him away, although I am sure I could do that if it were necessary for survival. It is strange to think about his getting stronger each day in his own personality, harder to reason with, harder to subdue if he does not want me to shift out for an evening's run in the dark fields. I wonder if I have created a monster, and the thought makes me smile into the terrified eyes of the rabbit I have just caught and am about to eat. The rabbit has not been much fun to catch, being a cross with the tame ones the people in the town raise for food. It is large, brown, and fat, with a wattle of fat under its neck, very unlike the lean, fast cottontails I would catch in Martin's hedge rows and creek banks. But it tastes very good, almost sweet like chicken or lamb. My tastes are becoming more fastidious also, I find, spitting out chunks of hide and fur. I no longer enjoy bolting small animals whole but find myself picking them apart for the good bits and wasting much of them. Perhaps I too am becoming civilized and will soon be eating Red Heart dog food in three delicious flavors out of a can.

But the warm summer nights retain their full, sensuous charm as I lope through the pastures and newly cut grain fields outside of town. I sense the sleeping cows under the dark umbrella of a maple tree in the corner of a pasture, and the muskrats are lying in the mouths of their tunnels in the creek banks, sniffing for crawdads and minnows; the cats are out, their eyes shining like lanterns as late automobiles pass on the streets and country lanes. The crickets and frogs make angular sounds along every ditch and stand of weeds. The earth is good to my feet as I pace quietly, feeling very much a part of life and breathing in scents of the crawling, hopping, running life of the night, the hungers appeased so easily in the summer nights, the animal feeling of fullness and happiness that forgets the freezing winter and the stupid torpor of a burrow under the snow with the stomach slowly shrinking in on itself and the cold making the heart slow and the brain numb and without even dreams.

I look up at the sliver of moon that barely makes shadows in the darkness. There is something else, something that has been growing and making my mind seem to itch strangely. I feel it sometimes even when I am trailing a fox and get a whiff of her musk. Robert feels it watching his beloved Vaire. It is like wanting to kill and eat luxuriously but without hurting the animal I am killing and eating. Indeed, it is a paradoxical feeling I have not had before, and can only attribute to Robert's growing strength as a personality, something humans experience that is spilling over into my own life. It is something then that I must deal with, for it seems now that I am committed to existence with the human. They are strange, terrible, suffering creatures, but I am one of them now that Robert has come into being. This feeling can be savored like any other sensation, and so I am content with it, even though it is an irritation. Any sensation, even pain, is to be experienced and is better than no sensation at all.

(5)

Willie Duchamps knew not to walk directly up to the Woodsons' porch. He had been shouted at several times by both Vaire and Walter for his meaningless cruelties and pranks. He had tied cats' tails together, put a firecracker under a dog's collar, told Anne some words with which she had innocently horrified her mother's friends, and worst of all from Walter's viewpoint, had in a random fit of rage chopped the Woodson garden hose into thirty-eight nearly equal pieces with Walter's own hatchet. Surveying his front yard full of what looked like red macaroni one Sunday morning, Walter had stomped back into the living room and said, "The Duchamps boy does not ever set foot on this property again."

The problem was made nearly insoluble by Willie's father, who, it was rumored, was a whoremaster besides being a late-shift bartender at the George Washington Tavern in downtown Cassius. He had the look of a shaved gorilla, when he shaved, and had got rid of his long suffering wife by beating her so badly that she was forbidden by the court to return to him and left forever to live somewhere in Colorado with her widowed sister. Bart Duchamps was not a neighbor one approached angrily or holding Bart's rascal boy by the scruff of the neck and uttering threats. Bart often beat Willie until he could not stand up or go to school for days, but he would, so he claimed, kill anyone who harmed a hair of his boy's head. All of this was neighborhood gossip and easily picked up from any of the many children in the two- or three-block area of the outlying district of Cassius the Woodsons lived in. Willie was nine and too old for either Anne or Robert to play with anyway, Vaire would say, and she had no idea why he hung around instead of playing with boys his own age.

It seemed pretty obvious to Anne that the reason he hung around was that he liked to bully and play tricks on the littler ones, and besides, she said to Robert as they sat in the porch swing and watched Willie throwing rocks at a cat he had trapped under his front porch, Shirley was his girlfriend. Shirley was a skinny black-haired girl of about six or so who lived two houses up the street from the Woodsons. She had no real mother or father, Anne told Robert, but lived with her grandmother and a middle-aged couple who said they were her aunt and uncle but who were not at home much. Anne made a lot of the fact that Shirley was almost a year older than she and yet was not in school and would not begin until fall when Anne did. She was sickly with some sort of recurrent weakness that put her in bed for a week at a time, and in Anne's opinion was not as smart as she seemed to think she was. Shirley was Willie's special friend, which meant she not only shared in the interesting games a resourceful nine-year-old could think up but also received second hand the overflow of the beatings he got from his father. She was a surly child with a pale face and dark circled eyes that most often looked at the world with ready rejection, since she had experienced more of that response herself, evidently, than any other. Her grandmother was of some foreign extraction and looked a lot like the witch in Anne's Hansel and Gretel book with drooping nose and hairy moles distributed in unlikely places on her face. She was not an unkind woman, Robert thought after she had given him half an apple one afternoon, but she did look terribly witchy in that black dress and with her gray hair hanging down like moss around her face.

Willie had spotted Robert immediately as a prime mark, as he was almost wholly innocent, small for his

79

age, pliable and gullible enough to believe the wildest tale Willie could think up. The fact was, Robert was intensely curious about Willie, for he had had no experience of such gratuitous meanness and found it both exciting and repulsive. After a chat over the back fence one morning, Robert managed to slip away from Anne and walked down the alley with Willie and Shirley to the river bank where the old storm drain emptied into the channel. Some ways back in the storm drain, which was over six feet square at the opening, they had a secret hideout. A large chunk of masonry had fallen out of the wall forming a cave that had obviously been used by tramps now and then. Willie had found a blanket for the floor and some candles, and he and Shirley had set up housekeeping in the musty but properly secret hideway. As for Robert, he found the situation so different, dirty, and forbidden that he instantly adopted Willie as his leader.

The three of them sat in the dark burrow off the storm drain eating an orange Willie had stolen from Capp's fruit stand. Robert could have brought some from the Woodsons', but it was more like bandits this way.

"Don't eat the white part," Shirley said in her squeaky voice. "G'ma says it'll give you worms."

"That's crap, Shirley." Willie said, tearing off a big piece of the white and eating it. "It's raw p'taters that gives you worms. Any dummy knows that." He split off a section and handed it to Robert who sat on the concrete edge of the cave opening. "Here, Robert, you're part of our gang now."

"Thank you," Robert said, taking the orange slice. "It's a great cave you got here. We can play robbers and nobody can ever find us."

"We do more than playin' robbers, don't we, Shirley?" Willie said, finishing the orange and rubbing his mouth on his sleeve. Shirley giggled and rolled her little dark eyes up so the whites showed, nodding her head so her black hair that looked like it needed washing flopped over her forehead. Robert hadn't the slightest idea what they were talking about.

"Do you want to be part of our gang and never tell anybody, not even your dad and ma, where the hideout is and what we do?" Willie said, holding Robert by his shoulders and looking into his eyes.

Robert looked back into the greenish dark eyes in Willie's narrow face and nodded his head. "You got to swear on the bones of your ancestors," Willie said, digging his fingers into Robert's shoulders so that it hurt.

"Ow. I swear, I mean how do you swear?"

"You just did. You just say, 'I swear.' "

"I swear. And you're hurting me, Willie."

"Okay. It's just a little hurt so you'll remember that anybody in the gang who tells any of our secrets get hurt real bad."

"I won't tell."

"Okay. Now you're part of the gang. But we got to do the initiating stuff to make you a member." He began unbuttoning Robert's shirt.

"Do you have to take your clothes off?" Robert asked.

"Yeah, we got to do a doctor's examination to make sure you're okay."

Willie helped Robert take off his shirt, pants, and underpants. They were always barefoot, so this left Robert naked, sitting on the blanket in the cave.

"Now lie down here so we can examine you," Willie said.

Robert lay down on the blanket and Shirley squatted down to watch as Willie began to poke various parts of Robert's body with his forefinger. Robert was interested, ticklish, and excited by this process, and it brought me to awareness also as his excitement mounted. Willie tickled and rubbed, talking all the time in a doctorish way as if he were checking things out. After a bit, Shirley, who was being his nurse, joined in by taking his pulse and looking in Robert's mouth so she could count his teeth.

"Now that you're all examined," Willie said, standing up and shucking off his clothes, "we'll do the sandwich game."

Shirley also undressed and Willie directed them so that he and Shirley faced each other and Robert stood behind Shirley facing her back. Then they all clutched each other and began a silly, laughing little dance, hugging each other and jumping up and down and squealing. After a bit they did it lying on the blanket, rolling over each other and tickling and slapping each other with loud smacks. They kept it up until all three were red-faced and panting and hardly able to move. All lay on the blanket in the now sweltering cave, breathing hard and looking at the scratches they had picked up in the struggle. Robert thought he had never done anything that was so much fun, and he lay on the blanket looking up at the clay ceiling blackened with the smoke of many candles and thought it was the best time ever in his life, he felt so good and relaxed, like a little pond of water that has come through a giant storm with white caps and whirlpools and now was relaxing out into little ripples that spread slowly into the evening surface until it was all smooth again and calm. I had been aware of the process, since Robert's excitement brought me to the surface for a time, and although I enjoyed the sensations, the game seemed peculiarly pointless, so I thought no more about it.

Robert did indeed feel like one of the gang now, but the good times in the cave took their place in his daily life as another new thing to do, another bit of wonder to be explored along with hikes with Willie to the bluff to drop stones on the tops of cars as they sped by beneath, or chasing the farmer's cows with Willie and Shirley and laughing at their stampeding with tails in the air and udders banging between their hind legs, or having an intricate game of hop-scotch with Anne and Shirley on the walk in front of the house. But the cave and the gang and the sandwich game did become something of a shadow side in Robert's life, as he began to realize that the reason he had not told Anne about it was that she was closer to the adult world, that she was intimate with her mother and father, and that the cave and the gang and their games were not things you told adults about, since they would probably find it dangerous and in some adult way would make it impossible. It formed a bond between the three that seemed for a time unbreakable and unshareable. Willie would tell them about making babies sometimes out of his wealth of knowledge gained from being with his father nights in the bar.

"You have to get some white pee called chissom from a man and some from a woman," he said one time as they lay in the dark cave. "And you take and put it in a corn shuck so it mixes together, and then you wrap up the shuck and put it in a dark place, like under the porch, and after a long time a baby grows out of it."

"Out of the corn shuck?" Robert asked, his eyes wide.

"Yep."

This never failed to make Shirley vaguely angry, since she thought there was more to it than that. She had seen her aunt with a big stomach before her little cousin was born, but she would not dispute with Willie. He was bigger and meaner than she was, and anyway, she didn't really care at the moment because the faintness in her stomach was hurting her again.

Robert, on the other hand, spent several times at the toilet in the Woodson house watching his urine to see if it was white. He thought it would be interesting to have a baby if he could catch some of his white pee in a corn shuck sometime. But here again, he was not interested enough to pursue the game very far. It was intriguing at the moment, but there were so many other things to do and think about that he could not often be bothered trying to make a baby.

The gang would probably have continued their fun through the end of summer if an accident of Shirley's health had not removed her from the gang. Robert learned one morning at breakfast that the little Stillings girl had been taken to the hospital and that they thought she had a liver condition. Robert did not grasp the significance of this until several days had passed and he and Willie had not visited the hideout. To his questions, Willie was vicious, cuffing him hard on the ear and calling him "queer" for suggesting they go and do the sandwich game by themselves. Robert was more emotionally wounded than physically, for he was used to Willie's rages and unmotivated blows.

"But I like to do it, Willie," Robert said, his ear burning red.

"We can't do it without a girl, stupid."

Robert thought about that and slipped away to look for Anne. There was more than one girl in the world, he was thinking, and it would be twice as much fun with Anne because she was nicer than Shirley, and he liked her more. He ran about the neighborhood until he found her riding her tricycle in front of the house. Breathlessly he told her that he knew a game that was more fun than anything they ever did, and he would show her how to play it, and Willie would too if she wanted him to play. Anne said she hated Willie because he was mean, but she would play a game with Robert if it didn't get her dress dirty. He said it certainly would not, but didn't mention the fact that they would have to take their clothes off, since that detail didn't seem important. They decided to do the game in the garage with the doors shut. Robert did his best to show Anne how the game went, but it was not the same. The garage was not close and secret as the cave was, the ceiling was too high, so they seemed to be at the bottom of a well instead of inside a cozy place, and he wanted to do it, but it didn't feel right. Anne did not object to taking her clothes off, but she thought the rest of it was kind of silly. She liked the tickling and running around the garage naked, but then she wanted to put her clothes back on and go in for lunch. Robert decided it was not the right place to play the game and that he would have to take her to the cave hideout and make her a part of the gang.

August waned in heat. The nights were sultry after the usual late afternoon thunderstorms, and then would come the baking afternoons that broke records all over the midwest. In the hot nights I sulk about, seldom hunting, although the game is torpid with heat and easy to catch, my mind seemingly preoccupied with internal processes, uncomfortable longings that I cannot identify and have never felt before. I spend some nights idiotically lying full length in the river shallows, content just to lie and let the water run over my body, smoothing my pelt into fine bronze runnels of fur in the moonlight. One night I actually catch fish that way, lying in the shallows of the river with my ears submerged listening for the delicate swish of fins as they search the bottom for food. I grab three that night, two of them only carp, but good enough for a few choice bites.

This night, waiting for the Woodsons to retire so I can slip out again, I hear something of that catastrophic morning a month and a half ago and perk up my hearing.

"They sentenced that Prokoff fellow to thirty years," Walter says around the stem of his pipe.

"Just a boy," Vaire says, sounding preoccupied.

"That guy Rustum will never walk again, it says. He's going to have to wear a brace, like the President," Walter says and chuckles.

There is no answer from Vaire, so he goes on. "The old man died last week, it says, and that big fellow, Hamner, they found out he had a family right near here, over in Grand Valley somewhere, wife and four kids."

"Walter." Vaire sounds as if she is about to cry.

"What? Oh, I'm sorry, dear." Walter has taken the pipe out and now sounds more normal. "That's stupid of me. I don't know what I was thinking of. Not thinking at all, I guess."

"Oh it's not that. It's Mother."

"Drinking?"

"Yes, that too. But mostly that strange person she's been seeing in Grand Rapids. I'm afraid she's going to get cheated some way or lose the farm or something. There are so many cheats and swindlers around. You read about them every day, that one in Chicago that took everybody's money."

"Sam Insull?"

"Yes, like him."

"What sort of person? First I'd heard about her

85

consulting someone." Walter sounded stiff. "I had always thought if she needed advice, I could help. After all, in my line of business I . . ."

"It's not that kind of person, Walter. It's, well, he's, he seems to be some kind of . . ."

"Oh what, for heaven's sake, Vaire?" Walter sounded irritated.

"A medium."

"A what? A medium? A medium what?" Now he was laughing.

"It's not a joke." Vaire's voice had a dangerous edge to it.

"Now dear, I'm not making a joke, but what do you mean?"

"A medium! A spiritual medium. A person who talks with dead people."

"Oh no."

"Well she's *not* crazy. She loved Dad very much, and it was all so, so unexpected and useless and wrong, and she's just gone off the deep end for awhile, but she's not crazy, and Walter, I won't have you thinking she is. She's my mother and she's the finest woman in the world, and . . ." Vaire is crying now and Walter has rustled his paper, put it down beside his chair. He is making scraping noises, his pipe.

"I didn't say she was crazy, dear. I suspect she will get cheated, since there are no such things as spirits that people can contact, and all that sort of thing. Of course it makes her feel better and helps ease the transition."

"Walter!" Vaire is standing up. I can tell by the closeness of her voice. "Damn it, Walter! Damn it! Damn it! Damn it!"

"Vaire! What in the world?" Now he is standing.

"Transition to what? She's not transitioning to anything! Her life is broken up, Walter, can't you understand how terribly this has changed her?"

"Now wait a minute," Walter begins.

"No I won't." Vaire is moving back and forth below me. "All I want to know is, will you help me get her away from a person I think is going to cheat her? That's all I want to know." I have not heard Vaire who is usually so calm and sweet talk so violently before. Walter is obviously shocked. Pause.

"Yes, of course I will, sweetheart. Of course I will."

There is silence below me as they embrace. Then they both sit down again.

"She's going to a medium to get in touch with your father?"

"Oh I don't know, really. She goes to see him a couple of times a week and tells me she feels so much better afterwards and that he's going to show everything in its true reality. I don't know what she means by that, but I'm afraid for Little Robert."

Listening to this, I wonder what a medium can be, what it can do.

"For Robert?" Walter has apparently forgotten the episode of a couple of weeks ago when his mother-in-law was drunk and accused the boy of being a demon. I begin to think about that.

"Walter, I do want to help mother, but I don't know how to handle it. What can we do?"

Walter's voice takes on an authoritative edge. "Well, we need to meet this person, to make some estimate of his character and his motive before we try to take any action. Then perhaps even legal action would be in order."

The rest of the conversation does not interest me, and I content myself later that night with a long cool swim across the river to tip over a late fisherman in the muddy shallows. I have not been much for tricks up to this time, but I feel this itchiness inside that seems to have no outlet, and it makes me do strange things. I find myself chuckling, lying on my back in the water, dark and invisible as an otter in midstream, listening to the curses and splashings of the fisherman as he wades ashore towing his boat. But then it may have been simple revenge, since the fisherman was running a nightline that I ran afoul of some time back, catching one of the hooks in my right hind foot. I do feel good watching and listening to him weltering in the dark water. The last thing I think before shifting back up in Robert's bedroom is that it is the boy's affair, not mine, and that distinction seems a new one also.

Trading Anne for Shirley turned out to be more complicated than Robert had thought it would be. Anne liked playing doctor with him in the garage, but it never got to be as much fun as the three gang members playing sandwich in the hideout, and Robert wanted that again. The trouble was that Anne hated Willie, and Willie was forbidden to come into the Woodsons' yard. Willie would not go to the hideout without Shirley, and he became increasingly vicious when she did not return from the hospital by the end of the week. Robert felt there must be some way to convince Anne that gang life was fun, that Willie was really an exciting person, and that it was worthwhile to have some secrets from one's family, since Anne was notorious even among other tattle-tales for telling her mother everything that happened. Finally it happened the day of the big hail.

Robert, in the relative security of his male sex, was allowed to play with Willie, even though Anne was not. He was at Willie's house right after lunch time playing with Willie in his large unkempt sandbox in the back yard, the house being too sweltering hot to enter, although Willie's father was sprawled in there somewhere asleep. He worked nights and slept most of the day until mid afternoon. Robert kept bringing up the subject:

"Why *can't* Anne be one of the gang?"

"She's a tattle, that's why."

"She won't if we swear her not to, I bet."

"She tells her ma everything."

"I bet she won't this time because she does things for me, and I'll ask her not to."

Willie thought about it for a moment. Apparently Shirley was in the hospital for a long stay, and the hideout was going to waste. School would be starting in two weeks. Two weeks! "Well, I don't know. She don't like me, and I don't like her neither."

The boys hardly noticed how dark it was getting

88

until Willie looked up and said, "Geezus, look at that black cloud."

Robert looked up at the huge thunderhead, purple-black on the underside, moving silently over them so that the sun had been blocked out and now the whole sky was being overspread with the black-purple pall. The wind had stopped so that every leaf and grass blade held perfectly still as if the transparent summer air had quietly and completely solidified into glass. Robert felt the stillness in his throat and for a moment he held his breath. There would be a big storm, and he felt goosepimples at the thought, since he had only recently begun to appreciate the awesomeness of nature and liked to watch the lightning and be scared by the thunder. Far off came the deep, husky rumble of the approaching storm.

"It's going to be a big rain, isn't it?" said Robert.

"Hey, you little farts get on in the house," Mr. Duchamps called from the back porch. "Goin' to rain like a cow pissin' on a flat rock here pretty quick."

Willie and Robert dawdled until the first huge drops came splatting down like little bombs, smacking into the sand like birdshot. The boys squealed and ducked as if rocks were being thrown at them. Then the wind hit, bending the trees over as if they had all been suddenly knocked to their knees, and the rain crashed down like a waterfall. They were both screaming, giggling wet before they could get across the back yard.

"Getcher asses in here," Mr. Duchamps hollered from the porch.

They made it to the porch wetter than if they had both been dumped into the river, and Mr. Duchamps agreed they couldn't get any wetter and let them play in the rain like a couple of skinny little satyrs, their clothes and hair plastered to them so they looked like stick figures prancing in the gray sheets of rain. Then it began to get cold all of a sudden and they ran for the house. It was like ice suddenly, and the hot air trapped inside the house was turning to steam as it flowed outward into the cooling rain. The ground, the sidewalks, the streets, automobiles, everything steamed as if the world were smoldering as the rain turned cold and hit the overheated August land. The rain began to slack back, and as yet there had not been much lightning or thunder, but now it began with a close hit: CRACK-BAMMM! and continued in a cannonade. The lightning flashed like a battery of 105's on the Duchamp's roof firing at will, the thundercrashes overlapping so you could not tell which flash went with which boom. It was deafening. The boys kept pretending to talk to each other, working their mouths in imitation speech while the barrage of sound blocked out everything. The rain and wind increased so that they fell silent, looking out across the humped tar street swept again and again by heavy sheets of rain. Mr. Duchamps continued to drink his breakfast beer and gaze out placidly at the storm. As the rain slacked again, and the thunder began to recede, the crashes further apart, Robert drew in a deep breath as if he had been living on sips of air for the past few minutes. The storm had been exciting, and he was sorry it was about over. The steam was disappearing as the land grew cooler, and it seemed to be getting lighter outside. At that point the paper boy rode by, tossing the afternoon paper into the grass beside the walk. Mr. Duchamps cursed and drained the can of beer.

"Little shit," he said. "Throw it in the wet grass." He opened the screen and clumped heavily down off the front porch and into the wet front yard. And it was as if the rain gods had been waiting for Bart Duchamps to get out from under his roof, waiting for his lumpy bald head and heavy round shoulders to appear in his front yard, flanked by protecting elm trees but open to the sky directly overhead, waiting and being deceptive about the storm being over. Mr. Duchamps had just bent over with great effort to pick up the folded paper from the wet grass when a great booming rattling crashing sound began so suddenly that both boys jumped as if they had been burned. It was not thunder, and for a second they could not believe ears or eyes, as what appeared to be baseballs came flying down through the air, hitting the house, smashing into the tops of cars parked at the curb, splitting off branches from the trees, making a mad dance of bouncing, splitting ice balls in the street and on the sidewalks, driving dogs under porches, people screaming into any shelter, booming on roofs, and on the other side of town destroying every pane of glass in three long greenhouses and every plant inside of them.

Out in the mad, bouncing, careening flurry of ice chunks, Mr. Duchamps lay full length, full width in his front yard, the prey of the worst hail storm in the history of that area since there had been a history. The first ice ball had been right over the plate, hitting Mr. Duchamps directly on the crown of his head, knocking him senseless and flat on top of the paper he had gone out to pick up. The rest of the brief flurry of huge hail had pummeled his body and head, even ankles, as he would find out when he awoke with bruises everywhere, but did no more damage than that first pitch.

When they had recovered their wits, the boys found the hailstorm over, the ground covered with unseasonable ice that was even now melting from record size to less than golf ball dimensions. Willie and Robert ran into the yard to the prone Duchamps who had a bloody laceration on the top of his head and several lesser scratches visible on his baldness.

"Dad! Dad!" Willie screamed, as if his father were the best parent in the world.

The skinny older boy knelt by his father just as the man regained consciousness and got to hands and knees. The heavy man shook his head, shaking blood on Willie's face as the boy tried to help his father to his feet.

"Oh, God," the elder Duchamps said, rolling to a sitting position and feeling around on his head tenderly. "What the hell?" He looked up at the sky, down at the scatter of melting hail amid which he sat like an old sea lion on a deserted rocky beach.

"Dad, are you okay?" Willie said, wiping his father's blood from his face.

"What d'ya think? Hell yes," said Duchamps, heaving himself up to his feet. "Get off yer knees, you dumb shit."

Willie got up, not yet restored to his usual sanity. "I saw you get clonked and I thought you was dead," he said, about to cry.

Robert was standing a few feet behind Willie, but when Mr. Duchamps slapped Willie in the face, Robert felt as if the huge hand had hit his own face. The smacking sound carried out into the street, as an auto accident is heard by a whole block of houses. Willie went down in the melting hail, put his arms over his head and curled up his body. He had found reality again very quickly.

Duchamps staggered back into the house, muttering about the boy wishing he was dead, and that he would teach his son better. Across the street a woman standing behind a porch trellis screamed at the departing figure, "Duchamps, God will punish you, you rotten terrible thing," and she would have gone on if an arm had not emerged from her front door and drawn her back to silence.

Robert stood beside Willie's curled up form until it uncurled and got to its feet. The large ruddy mark of the father's hand covered the left cheek giving Willie a birthmarked appearance. He squinted up his left eye in pain and then smeared the tears away with a quick wipe.

"I'll meet you at the hideout if you bring Anne," Willie said out of his squinted up face. "And if you don't bring her, you're not part of the gang anymore."

"Aw, Willie," Robert began. But he stopped as Willie turned to walk around to the back of his house. He felt now the whole thing was broken, but he didn't know. Maybe it would be all right. He would talk Anne into doing it, and she would like the game, and Willie would have a good time, and it would all be right again. He turned and ran out of the yard, sliding in the almost melted hail, and ran for home.

But it wasn't all right. Anne had been reluctant, but she liked Robert more than even he supposed, and she went with him, marveling at the old storm drain that was still running knee deep that afternoon with the runoff from the cloudburst. They walked barefooted into the darkness of the drain, listening to the hollow splashing of little waterfalls back in the blackness where the drain tiles and storm sewers from all over town emptied into the main tunnel. Anne was frightened and held to Robert's shirt with both hands, making it twice as hard to get to the cave, but also giving the little boy his first taste of being a leader and protector. He liked it. When they arrived at the broken out place, they saw candles burning. Willie had got there before them and had set up four candles, one at each corner of the little cave. Robert thought he had never seen it look so cosy and secret, although the storm had raised all sorts of decay and old rotting things from the drains, and the smell in the tunnel was rank enough to turn an adult stomach.

"Here it is. See, Willie's got candles," Robert said, helping Anne with a boost to climb up over the broken places into the cave.

Willie looked sourly at both of the smaller children, his face dark purple under the left eye. "You can't tell anybody about our hideout," he said harshly to Anne, "or a terrible thing will happen to you."

Anne looked at the larger boy with fearful eyes, but she was not going to be cowed. "I promised Robert I wouldn't tell as long as you act nice."

"See," Robert said excitedly, "this is our gang hideout, and we make raids and steal from the rich so we can have it in our cave." And he went on telling how they would be outlaws like on the radio until Willie stopped him.

"Time for the initiating," he said.

But this time it was not the same. They took off their clothes and examined Anne much as they had Robert, but Robert felt that Willie was being more rough than he had to, and a couple of times he pinched instead of tickling so so that Anne got tears in her eyes, but she held her lips tight and did not say anything. Then she got to laughing, and Robert thought it would be all right again. But when he wanted to sandwich game and

93

dance as they had before, Willie seemed reluctant. He wanted to lie down first. Finally Robert got his way, and they sandwiched and danced, hugging each other and laughing and slapping and tickling until one very hard slap caught Robert squarely in the nose and made stars go off in his eyes. He felt gone for a moment and sat down on the floor. Willie, who had hit him, stepped back from the game, and Anne turned to look at him in horror.

"Oh, Robert," she said. "You're bleeding a lot."

Robert put his hand to his stinging nose and drew it away with a large streak of blood. He looked at it in disbelief. It felt bad, but it didn't feel *that* bad. It looked as if in a few minutes he would run out of blood if it kept coming out like that. Willie handed him a rag from the floor and told him to sit down a minute while they finished the game. Robert sat and watched, holding the dirty bit of blanket over his nose and snuffing up great quantities of blood which he partly spat out, partly swallowed.

Anne was more concerned with Robert than she was with finishing the game, but Willie was holding on to her tightly and doing something she didn't like. He panted a lot and kept doing it, holding her down while she wiggled, and Robert was just going to say, "Don't," when Anne screamed as if she had been stabbed. Willie drew back quickly and got his clothes in his hand.

"You're not part of the gang, you little bitch," he snarled, and stepping into his pants, he stuffed his shirt in his back pocket and leaped out of the cave into the drain water.

Anne was crying and holding her legs together. Robert waited until she stopped to look at herself, between her legs, and he looked too.

"Hey, Anne," Robert said in awe. "You're bleeding too."

Anne looked at herself and then began to gather up her clothes. She stopped crying, but her lips were thin with pain, and her face was white. Robert's nose had stopped bleeding but two large clots and smears made his face look much worse than it was. Anne got her clothes on, and her white pants showed a blood mark when they looked later, but then it stopped bleeding before they got home.

They were walking down the alley toward their backyard when Robert thought about the "swearing" they had done.

"I don't like Willie anymore," Robert said. "And he hurt both of us, so I don't think the swearing counts now."

"I'm not going to tell," Anne said.

"It's all right," Robert said as they paused at the gate. "But I'm sorry anyway, and if you want to tell, it's all right."

Robert felt downcast, and his nose hurt, and he looked at Anne, wondering if between her legs felt like his nose. He felt at that moment that he wanted to be as big as Willie because he wanted to hit Willie, hard.

Perhaps if it had been a different night that Mr. Sangrom had come with Aunt Cat to visit, Vaire would have noticed the bloody little white pants at once. As it was, the family had been engaged in a tight discussion that had everyone on edge, Walter having come home from work early on that Friday, Vaire and her mother looking at each other from distances they had not known before, and the suave, undertakerish Mr. Sangrom in the midst of it all with his fixed, thin smile and his narrow dark eyes and the black smooth hair that Robert thought looked like a polished car fender. The situation was such that Anne and Robert were told to go upstairs immediately and get washed and dressed in clean clothes. Robert's nose was given a perfunctory look by Walter who pronounced it nothing more than a boyish accident, after which he gave it a tweak that made Robert wince.

Having dinner with a spiritualistic medium, as Mr. Sangrom called himself, was not Walter's idea of an enjoyable evening. The man seemed to have nothing to his face but that damnable smile, and he obviously had insinuated himself into Mrs. Nordmeyer's good opinion by some sort of chicanery. Such things always made Walter clench his teeth, for he could not abide

95

people who tried to do business with spirits and ghosts and all that jiggery-pokery. Mr. Sangrom seemed quite comfortable, but his eyes would move often to fix on Little Robert who sat across the table and ate what he could with his nose hurting every time he chewed. He noticed the adults seemed more than usually interested in him that night. Aunt Cat and the stranger especially looked at him when they didn't think he saw them. It began to make him uncomfortable so that before the others were finished, he asked to be excused. Walter excused him and said almost as if it didn't really matter, "Stay around after supper, kids."

Vaire served coffee after the children had gone upstairs to play in Anne's room, and it seemed as if they had been waiting for the coffee to begin the real business of the evening.

"You have to know, Mr. Sangrom," said Walter stiffly, "that I don't believe in your work, and I don't particularly like what you are proposing to do with the child."

"Mr. Woodson, if everyone believed in what I do," Mr. Sangrom said sadly, "this world would be a paradise." And he dropped his gaze to his coffee. "A paradise," he repeated in a lower tone.

"Did you feel anything during supper?" Aunt Cat said.

"It is difficult with so many contradictory vibrations at the same table," the medium said in a low voice. "But I detected certain emanations, and once I saw a strange glow in the little boy's aura that was not a natural one. Yes, Mrs. N., I think I can say that this will be a fruitful experiment."

Walter turned away in disgust, lifting his eyebrows at his wife.

"Mr. Sangrom," Vaire began in a nervous voice, "just what is it you are planning to do in your experiment? We really can't allow the little boy to be frightened to death because of some, well . . ." She looked at her mother in embarrassment.

"Vaire, you can't insult me this evening," Mrs. Nordmeyer said. "Tonight we're going to see the proof of what I know is true." Her long, homely face was thinner than her daughter had ever seen it, and her lips did not smile at all, although they turned up at the corners. It was as if her mother had renounced the living, Vaire thought, feeling a chill in the hot, humid August twilight.

"There is no danger to the child," Mr. Sangrom said with his fixed smile. "I am only proposing that Mrs. N. and I be allowed to ask him a few questions about the terrible incident that culminated in Mr. Nordmeyer's murder."

"I think Walter and I should be here," Vaire began.

"Of course, Mrs. Woodson," said Mr. Sangrom. "Your presence is essential. After all, it is your skepticism we are seeking to allay."

Vaire felt relieved, but thought that if he got to calling her Mrs. W., she would throw a coffee cup at him. She looked at Walter who was being stern and realistic and thought that at least none of this had touched his calm strength, but then he had not seen . . . anything. And she felt her reserves of strength and love for Little Robert melting away.

It was around eight, the children's bedtime, when Mr. Sangrom stood up and announced that he was ready to begin the questioning. After putting Anne to bed hastily, Vaire brought Robert downstairs in his nightshirt and asked him to sit at the table with Aunt Cat and Mr. Sangrom. Robert said hello to Aunt Cat and looked at the thin dark haired man with the smile printed on his face who got up as he entered and moved to the other side of the table so that he faced the boy directly.

"If you will turn off the overhead lights, Mr. Woodson," Sangrom said softly, watching Robert as if he might disappear. "We will have just the one light, that one on the sideboard, if you please," he said, indicating an ornamental lamp behind him so that from Robert's point of view the only light in the room was behind Mr. Sangrom's head.

"Now, young man," the dark man said in a thin but kindly voice, "you mustn't be afraid, for we are only

97

going to ask some questions about the day the bad men came to your house."

Robert sat on top of the big medical encyclopedia which made him feel tall, his eyes widening in the dimness of the dining room. Yes, he could bring back very clearly that day in the farm dining room when he had sat at the table and waited while the men were mean to the family, and waited for what he was not sure, but waiting all the same. He looked across at the face of the black haired man whose smile did not change and whose upper lip remained stiff when he talked. This man seemed dangerous too, but not in the same way, so that the scene began to seem mysterious, interesting, like an adventure. Robert almost smiled as he thought that, and the familiar thrill of goosepimples raised up on his skin. No one could hurt him with Vaire and Aunt Cat and Walter there, so it was going to be all right.

"That's fine, Robert," Mr. Sangrom said, stretching his arms out so that his two long, white hands rested directly in front of Robert. "I'd like it if you would put your hands on top of mine, Robert," he said. "You see, I am able to feel the magnetic currents in your body, and I will be able to understand your answers better this way."

Robert put his hands on the backs of the long, white fleshed hands that rested before him like plaster casts. They felt soft and wrinkledy and cool, like a toad's back. He heard Walter make some sort of coughing sound from his chair in the corner of the room, and looked at the window seat where he could see Vaire's silhouette against the bow windows still gray with twilight. She was sitting sideways with her hands in her lap, and it made Robert feel brave to see her sitting there. He looked at Aunt Cat, but she was in a shadow and was only a tall, angular form like a black paper cutout sitting at the other end of the table.

"Now, Robert," Mr. Sangrom began in a very steady voice that seemed to be speaking only to Robert so that only he could hear it. "You are very comfortable here with your family, and you are safe here, and it is getting late in the evening, so I would not be surprised if you were to get a little bit sleepy sitting here in this dark dining room."

Robert felt that he was a little bit sleepy, even though his nose still hurt and he worried about Anne. He did feel safe here, and he was not afraid of the man with the polished hair, and so he listened to what the man was saying. It seemed to be making him more sleepy all the time, but he wasn't going to sleep really. It was more like he was thinking himself into a dream, maybe letting the words make a dream for him, since that was easier, and then he was really dreaming, but he was still listening to the man's words which seemed to be taking his hands and leading him along somewhere in the dark.

"You remember that morning when it rained, don't you. And you remember coming downstairs that morning and the man that grabbed you and made you sit at the table, don't you, and that there were bad men in the house who were going to hurt your Uncle Martin and Aunt Cat, and then Aunt Vaire was there too and the men were going to hurt her too. You remember it all, don't you. And you didn't like those bad men."

Robert, listening, felt being led back into the farm kitchen, as if he could see the scene again, being grabbed by the chicken faced young man and sitting at the table. Now Vaire was there, holding his hand, and the tramp in the torn coat was making her red in the face, and his blood was pumping hard in all of his body. He wanted something very large and strong and vicious to come and help Vaire because the man was going to hurt her. It was coming, but he was afraid. It was coming and he wouldn't stop it anymore. But if it came, he would not be able to stay, and Martin would be killed. Robert fought the power for a time, watching the red haired man hurting Vaire. And then all motion slowed as he felt his wanting torn in two directions. He would not let the bad man hurt Vaire. But he couldn't let the great power come out because then Uncle Martin would get shot. So it all had to stop. But he couldn't know about that. That didn't happen yet. So it was all right and he couldn't help it anyway. The

99

power pushed against his will to stop everything. A voice said, "That's it. Let it come! Let it come!" And time began to move again. The red haired man pushed Vaire against the table. Things moved faster now, his hesitation gone like a still movie frame lost into the past as the projector started again. Time was moving, and the red haired man was taking Vaire away to hurt her. Someone said, "She needs help! Robert! Help her! Help her!" And now the man is pushing Vaire past his chair. It is really happening. I have to save her. I will bite. . . .

I wake at the shift, feeling disoriented and outside myself as I have never felt before, the room emerging into existence unexpectedly as if I had been wakened from hibernation too soon. Strange people in the room, dangerous people. I cannot be here. I push against the table, where is it? The kitchen of the farmhouse where Rusty, no, the dining room of the Woodson house, who is that dark man with his mouth stretched wide as if he will scream? I push back hard on the chair and forward on the table and think hard, Robert!

Aunt Cat and Vaire screamed in the same key harmonically, the older woman standing up so that her chair smacked backward onto the floor, at the other end of the room Vaire standing at the window seat with her hands over her mouth, Walter knocking his head back against the wall behind his chair and uttering some curse. Now the man with the polished hair pulls his hands out from under something on the table and screams falsetto as the table moves screeching across the polished floor, Robert's chair crashes over with the weight of something much larger than he.

Mr. Sangrom fell as he pulled away from the table, hitting the sideboard hard enough to knock the ornamental lamp off onto the floor where it smashed and the electric filament went out in a blue glare, leaving the room dark.

"Get the lights!"

"Help! Help! Help me," cried an unfamiliar voice from the floor beside the table. Mr. Sangrom was on the floor.

The lights went on as Walter got to the overhead light switch. The dining room flooded starkly with light. The two women stopped screaming. Mr. Sangrom lay tangled on the floor with his chair and the shattered lamp. He was wringing his hands tenderly. The two women stood at opposite ends of the table looking at Little Robert who stared across the table blankly as if still in a dream.

"My hands," Mr. Sangrom said in a pitiful voice, holding his hands up for the women to see. "It has clawed me, the demon has clawed me," he whined.

His hands were bloody with several long, deep scratches on the back of each one. Walter walked to the table. His face looked stunned as he took Mr. Sangrom's hands and looked at them wonderingly.

"Jesus," Walter said stupidly, holding both of Mr. Sangrom's hands as if he and the other man were preparing to dance. "Look at this."

Robert sat down weakly on the floor. He was just waking up. What had happened? I too am dazed, wondering if I shifted or not. I have been asleep, and I have shifted in my sleep? I have never done that, and I think it is impossible, but something has startled me into full awareness while Robert is still present. Robert felt light, as if he could drift away on a breath of air. He stood up, looking at the adults in the room. They were all looking at him with horror on their faces, and the dark haired man was waving his bloody hands at him.

"Now will you believe me?" Aunt Cat said, standing very straight at the end of the table. "Now that you've seen with your own eyes?"

"Look what the demon did to me," Mr. Sangrom wailed, his smile turned upside down, his polished hair in sticky disarray over his forehead. "This is not work for a spiritualist," he said in his high, hurt voice. "You need a wild animal trainer, Frank Buck, a cage." He kept walking back and forth, holding his wounded hands up for everyone to see while Walter turned back and forth mechanically, like a tin target in a shooting gallery.

"Here, Mr. Sangrom," Vaire said, coming back from the kitchen where no one had seen her go. "Wrap your hands in this wet towel. I have some mercurochrome upstairs. I'll get it."

But Mr. Sangrom wrapped his hands and did not want to stay in the house. He walked unsteadily to the front door, making a wide detour around Little Robert who stood beside his fallen chair in his night-shirt which had a long tear down the front.

"No. No, thank you, Mrs. Woodson," Mr. Sangrom said. "I am finished with this case. Mrs. N., I am afraid I am not the one you want. I am a spiritualist and a worker with hypnotism. I am not an exorcist, I am not a dealer with such things as I have seen and felt to-night. I am not accustomed to dealing with such phys-ical, such *awful* things." He continued to stand at the door, aware that Mrs. Nordmeyer's car was his only hope for quick escape, and yet wanting to bolt away from the house as if it were on fire.

Robert was awake now, looking from Aunt Cat to Vaire to the discouraged Mr. Sangrom, now so different from the suave, dark man who had put his white hands on the table for Robert's own hands to rest on. He felt sad, looking at these people, at beautiful Vaire who looked sideways at him but not directly, at Walter, whose head was cocked on one side with his face drooping as if he were still stunned and who did not look at Robert at all; and at Aunt Cat who looked him in the eyes with a hard, impenetrable stare, as if she were trying to hate him. He understood what had hap-pened and also that he could not stay here, perhaps could not stay himself, understood that perhaps this was the same as his last night on earth, for only with these people could he be himself. And he had done something unforgivable to these people. He wanted to cry, but he could not. He stood there watching the peo-ple wake up to themselves, begin to be their own per-sonalities again after such a shock as he had acciden-tally given them. Walter's eyes came back into focus, and he began to speak in the old way, the confident, masculine way he had, of mass hypnosis, and how Sangrom had put them all under, and Aunt Cat began to shout at him, cursing as Robert had never heard her do, and Vaire speaking comforting words to Mr. Sangrom who was still standing in the doorway, wanting to get away and looking with fear at Robert. And Robert listened to all of this, his fingers feeling down the long rip in the front of his nightshirt, a rip he could not have made with both little hands, knowing how that rip had happened, and knowing it was not his fault. He began to be angry, very angry at these grown-up people who would now do something terrible to him when he had only wanted to live among them and love them and learn about what it was to be a little boy growing up with other children, wanting to be a little boy and be loved. He grew angrier so that his face suffused with blood, and he thought about Mr. Duchamps getting hit with the hail and about Willie crying over him and the big shouldered man getting up in the icy grass and hitting Willie and knocking him down on the ground and Willie hurting Anne, and Martin's face with the rain streaking his gray hair across his dying eyes, and Aunt Cat staring at him in horror, and the need he felt to come back to them all, to his beautiful Vaire and brave Anne, and how he wanted to love them if he knew how, if only he could know how to do it, and now he would not ever be able to do it, and he must run away in the night and hide again, and he thought about the dirty men under the railroad bridge and their sickness and cruelty, and about the dogs on the farm and the snakes in the chickenhouse and being in the cowbarn with Martin and the cats getting squirted with milk and now it was all gone, and about Rusty and the smell of him and his cold hatred that smelled like rotting fish, and remembered what it was like in the cold rain dancing with Willie and the sandwich game and Anne reading to him from the book about Happy, and now he had to run away again, be something else, someone else, forever, because they had made him do something he didn't want to do, and that Mr. Sangrom, he was glad of the claws that had sprung out by accident, because there was no way now to get back into the family again, no way for them to know him, Little Robert, because they had pushed him into something else, no way for it not to be; there was no way to go back even to this afternoon and not go to the hideout and not want ever again to play the game with Willie, and not even come in to supper but run and hide under the porch so Mr. Sangrom would go away and it all would not have happened, no way for it to be anything but right now with all these suddenly strange people hating him, afraid of him, no way for it to be anything but now, NOW!

Little Robert screamed and ran directly at Mr. Sangrom who shrank back so Robert slipped past, through the screen door and down the porch steps into the warm darkness. As he ran down the black tar street toward the hanging light at the far corner, his tears making the light all glittery and bouncing, he heard a woman's voice calling his name.

PART II

SECOND PERSON

(1)

There is much I do not know about the world I have been living in. I must learn to read, know more about humans and their ways, what they are capable of. Now I keep alert, travel at night, do not attempt to shift. I sense no feelings of fear or alarm in the houses I pause near at night. There is no general alarm in the countryside. Whether they are looking for the boy, I do not know, nor can I at this moment care. I travel southwest, following a feeling that I do not question. I do not pause long enough to consider making a burrow or hideaway, only sleep at night in thickets, hedges, empty outbuildings, and one night in an abandoned house on an old mattress. The tramps who had been living there thought I was a large wild dog in the dark when I woke and growled at them. But it is not pleasant, and for the first time I do not find it fun to run at night. The weather continues wet with thunderstorms and showers night and day soaking the ground, and I cannot avoid leaving tracks sometimes. There are so many fields being harvested of hay, so many creeks and rivers to cross, fences, towns to be avoided, farms and their ever present dogs.

Tonight I am curled up in a large concrete drain tile hanging from a sand bank over a vast lake of water that I cannot see across, and although it is comfortable to lie and watch the lightning streaking from cloud to cloud out over the lake, there is a feeling of irritation that I have not felt before, as if I had a wound somewhere that ached. I will know when I have arrived at the proper place, however far that may be, and there I will attempt to shift into an appropriate form to continue my human life.

Judging by the children I have seen, this boy must be between nine and twelve years old. He sits in the back of a half sunken old rowboat that is tied to a large willow tree and sticks out into the river. He wears a straw hat and the bib overalls all the farm boys wear, and his fishing pole is a length of ordinary sapling with string tied to the end of it. While I watch, he catches two fish that have whiskers and apparently bite or have stickers. I am not familiar with this fish and almost fall into the river straining for a better look at them. They are greenish black on the back and straw yellow on the belly and have wide mouths. The boy seems dissatisfied with them but puts them on a string he has dangling in the water so they cannot get away. I have studied him for some time, allowing his personality to shape my feelings, and now I am almost ready. I extend my perceptions but find not even a dog near, only squirrels and at the farthest extremity, the bend of the river, a couple of ducks in the reeds. I begin my concentration, the name comes closer as I feel my self contracting to a fine point like a brilliant spot of light, and it says itself in my mouth as the shift occurs: Charles Cahill.

I am still present at the shift, as I usually am when a new person arrives. Charles holds the overalls I have stolen for him in his hands looking at them. They are smaller than they should be. He is bigger than I expected him to be, a bit larger I think than the boy in the boat down below the bank. He gets to his feet and walks unsteadily back to some bushes and tries to get into the overalls, but they are much too tight. I wonder as he is struggling and laughing to himself how I have shifted into so much larger a human than I had anticipated. For a moment I have the impulse to try again, as this person seems foreign to me, but I recall that for more than three months now much of my existence has been in a very different person, much smaller and younger, so perhaps I am only reacting to the change. I do not see how I could possibly shift into a person antithetical to myself. But he needs some clothes. I am about to take action on that matter when suddenly, before I can stop him, he has dropped the overalls and is running toward the high bank where I had lain hidden. I gather myself to shift back, but hesitate to perform such a thing in midair, for we are sailing off the bank, over the head of the startled boy in the old rowboat, and crashing into the river head first.

Charles Cahill comes to the surface blowing a spout of muddy water in the air. Apparently he is as comfortable in the water as I am, swimming easily out further into the current before looking back at the white faced boy in the rowboat who has dropped his pole in the water and is watching it float away.

"Hey," Charles hollered, "did I scare ya?"

"Yeah, and it's not funny. That's the only line and hook I got, and there it goes," the other boy said with anger.

"Jump in and get it then."

"I can't swim."

Charles swam back toward the boat, kicking powerfully against the current, picked the fishing pole out of the water, watching for the hook on the end of the line. "Here." He handed the pole to the boy in the boat who eyed him curiously.

"Thanks. Who are you?"

"Charles Cahill. Who are you?"

"Douglas Bent. I live up on the rise back there in the white house with the big double silo barn."

"Yeah, I seen it," Charles said, hanging onto the boat and drifting his legs out in the current. "Sure is a big place. How come you ain't hayin' like everybody else?"

"Oh, my Pa lets me fish when I want," the boy in the boat said, looking away.

"Must be a swell Pa you got. I seen a bunch of men and boys out in the oat field that must belong to your farm. They was workin' pretty hard, it looked like."

"I don't do so good in the hayfield," Douglas said, looking straight at Charles as if he wanted to hit him.

"How come is that?" Charles said, rocking the boat and sloshing the water in its bottom from side to side.

"Quit it," Douglas said. He raised one leg and laid it on the gunwale of the boat. It looked like he had a silver bolt through his foot. " 'Cause I'm gimpy."

Charles examined the bolted foot, discovering it was a U-shaped brace that extended up into the boy's pants leg. The foot had a shoe on it and looked rigid. "You got a crippled leg?" Charles said as if it were a marvelous new invention.

"I had infantile paralysis when I was little," Douglas said, putting the leg back into the boat. "I can get around okay, but it's no good for workin' hay or like that."

"Well then, you don't have to sweat yer ass out in the fields or carry them heavy milk cans or any of that stuff," Charles said eagerly.

"I'd rather," said Douglas. "But Ma says you don't always get your druthers." He smiled crookedly as if he wanted to cry.

Charles realized he could not make a good thing of it, and that probably Douglas didn't spend much time thinking about it. "Well, at least you got a family and a place to sleep," Charles said, chin on the back of the boat. "I ain't got nothing, not even any clothes now."

"You haven't got any clothes?" Douglas said, his eyes big. "What happened?"

"Oh I stopped to swim back by the railroad bridge this morning, and I know better than to leave clothes around like that, but I just hopped off a freight, and I was hotter than a hot box, so I shucked 'em off and dived in, and I swum right back, but they was gone."

Douglas took his hat off and wiped his forehead. His hair was shiny black, plastered to his head with sweat. He had deep brown eyes and a kindly face with an unfortunate turned up nose that seemed out of place with his broad upper lip. Charles studied his face for a moment. Douglas looked more like a frog than he should, Charles decided, and at that moment, Douglas smiled happily and then opened his mouth and laughed.

"And you been running around all day from here to the railroad tracks without any clothes?" Douglas laughed tentatively, then found it really funny and rocked back in the boat, fanning himself with his hat. "You went right by old lady McGee's place, I bet," he said, trying to catch his breath. "And if she saw you sneaking around her place naked, she'd call out the National Guard."

Charles got to laughing too at that, and he swore he had danced in old lady McGee's front yard using rhubarb leaves for fans like Sally Rand at the World's Fair. Douglas laughed until he cried, Charles watching and liking the smaller boy for his humor. After awhile they got quiet.

"Don't you live *any*where?" Douglas said.

"Oh sometimes I sleep in a drain tile, sometimes in an old house like a hound dog," Charles said truthfully. "I ain't got no real home."

Douglas thought about that for awhile, looking Charles in the eye to see if he was kidding.

"What grade are you in?" Douglas asked, trying to trap the other boy.

"Never been in *no* school," Charles said. "But I'd sure like to go."

"Never?"

"What grade are you in?"

"I'll be in fifth this year. I skipped a grade last year, and now I'm in the same grade as Rudy. Rudy's my next older brother," Douglas added.

"I bet old dumb Rudy likes that," Charles said, grinning. He was beginning to feel cold in the water.

"He's not really dumb," Douglas said. "But how'd you know he didn't like it?" Then his face lit up. "Oh, yeah, I see." He looked at the other boy with a more respectful eye.

"I don't s'pose you could give me a hand," Charles said, shivering a little.

"You mean to get out? Oh, you mean to get some clothes and like that?"

111

"Yeah. I'd work for 'em, or pay you someway. But it'd have to be after awhile, 'cause I ain't got anything now except my good looks." And Charles grinned.

Douglas looked thoughtfully at the bigger boy, so comfortable seeming in his big strong body, a smooth swimmer, smart about people, and had probably had thousands of adventures. He took a deep breath. "I'll get you some of Rudy's or Carl's old ones. Carl is my oldest brother," he said.

"Lord, how many brothers you got?"

"Just two, but Ma's pregnant and we'll probably have some more by Christmas, Pa says."

"Well, I'd be your friend forever if you could get me decent," Charles said, putting his feet down and squishing through the mud toward the bank. "If old lady McGee sees me in her front yard again, she'll just die of fright."

I have been comfortable in this large, airy barn that is filling up with hay and has a dozen fine Holstein cows in its stanchions and two horses and a yearling colt at the other end. There are all sorts of nooks and doorways I use, and the dogs quickly learned they must leave me alone. But the situation has been strange. I find myself in a double-double life situation, with Douglas bringing clothes and food to Charles whenever he can, pretty much in return for the stories Charles tells him of his adventures, although where he has picked up these tales is quite beyond me. I seem to have shifted into a person with an endless gift for lying entertainingly, and that is exactly what the young Bent boy likes. Now I will make arrangements for attending school. It begins week after next, and I am determined to learn to read. I had thought that perhaps Charles with his facile tongue would lie his way into a place in the one-room brick schoolhouse that is less than a mile down the road from the Bent farm. But as it turns out, no lying is necessary, thanks to Mrs. Stumway, a widow living alone in her large stone house not more than a quarter mile from the school.

She was pointed out to Charles one day when he

and Douglas were slipping through the fence into her apple orchard. It was no longer an orchard, really, only a few straggly trees with wormy apples, but it was safely away from the house and hidden in the five-acre forest which was what the old lady had left of all the land she and her husband had once owned. Her house was invisible from the road, the whole five acres surrounding it being covered with oak, maple, fruit trees, some pines and other evergreens, buckeyes, lilacs grown into eight-foot hedges, and hazel bushes. Dense thickets of raspberries and gooseberry filled in the chinks, so that Mrs. Stumway lived like an old widowed rabbit in the midst of an inaccessible briar patch. Her neighbors had long ago given up trying to be friendly or even communicate with her after her husband had died some fifteen years past, and for most of them it was of little interest whether she lived in that impenetrable tangle or had died and been absorbed by it. Except that she appeared at her mailbox every few days in good weather, they would have believed she no longer existed. She was sharp tongued with those who professed good intentions and violent with those who professed anything else. An itinerant scissors sharpener and odds and ends salesman who occasionally visited the area told a tale of being beaten with a mop handle for trying to flatter the old lady into buying a bar of scented soap.

Charles listened to Douglas telling about the old Stumway widow, eating his fill of her apples while sitting on a low branch and studying the back of the house which could be dimly made out through the dense tangle of trees and undergrowth. It seemed to him there might be a possibility in such an old lady if she were approached right. Douglas said she had given him a piece of cake once because she felt sorry for his having a bad leg, but that she didn't like either of his brothers at all, and was probably not fond of his family in general. Charles thought she was showing nothing but good taste in that, for he did not like either of Douglas's brothers either, finding both of them surly prisoners of the farm work, practically slaves of their father, working alongside the farm hands Mr. Bent hired, but getting no pay for their work. They were both in a perpetual state of suppressed rage that left them either exhausted or dangerous most of the time.

"Doug," Charles said, putting his hands on the smaller boy's shoulders, "you are going to find me a place in the world."

Douglas looked doubtful. "If you're thinking about living with Mrs. Stumway, you'd better forget it. She's about as friendly as a gar fish."

"Maybe so, but I think a person living like she does needs me around to help 'em, especially since I'm so handy and could fix things up and clean up that rat's nest she lives in."

"I think she likes it that way," Douglas said.

But there are factors Douglas knows nothing about. The next three nights I sneak into Mrs. Stumway's woods, make my way to the old stone house sitting in its welter or maples and oaks and raspberries, and the one faint oil lamp burning in an upstairs window, and I wait until that lamp is turned down and blown out. Then I leap silently to the porch roof, old, sagging, but still sound, creep along the side of the house to the old lady's window and listen through the screen until she breathes regularly. It is quite easy to tell when she is sound asleep. She snores like a rusty windmill. Then I insert one long claw, flip the hooks on the screen and slip into the bedroom, crouch down beside her bed on the nubby hooked rug that pictures curly flowers in a circular garden, and I whisper in her ear. She is between seventy and eighty years old, pure white hair, some of which has fallen away and left a bald spot on the crown of her head, no teeth at night, a high broad forehead with fine wrinkles, a long thin nose and a sharp chin that points at the ceiling as she sleeps among her big pillows and snores great long squeaky windmill snores. Her hands are large with long fingers that have not lost their look of grace in age, although they are covered with brown patches. The hands look as though they might still play a piano or some stringed instrument. She sleeps on her back, her hands lying on top of the patchwork quilt.

I whisper Charles's name: "Charles Cahill, a good boy." Over and over I whisper it, thinking how absurd this is, and yet something prompts me that the procedure is not without effect. I have resisted the impulse to explore her house at night, for if she should wake and hear me, she might suspect a prowler, and I do not want to frighten her. That, I believe, would be the wrong approach, although I had thought of frightening her so that she would need a protector. The whispering campaign I am conducting in Charles's behalf is an interesting experiment, and it pleases Charles.

The two boys turned off the road into Mrs. Stumway's driveway which was not really a driveway anymore since a cottonwood tree had fallen across it years ago and had not been removed. It was a twenty-foot-long turnaround where the grocery delivery man's truck pulled in once a week to bring the old lady's provisions. Charles carried a watermelon, one of the long light green ones, as a propitiatory gift. Douglas was full of doubt, but rather excited about what Charles was attempting. As they crashed through the underbrush toward the back porch, Douglas expected any second to be shouted at. He was jumpy and irritated at catching his brace in the raspberry creepers. When the voice did come, it startled him so that he fell to one knee.

"Get out of there, you damned kids!" came a strong voice from the dimness of the back porch which had curtained windows all around it.

"Mrs. Stumway," Douglas called, getting back to his feet. "We brought you a melon."

"You got no business botherin' me, you damned kids," the voice shouted again. "Now git, before I get my rock salt after you."

As far as Douglas knew, the old lady had no rock salt, nor a shot gun to fire it in anyway, but she was full of threats.

"This is my friend, Charles Cahill, Mrs. Stumway," Douglas shouted at Charles's prompting. Charles held

115

the green melon in front of him like a sacrificial baby held out to the wrath of Moloch.

There was silence from the porch, and Charles wondered if the nightly whispering sessions had made some difference in the old lady's feeling about strangers.

The back door opened with a creak of the spring and the old lady appeared, wearing what looked like an aviator's helmet minus the goggles, so that her white hair stuck out like little cold flames all around her face. She wore a long, featureless brown dress that fell straight from her neck to her ankles, giving her the look of a fake tree trunk with an old lady's face peeping out of the top.

"Douglas Bent," she said, as if naming the boy for the first time in the history of the world. "Come in here, and bring your melon friend there too."

The boys walked into Mrs. Stumway's kitchen, expecting to find an indoor counterpart of the wilderness outside, but the kitchen looked like any farm kitchen, perhaps cleaner than most, with a serviceable sink and pitcher pump, a kerosene cook stove and an enamel top table that looked surgically clean. The light was dim because every window was grown over with ivy, four o'clock vines, and ornamental bushes gone savage. In Charles's mind it seemed almost like an undersea cavern with the greenish flickering light from the wobbling leaves and intermittent sun.

"You!" Mrs. Stumway said so suddenly that Charles jumped. "Put that melon on the cutting board. I suppose you kids want something, bringing me a melon. But I can't imagine what it would be. You steal my fruit soon as it comes on the trees, worse than jays and magpies."

Charles tried to think of some way to put the old lady in a better mood, but every time he opened his mouth to speak, she shot out something of her own that silenced him. Douglas was turning back and forth as the old lady went from cupboard to table, getting out plates and forks, trying to get some word in also. He was about to leap into a silent space in her monologue when she bent over the kitchen cabinet, but as he was about to say Charles's name, Mrs. Stumway straightened up, pulling something long and gleaming from beneath the silver drawer. She whirled about swinging a giant blade that looked as long as her arm.

"Ha!" she said, swishing the blade back and forth.

"Charles!" Douglas screamed involuntarily, stumbling back and bumping into Charles who was also moving backward.

The old lady looked at the boys over the long blade and grinned so that her artificial teeth shone like a row of skulls. "Scared you?" she said. "This is from the Philippine Islands. My baby brother, Adam, brought it back with him from when he was there fighting the Moros. It's called a bolo knife." She waved it again, but a bit less militantly.

"And it's very good for melons," she said, walking to the cutting board. She raised the long knife in both hands and brought it down clean and hard, right through the middle of the melon so that it stuck in the cutting board. "Damned knife. Haven't had a melon for a ugh, long time, ugh." She could not pull the knife free.

Charles came forward and worked the long blade loose from the cutting board and handed it back to the old lady. She sliced circles of melon for all three, and they sat at the enamel table and ate them with old iron forks with black wooden handles and long tines like pitchforks. The old woman studied Charles quite openly as they ate, asking him about his home, parents, whether he went to school, and Charles did his best to charm her and play on what he imagined were her sympathies.

"I never did know any father or mother, ma'am," Charles said, his face looking as if he were about to cry. "My uncle used to make me work in his store till nine o'clock every night, and then I had to sweep up and wash floors and windows on Saturday mornings, so I just ran away one time when I got sick of it."

Douglas looked at Charles with amazement. He had never heard that version of the other boy's life, and he didn't know whether to believe any of his tales now or whether to be angry or delighted at Charles's facility at lying. Mrs. Stumway nodded her head in the aviator's cap and clucked disapprovingly at appropriate points in the story.

"So you ran off when the work got hard?" she said, astonishing Charles who had thought he was getting her approval.

"It was awful hard, ma'am," Charles said, at a loss which way to proceed. "And sometimes he licked me with a strap."

"Some boys need it," she said, smiling her even false teeth at Charles who felt less certain of himself now.

"Charles would like to go to school and learn to read and write, Mrs. Stumway, but he's got no place to live," Douglas said with a desperate edge in his voice. "He's been hiding out in our barn, but if my Dad finds out about him, he won't be able to stay."

"Maybe your father could use an extra hand with the hay, Douglas," the old lady said, spitting a line of melon seeds into her plate.

"But Charles said that he didn't . . ."

"Didn't want all that work, hah?" the old lady broke in. "Well, I'm not surprised."

"Wait a minute," Charles said. "I'm not afraid of work. I worked plenty where I come from. But I don't want to get Douglas in trouble with his family. He's been a good friend. I thought you might need someone around to kind of straighten up outside, get that brush out of the driveway and such."

"Oh, you're welcome to stay here and go to school, Charles Cahill," Mrs. Stumway said, looking directly into his eyes. "I just didn't want you to think a couple of sprouts like you could put something over on an old lady." She put her hands on the table and looked at Charles, the corners of her long mouth turned up sharply. Her face, seamed and foxed with age as it was, reminded Charles of someone, but he couldn't say who. He smiled at her with what he imagined was his most winning and ingratiating smile. He had a place.

Charles found that although the old woman had an

118

acid tongue and sometimes accused him of being lazy, she did not often lose her temper, and did not insist that he do much work around the place. On the following Tuesday when school began in the one-room brick school just across the road and down a bit, Charles felt quite at home with Mrs. Stumway and was looking forward to learning to read.

It was no surprise to Miss Jessie Wrigley on that first day of school to find Charles applying for entrance to the first grade. He was as big as any twelve-year-old and could not read his own name or even spell it properly, for that matter. She had signed up William Seaboldt last year for first grade, and he had been fourteen. He had attended no more than a month before he ran away, and she hoped that this poor orphan boy whom Mrs. Stumway had taken in would stick to his studies. Certainly he was promising looking, but then she read in the note from Mrs. Stumway that he had good looks and a winning manner, but was not a worker or very persevering. She looked at him, standing in front of her desk amid the other children in all eight grades who were signing up for their year's school, and she wondered if his good appearance would not work against him. He had obviously got the little crippled Bent boy in his spell and was earnestly working on some of the other boys, telling them some outrageous story about his days riding the freights.

"Charles Cahill," Miss Wrigley said, "will you move one of the larger desks over into the first grade row? We don't want you breaking one of our little desks." She smiled at him to help soften the disgrace of his being in first grade row, but he appeared not to have the slightest embarrassment at his position. An unusual boy, she thought, watching his easy way with the other children. Different from most of these farm children who are so shy and wordless, she thought. I wonder if he is a fast learner?

For his part, Charles was as delighted with Miss Wrigley as he was with having a home and being accepted in the farm community. He had walked in with Douglas that Tuesday morning and joined the circle

119

of children around the teacher's desk expecting to confront some old crone of a spinster woman who would smack his hands with a ruler if he did not do as she said. Instead he found a young, mild looking woman with short brown hair and a direct manner that made the children feel at ease because they always knew how she felt. If someone did poorly on a lesson and Miss Wrigley was displeased, she would say to that child, "That bothers me, Mary, because it makes me feel that you don't care about learning to be a civilized person." And the child would usually feel that it was only right that Miss Wrigley feel that way. Charles admired this approach to the manipulation of others, which was how he felt about it, and learned to use it himself as best he could. He was also rather taken, even on that first day, with Miss Wrigley herself. She was short, not much taller than Charles, with a compact, efficient looking body that Charles liked to watch. Her school clothes were ordinary enough, even drab, some browns and dark greens with an occasional white blouse to set off, but she seemed to Charles to possess a quick grace that did not need ornamentation. And most of all he admired her learning. She seemed to Charles to know everything in the world, and he wanted passionately to know what she knew, to move with her assurance through the stories, the histories, the mathematical problems he watched her doing for the higher grades. And although he was not, as Mrs. Stumway had surmised, a willing worker in the fields or around the house, he worked for Miss Wrigley in the name of learning.

(2)

I have, of course, noticed the increase in my own size. That is no surprise; and the other changes, the strange sort of itching I feel that must be the beginnings of sexual need, the impulses I have to pull strange pranks and tricks on humans when I am hunting at night, these might be expected in a growing creature and are reflected by Charles's behavior in the human world in daylight. But there are other changes in my world less explicable. For one thing, some mysterious force has made it impossible for me to enter the old Stumway house without shifting back into Charles. This is baffling to me, as I cannot imagine anything that would prevent me entering any human habitation unless it might be armor plate and giant locks. In the second week of my living there I slipped out at night as usual, and upon my return, I was unable to cross the threshold of the back door. I tried a window downstairs, my own room window upstairs, and all was the same. Something I could not even imagine kept me from entering. As I would put my head through the window, I would feel faint, and my heart would begin to pound in my ears, a sensation I have never had before would twist my guts, and only my moving back from the house would relieve the feelings. And yet, once I had shifted to Charles, I walked in through the door with no harm or adverse feelings. The danger here is something to ponder, something to find out about, but as long as Charles is immune to this force, I feel relatively safe. It is only that, among the other changes developing in my life, this one is the more worrisome, the more nagging because it is inexplicable, and I do not know if the old woman is responsible or if it is some effect of which she is unaware.

The other change is even more surprising, and is much more pleasant. I am crouched in the weedy corner of a field with a huddle of sheep about twenty yards away beginning to make their loose fright noises in the darkness. I expect any moment to have to take care of the dogs that are inevitable in such a situation. I do not often go for a lamb now, but this night I am hungry and not in a mood to make do with rabbits and chickens. I wait for the dogs and extend my spatial sense to find them. They are there at the corner of the tall manger affair from which the sheep get their hay. There are two of them, sheep dogs of some sort, large quiet beasts that creep up on one and bite suddenly without barking. I will have to deal with them, for they have scented me. I feel their arousal and fear as they come creeping along the fence row in the weeds. I will deal with them quickly, for they make me full of rage, and I am hungry. I sense them clearly now as their vibrations reach my spatial sense, and I feel myself repelling them, hating them for interrupting me. Suddenly I am startled, for they have stopped coming toward me. They are turning about, standing up and trotting away back toward the distant barns. I stand in the weeds, showing myself, but they do not turn. In fact they are running away now, dashing as if in a race to see who can most quickly leave the flock unprotected. Can they be going to get the farmer? I stand as quiet as a tree stump listening, reaching out to the distant barns with my senses. They reach the barns and crouch down facing the fields. They are more than a thousand feet away now, at the very limit of my perception, and they are lying down as if nothing was happening. I keep them in the corner of my perceptual field and walk among the sheep who are petrified, of course, and pick out a fat lamb. The dogs have not moved. Amazing!

I move to the next field, across a small creek, and

have my meal. The lamb is delicious. No sign of the dogs as I dig a small hole to bury the leavings. It will not do for the farmer to know that something has eaten his lamb. Better to let him think it was simply stolen. Perhaps the dogs are cowards, but I must know. On the way back to the Stumway place, I try it again: slipping up to a barn, I wait until the dogs begin sneaking around sniffing for me, and then I make the feeling of repulsion toward them. They stop, stand up as if in broad daylight, and walk back to their beds under the back porch of the farmhouse. Perhaps there is more to it than this. I extend my senses for animal life and find a cat sneaking about in the barn looking for mice. I make a feeling of greed, of hunger strong in my already sated body. I feel that the cat must come to me. I watch carefully, feeling for where the cat is. She stops stalking the mice and comes obediently out the barn door, tail in the air as if she were going for a saucer of milk, out the big door, tail waving gracefully and steps right up to me where I crouch in the shadows. I could have picked her up and eaten her, although I detest eating cats. She stands there looking around in the darkness, oblivious of me. I release the feeling from my mind, relax the feeling of attraction in some way, I am not quite sure how, but I feel the spell is broken. The cat suddenly bristles and blows up like a balloon, every hair erect, spitting her fear at me, backing up in terror. I laugh softly and she turns and races across the yard to a tree and vanishes up the trunk.

The implications of this new power are enormous. I must try it out carefully to determine its limits. Could I, for instance, make a larger animal or a human obey my feeling? One thing it does ensure is a ready supply of food without my having to run after it.

Charles picked up the knack of reading as if he had only forgotten it for awhile instead of having to learn it from the beginning. By mid-October he had finished Elson Reader, Book II, which was what the second graders were using, and he could do carry addition and mark-off subtraction, and Miss Wrigley considered him her star pupil among the twenty-seven students. Some of the other students were not so happy with Charles because he made them look less than intelligent with his pertinent questions and his astounding progress, but most of them liked his fresh, outgoing manner and his willingness to try any game or feat they could think up. A tribute to Charles's good nature, Miss Wrigley thought, was the fact that he had not to her knowledge had a single fight since coming to the school, something of a record for new boys. Charles's secret on that subject was simple. He told the challenger, and there were several in the first week of school, "I don't know much about fighting fair, 'cause I always had to fight guys with knives and stuff. So if we fight, I hope you fight dirty, 'cause that's what I do." His opponent usually had second thoughts at that, recalling Charles's gory tales of battles among the tramps on the railroad and in the hobo jungles. So far, Charles had not had a battle, and he could usually kid his enemy out of his anger and save both their faces.

At softball, which was the only game the farm boys played, besides such chase games as cops and robbers and red rover, Charles was an apt learner, but was somewhat slower than in the academic field. It was at softball that he learned that some of the strange power I had discovered that night in the sheep pen carried over to his life. The star pitcher in the school was Ronald Borsold, called "Runt" because he was small and compact. Runt Borsold was thirteen years old with powerful arms and a sharp eye, and he was known for fanning the softball batters on the opposing team. Charles happened to be on the opposite team one afternoon when Runt was pitching and was finding it humiliating that he could not hit the ball. After two strikes of his second time at bat had gone by, he was beginning to get angry. The infield chatter was getting to him. He was sweating out the next pitch, knowing it would zip by as the others had, and he suddenly thought strongly, "Pitch it to me easy!"

The next pitch sailed in like a feather and Charles smacked it out into the tall grass around the old outhouse, a home run off Runt! Charles's team bruised him considerably with pounding on the back and head when he crossed home plate well ahead of the long, bouncing throw from a suddenly awakened left fielder.

Runt Borsold was standing on the pitcher's bare spot in the grass looking at Charles as if he had just levitated himself six feet in the air. The next batter benefited somewhat from Runt's astonishment and got a single off a bouncing ball past second base, but the rest of the batters had the same difficulties hitting him as they usually did. By the time Charles came to bat again, he was wondering also what had happened and allowed the first strike to go by without trying the command he had used before. But at that point, I am aroused by the emotional effect the game is having on Charles, and I force the feeling I had used on the animals to emanate, an effect that made Charles feel a strong emotional reaction, an emotional "command" to the pitcher to "throw it easy!"

And here it came, like a piece of cake, sailing in. Charles got set and whammed it over the far left field barbed wire fence, another homer for sure, as that fence was so seldom hit that any ball going over it was an automatic home run. Both teams were screaming now, some of the players on Runt's team supposing he had sold out for some secret reward from Charles. It did look bad for Runt, but in the next minutes he redeemed himself from that charge by leaving the pitcher's spot in tears, an almost unforgiveable expression of emotion among the boys. Obviously, he was not selling out, but had been the victim of some unaccountable lapse.

Charles was freely said to have given Runt the evil eye, and his stock as a softball player went up a thousand points. Charles, when he was able to get a thoughtful minute to himself, felt the reality of his power over the other boy and wondered how he could make it work for him. He decided to try the big experiment at once. He tried to command Miss Wrigley, and it didn't work. It was simply a failure. He worked himself up to an artificial pitch of emotion and silently commanded her to walk over to his desk with a book he wanted from the "library," a single set of bookshelves in the front of the room by the piano. Sitting at her desk marking papers from the seventh and eighth grades, she look up once and, catching Charles's eye, smiled faintly at him, but she made no move to get the requested book. Charles was heavily disappointed at the failure of what had seemed to him an easy road to getting whatever he wanted in the world. His experiment that same evening with Mrs. Stumway he counted worse than a failure. It had a reverse effect, causing her to get angry with him over his not having carried the kitchen garbage to the pit behind the house. And when Charles tried it a second time, thinking with all his will power that the old lady should fetch him an apple from the kitchen, she looked up from a long letter she was reading, just as if she *had* felt the command and said, "Charles, I want you to paint the outhouse this weekend." He retreated to his homework, thinking angrily that the power over Runt had been a fluke. I know differently, but Charles does not understand when I try to tell him that the power is functional rather than whimsical.

Charles and Douglas Bent hitched a ride with the grocery delivery man one Saturday in October for a fishing excursion. They got off near the dam just inside of town and climbed down the jutting stone ledges beside the old power house on the north side of the river. The river was higher now, with a solid green sheet of water pouring over the full width of the dam and frothing down the fish ladders on either side. Across the river they could see the public landing below the new power house with its line of fishermen and were glad they had come to the north side where only a few kids were fishing. They noticed that no one was catching much on this side, but they baited their hooks with worms and tossed them into the calm, deep water between the end of the dam apron and the old sandstone wall of the abandoned power house.

The water looked metallic and dangerous with deep eddies.

"There ought to be some bass in there," Douglas said.

"I'd settle for a red horse or maybe a buffalo," Charles said. He had picked up the fish names rapidly from Douglas, but had never caught anything. "Or maybe a blue pig or a green sheep or a purple chicken," he said, making Douglas laugh. Charles liked to make Douglas laugh, and the smaller boy in turn enjoyed Charles's ability to do so, often ending with tears in his eyes from his friend's absurdities.

After they had fished awhile in silence, Douglas said, "You getting along okay with Mrs. Stumway?"

"Yeah. She's not so bad. I'm supposed to paint the outhouse this weekend, but she didn't say anything when I asked if I could come fishin'."

"Does she make you work much?"

"Nah. She's funny. Y'know, I'm living there and eating her food, and she don't really make me do much at all." Charles said it as he thought about it, and realized it was true, and that he hadn't really thought about that. Maybe she's rich, he thought, and said, "Maybe she's rich, you think?"

"I don't know. Ma says her and Mr. Stumway used to own all the land around where her little woods is now, and where the school is and everything, but that they sold it all and quit farming even before her husband got sick."

"She must have some money," Charles said, not really interested. "I think she gets checks in the mail, 'cause she gives an envelope to Mr. Graham every week, and always talks to him about it for awhile."

"That's probably just his pay for the groceries," Douglas said.

"No. She pays him cash money for those," Charles said, watching the swirling water. "Anyway, she's okay if you like eggs for breakfast every morning of the world and sardine sandwiches for lunch and pork chops for supper."

"That's not so bad," Douglas said. "You don't have

127

to pick peas and tomatoes or shuck sweet corn if you don't want to, and I have to, and I don't get much better food than that."

"You don't have to paint a dirty old outhouse that's so rotten the flies all moved out last week."

Douglas laughed. "That's nothing. I had to paint all the storm windows last week, and that's a bugger because you gotta watch the glass, and . . ."

There was a sudden fountain of water from the pool where they had dropped their lines. For an instant, Charles thought a giant fish was coming out after them, but then both boys realized someone was rocking them. They looked around at the few other boys lined up along the ledges, but none of them looked guilty. The water rose up again in a huge splash, getting both of them wet. They heard laughter from overhead and looked up. On the ledge of the old power house building, some fifteen feet over their heads, a face peered, laughing evilly. The hair was red and stuck up in every direction, and the face looked unnaturally pale.

"Look out," Charles said as another piece of sandstone came plummeting past them into the pool.

"Hey up there, you damned idiot," Charles yelled at the white face, "we're tryin' to fish down here."

Another stone followed, this time missing the river altogether and smashing into the ledge not a foot from where Charles sat. "Hey, goddammit," he yelled, "you gonna hit somebody."

"It's a city kid," Douglas said, and there was fear in his voice. "They do things like that for fun."

"You sound like you're afraid of that red headed piece of horse apple up there," Charles said, grinning. He put his pole down and scrambled up the ledges toward the corner of the old sandstone building where projecting flagstone-sized steps led up to the ledge where the rock thrower was hiding. As he grabbed a projecting stone to begin the climb, Douglas shouted, he glanced up just in time to see the white face and red hair again, but not in time to duck away from the stone that hit his left arm a numbing blow at the elbow.

Charles sat down hard on the ledge, holding his arm. It felt like a baseball bat had hit it. His rage flared, and with the pain in his arm running up into his neck he thought savagely, "Jump in the river, you sonofabitch," and said aloud, "Oh, goddammit!"

Douglas shouted again, and something hit the water at the same time, something a lot bigger than the rocks that had been coming down. "He jumped in," Douglas shouted, and the other boys along the ledges were all standing up now too and pointing into the roiling backwash at the end of the dam apron beyond the fish ladder.

"Look at that. There he is," they were shouting.

Charles looked and saw the white faced boy being rolled in the heavy backwash below the dam. The crazy fool had leaped all the way over the pool where they were fishing and right into the worst part of the river, the wash below the dam where the falling water hit and curled back on itself. Sometimes barrels and old logs would be caught in the wash for days before they got loose. He would drown sure.

"He must be crazy," some of the boys were saying. "Go for a float or something. Get an innertube, a rope," they shouted, and some of them ran off up the bank looking for something to throw in.

"He'll drown sure," Douglas said, watching the boy's white face appear and disappear in the billows of water and foam. The boy was a swimmer and was trying hard to get out of it, stroking for all he was worth, but he was taking in water too when the undertow caught him and rolled him under.

"Damn," Charles said. "I got to get him out." He slipped out of his shirt and stood in his cutoff overalls watching the boy go under again. "I wish I didn't have to do this," he said to Douglas as he unhooked his overalls and dropped them around his feet. He took three running steps along the ledge and launched out in a long flat dive that took him below the apron of the dam. His naked body flashed brown in the sun before he hit, and he heard Douglas crying after him as the water crashed into his ears.

Charles was a good swimmer, but not that good. He made it against the current into the thunderous roil of the backwash, but then he could not see the red haired boy in the great waves and spume. He had to fight hard to keep from being drawn into the powerful undertow that would sweep him around underwater into the smashing power of the flood pouring over the dam. Twice he fought his way to the surface after being pulled under so hard that his body was actually hurled against the bedrock of the river bottom. He hit the bottom hard with his thrashing legs and knew he had lost some skin. He pushed off hard trying to get out of the wash and get to the top for a breath. He made it, only to be pulled under again instantly. He hit bottom with his shoulder and the side of his head, lost his breath and gagged on incoming water. He felt his fingers holding to a crack in the scoured rock bottom, the only thing keeping him from being drawn under the falls, and then he lost more breath.

Shift.

I force water out of my throat and let the roil carry me back almost to the great pressure of the falling water. I push upward from the bottom right at the edge of the fall, the weight of water just grazing my back. I look but can see nothing in the gray haze of spray. I duck under, letting the water push me to the bottom where I curl up tightly, holding to the edge of the dam apron and feeling through the water with my spatial sense. The buffeting of the water is strong and terrible. There he is. A limp thing with little life left in it, turning over and over at the inner edge of the roil like a drift log. I fix on it and push away from the bottom. It seems that the water is fighting my every movement, but I grab the boy's body from beneath and give a great thrust of my hind legs to reach up for air. The roil pushes me at the same time, and I seem almost to leap full length from the water with the boy under my arm. I take a deep breath and go under where the roil catches me again. I hit for the bottom, extending my hind claws and scratching on the rock for a hold. The water pushes us back until I feel my claws slide into a crevice. I double up on the bottom and push violently, clawing with one arm and both hind feet. Two of the claws on my left foot snag in the crevice, and I pull away without them. I feel nothing, but the quiet part of my mind tells me it will hurt later. We are off the worst part of the roil, and I head upward, lungs almost empty now, and I feel the downstream current carrying us away from the dam. I hold under the water one more instant, and as I surface, well down into the swift current, I concentrate hard, Charles Cahill, and shift.

Charles rose in the free current, the red haired boy loosely in the crook of his left arm as he took breath, gasping and looking to the shore. Along the downstream bank he saw a running, confused mass of people. They were shouting and waving their arms.

Charles grabbed the boy by the hair and jerked him along as he swam sidestroke toward the near shore, his breath panting faster than he thought he was able to breathe. He felt the bottom and tried to walk and fell. Then hands grabbed at him, holding him up, yelling in his ears, the noise sounding like the dam exploding, and he thought he would faint, but he did not.

When he got some of his breath and awareness back, he was lying on his stomach on the pebbles of the shore halfway between the old power house and the highway bridge. The red haired boy was stretched out on some boards while a muscular looking man gave him artificial respiration. A siren was approaching. Douglas had thrown a shirt over his shuddering body and was saying something, but for a time Charles couldn't make sense of the words. It seemed to be the same thing over and over.

"Why'd you do it? Why'd you do it? You could of got killed."

Charles felt as though he had been run through a giant egg beater. Pains were appearing like magic, elbows, knees, back, forehead, nose, chest, and his head felt full of water, making all sounds reverberate. It was as if he were wearing a bucket on his head.

He turned on his side to look into Douglas's anxious frog face and grinned.

"I couldn't just let the little shit get away, could I?"

The ambulance took both Charles and the red haired boy whose name was Wayne Ritter to St. Luke's hospital where Charles was found to have what the reported for the Beecher *Republican* called "multiple bruises and minor lacerations." The Ritter boy was described as being "recalled from a watery grave by the heroic efforts of his playmate," a misnomer that made Charles laugh until his minor lacerations hurt. The doctor at St. Luke's was interested to find out how Charles had lost two toenails entirely from his left foot, but Charles could only respond that it was an awful mess and he didn't know how he even got out alive .

The officials of the B.P.O.E. chapter who announced that Charles was hereby nominated for their "Young Hero of the Year" award thought it would have made a better story all around if the principals in the adventure had been socially more prominent, or at least less obscure. Charles was assigned "shirt-tail relation" by a dour Mrs. Stumway who would not allow reporters or Elks in her door and talked to everyone through the back screen. So Charles was written up as the "grandnephew of Mrs. Laura Stumway, residing at her farm three miles south of Beecher." Wayne Ritter's family was more of an embarrassment by being present: mother an obstinate alcoholic, father a sometime WPA shovel leaner, one brother in CCC and unavailable for comment, the other in the Army. The Ritter listed as being in the Army was a promising candidate for the public platform until it was learned that he was in the Post Stockade at Fort Sill, Oklahoma, serving six months AWOL time.

The rescued one was no better to deal with publicly, being a filthy mouthed and undernourished twelve-year-old who maintained amid a string of obscenities that Charles had thrown him into the river and tried to kill him. Fortunately this was contradicted by all witnesses who agreed that Charles was at least twelve vertical feet away from the Ritter boy when he leaped from the ledge into the water. The only adult witness, the muscular man who had given Ritter artificial respiration, admitted to being puzzled by the accident, since it appeared to him that the Ritter boy had leaped off the ledge from a kneeling position, shooting out horizontally almost fifteen feet as he dropped into the roil of the dam. This witness thought there had to be someone else on the ledge who had thrown the boy with considerable force, but this was contradicted by all other witnesses and by the victim himself.

Charles also thought about the horizontal distance the boy would have had to leap to land in the roil, and it seemed to him that he must in some way have helped to propel the boy off the ledge, aside from merely forcing him to do something as he had forced Runt Borsold to pitch him a setup. He understood now that strong emotion was needed to affect the actions of others, and it seemed a less useful thing to have than it had seemed before, because the strong emotion necessary to the power would dictate the nature of the force applied. Charles was disappointed.

At the PTA special reception and party for "Our Hero" at the red brick schoolhouse, Charles felt there was little else wonderful that could happen to him, with newspaper clippings of his exploit tacked up on the school bulletin board and old Mrs. Stumway coming out of seclusion to attend the reception dressed in a cloche hat and an ankle length Panama print of tropical flowers that made her look like an old wrinkled aviator wearing a trellis in full blossom. Mr. Safford, the local school superintendent, and the three farmers who constituted the school board all shook Charles by the hand, admiring his strength and courage, and the girls looked at him with new eyes now that he was more than just the handsome dolt who was the only twelve-year-old in first grade ("second going on third," as Miss Wrigley put it).

The only dissenting note Charles heard was from the real hero of the great river rescue who had lost two hind claws and who cautioned our hero in explicit terms not to be such a fool again, as he *and* the real

133

hero might well have drowned for Charles's grandiose gesture.

Certainly if it had not been for the rescue, Charles would never have been invited to Betty Bailey's Halloween party a couple of weeks later. Amid the social desert of the rural Illinois cornbelt, Betty's family had the reputation for being "smart." Her mother, Cora, was considered a flashy dresser, and her father, Edward, was "fast" as well as having a profile that reminded some of Douglas Fairbanks. Edward Bailey was more nearly a gentleman farmer than most of the other families in the district, having real estate interests in Beecher and some of the small towns in the county so that, in general, to be invited to the Baileys' was to have arrived socially. Betty Bailey was, as her parents had taught her to be, beautiful, poised as a girl can be at fourteen, and socially at ease. Her older brother, Edward Junior, had just entered Northwestern University, at great expense, it was said, and constituted the family's most glittering social asset at the moment. If there had been a "coming out" for what were later to be called "sub-debs," Betty Bailey would have come out. As it was, with the country yet in the fluctuating coils of the Depression, the Baileys in their modest way provided the country community with a social goal to which others could aspire.

Betty was, of course, sought after by those who imagined themselves to be in her social sphere, dreamed about by those young men and boys beneath her socially, and actually courted by one Alfred Kearney, the offshoot of a local farm family who had taken a job in a grocery store after his graduation from Beecher High with promises of a partnership someday. He owned a 1932 model B coupe with a rumble seat and a V-8 engine, and had painted its hood slats in alternating red and white stripes and had a vacuum wolf whistle that he exercised when he came to pick up Betty at school on Friday afternoons. Additional ornamentation on this chariot was provided by the scrolled name "Betty B." on the right hand door. Alfred affected polo shirts and an occasional silk scarf, and was far and beyond the grandest thing any of the farm boys had ever seen.

Charles had admired Betty, of course, but in a comfortably distant way, as she was two years older than his putative age and miles above in social station. Alfred, he thought, did have Clark Gable's big ears, but the rest of him was nothing more than big nosed, gangly farm boy. He also seemed of an advanced age to be coming around to a country elementary school to pick up a seventh grader on Friday afternoons.

Charles was astounded, then, to see Betty Bailey stepping across the school yard one lunch time with an envelope in her hand and a smile on her face. She is pretty, Charles throught, hiding the hand that held his sardine sandwich inside his lunch box. Her lips were red and perfectly outlined as if with a sharp pen, and she had her head cocked on one side, her heavy auburn hair hanging to her shoulders. Charles felt an increasing receding of reality as she approached him, her dark brown eyes looking directly into his own. As she stopped in front of him, her skirt still swinging from her parade across the school yard, Charles felt quite hypnotized, and could not have told if he was sitting right side up or if perhaps someone had turned him on his head.

"Charlie," Betty said. No one had ever called him Charlie. "I'd like to invite you to my Halloween party next Friday. I hope you can come."

She cocked her head the other way, trying to see if Charles was awake or had suddenly become unconscious. "You will try to make it, won't you?"

"Uh." Charles said. "Yeah." He recovered, taking in breath as if he had been under the falls again. "Oh, yeah, Betty. Thanks a lot for the invitation." He extended a hand to take the envelope, but the hand was unaccountably full of sardines and squashed bread.

Betty laughed brightly. "No thanks, Charlie," she said. "I've eaten my lunch already."

Charles looked at his hand, jerked it back and began to laugh. "I'm so surprised," he said, copying Miss Wrigley's style, "I feel kind of embarrassed I guess."

Then they both laughed, and their eyes met, a trick Betty was good at, and Charles felt that strange sense of unreality come over him again. Betty turned and waved after slipping the envelope into the bib pockets of Charles's overalls. He watched her swinging skirt as she paraded back to the coterie of girls under the big cottonwood beside the ocean wave swing. He found himself saying something under his breath and wondered if he was saying poetry.

"Oh Charlie," said a falsetto voice next to him. "I hope *you* will be able to come to Hollow weenie." It was "Kick" Jones, the tall bony sixth grader who had been eating lunch with Charles before the world disappeared.

"She was wearing perfume," Charles said, ignoring Kick's remark.

"Yeah, her and her family and their Packard," Kick said.

"They got a Packard?" Charles said absently.

"Yeah, and Betty says they might get a sho-fur," Kick said in disgust. "Geeze, they ain't that rich. My dad says Ed Bailey has got bills all over the state that he can't pay."

"Well, who cares," Charles said, stuffing a sardine into his mouth. "She doesn't need money. Wow, she's really something."

"You better not look at her crosseyed," Kick said. "Alfred'll turn you inside out. She's his girl."

"Oh, who's thinkin' about stuff like that," Charles said. "I just think she's a real knockout. Who wants a girlfriend anyway?"

(3)

In the days before Halloween, Charles made a few dollars husking corn for some of the local farmers so that he could buy a new shirt for the Bailey party. And then, like a giant distorted mirror image of the elegance the Baileys were to have on the night of the thirty-first, came the annual PTA Halloween party held on the preceding Wednesday night. School was dismissed at noon on Wednesday so the school room could be got ready with streamers of orange and black, arched black cats pasted on all the windows, orange witches on the blackboards, and crude skeletons on strings hung from the ceiling lights. There were also tubs of water to be brought in for apple ducking, the desks to be moved down to the basement so ring dances and games could take place, and a little stage with curtains prepared in the front of the room so that the third, fourth, and fifth grades could act out the ghost story chosen for the occasion. Costumes were optional now, since the party three years ago when the teacher who had retired before Miss Wrigley came demanded costumes and got a schoolhouse full of old sheets of various sizes and degrees of yellowness. Even the poor little Ricci boy whose family lived in an abandoned clapboard church building two miles down the highway was wearing a sheet. The scene had produced a ghostly effect all right, but in the course of the evening all the sheets had been shredded, and the families had complained of the expense. Now it was thought funny to come in a sheet, but the joke was getting old and few families had the imagination or drive to produce their own costumes. Store bought costumes were, of course, out of the question.

The play turned out to be an elaborate farce involving a knight, a witch, a bumbling king, and his silent (forgot her lines) queen, and any number of retainers dressed in pointed hats and cued for movement by a laughing and harried Miss Wrigley who prompted, pushed, pulled off stage, and supplied props from the wings at stage right. In between times she played appropriate ghostly music at the piano while the witch's cornsilk hair fell off, the king's crown came unpasted and drooped into his lap, and the knight kept knocking people on the head with his lance (the window stick). Just as the witch seemed about to triumph, partly because she had remembered all her lines and most of her costume had held together, the knight stepped forward and threatened her with his lance, a not altogether idle gesture, since he punched Mary Mae Martin (the witch) with considerable force in her plump stomach while he rendered his victory lines. Mary Mae retired defeated with a vindictive look at Harry Bennett (the knight) and a muttered threat about what he was going to get for hurting her with the lance. Harry was victorious, nervously, for a threat from Mary Mae was not brushed off lightly when one was six inches shorter and two years younger than she was. And so, virtue triumphed as Miss Wrigley played a victorious march on the old upright and the audience clapped and laughed appropriately.

Then the chairs were cleared away and the stage dismantled for the games, the traditional ducking for apples, blindfold games, and string chewing contests where each of a pair of players tried to get the candy tied in the middle, and the flirting game called "wink 'em."

Charles was having the time of his life, laughing so hard at the play that he and Douglas knocked their chairs over and were reprimanded by the elder Bent. During the pairing for the string chew, Charles didn't watch what he was doing and got paired with

Mary Mae, still in her witch hair and costume. Her eyes were bright as she grinned widely at Charles, now considered a "catch" at parties and box suppers. Charles took the other end of the string in his teeth, looked into Mary Mae's little round blue eyes beneath the gray frizzle of cornsilk witch wig and smiled.

"I liked the way you did in the play," he said around the string.

"Thank you, Charles," Mary Mae said around her end of the string.

Charles looked down the double line of kids with strings in their mouths, boys on one side, girls on the other, strings hanging in a V shaped canyon between them with a piece of homemade taffy at the vertex of the canyon. Charles vowed he would play the game fair and try to get the candy, even if it meant meeting Mary Mae in the middle, for she was no slouch as a competitor. Tenison mounted as last-minute adjustments were made, hands were placed behind backs, somebody's string got tangled and Miss Wrigley had to undo it, and finally she cried out, "Go!" and everyone began eating string furiously.

Paul Holton was disqualified for illegally pulling the string in his teeth, thus pulling the whole wad out of Sally Marshall's mouth, little Joe Ricci was winning until he choked and Miss Wrigley discovered to her horror that he had swallowed all the string on his side of the candy, Douglas Bent and Martha Portola got to their candy at the same time and Douglas got a bitten lip, and Charles found himself nose to nose with Mary Mae as they came down to the candy exactly together. He did not flinch but pushed on bravely as Mary Mae's lips had almost closed on the prize and got his teeth in the taffy. He and Mary Mae had their faces mashed together, spit on their cheeks, Mary Mae's red blushing face panting with excitement, her blue eyes crossed, Charles's panting breath whistling through his teeth that were locked on the taffy, sounding like a stud horse (as Paul Holton later said), until Mary Mae in a frenzy gnashed her teeth against Charles's teeth, and in surprise he let go. The string came reeling out of his mouth as Mary Mae straightened up and pulled back with the prize. The candy piece, with Charles's tooth marks in it, was hers. And only then did they realize that the rest of the contestants had finished and everyone had been watching them and cheering.

While the apple bobbing was going on, Charles and Douglas and some of the other boys walked out into the dark playground. Paul Holton had a cigarette and lighted it and passed it around. When it came to Charles, he took it, dragged the smoke in and choked so badly he thought he would vomit. The other boys laughed tolerantly but did not make fun. It was too easy to do the same thing, and besides, Charles was almost above being laughed at for something like that. On the other hand, he was vulnerable where girls were concerned.

"I thought old Mary Mae was gonna eat your face off," Paul Holton said, dragging expertly on the cigarette.

"They was tradin' spit," said Carl Bent, at fifteen the oldest boy in the school.

"Oh come on," Charles said, wiping his face again. He had ducked it in the first apple tub before he came out just to clean himself up.

"I didn't know you was so bad off for a piece . . . of candy," Kick Jones said, making an allusion only he and Carl knew. They laughed nastily, making Charles feel stupid.

Charles thought about going out into the dark and shifting and coming back as if he were in costume. That would be funny, he thought, smiling, but then I'd have to show people the costume. He giggled involuntarily, and Douglas said they'd ought to go back in before they all got caught. Charles said that was okay if someone would lend him a sheet so he could hide from Mary Mae, and they all laughed.

In the wink 'em game, Charles began to feel good again, and found himself forgetting the leers of Mary Mae who tried to get into his chair even though he had not winked at her. His chair was empty. He looked

140

around the circle of girls, big and small, pretty, not pretty, fat, bony, all looking expectantly while their guards held their hands at the ready like Western gunfighters waiting to shoot it out with a faster gun. Betty Bailey sat almost directly across from him looking rather bored with half shut eyes and her hair curled perfectly. She wore a jumper that emphasized her precocious bust development, and Charles thought he had never seen a more beautiful person in his life. He looked along the line to distract Kick who was her guard, and suddenly glanced back at her and winked. She tried to get up, but in a slow and genteel way so that Kick had her by the arms before she could even lean forward. Charles looked along, passing over Mary Mae, Kick's twin sister Carol, little Ellie Gustafson a second grader, came to Brenda Gustafson, her older sister, a sixth grader, and winked. Brenda lunged forward and bashful Kenny Grattan missed her completely. Brenda eased into Charles's chair as if she felt at home, looking around with quiet triumph. She was a calm, plain faced girl who was good at sports and sometimes got chosen to play softball with the boys. Charles liked her in a comradely way and managed to hold her while the battle raged around them. Part of the game, of course, was to offer an excuse for boys and girls to make some physical contact. Dancing was practically unknown except for formalized round dances and an occasional square dance formation, so there were hardly any legitimate ways boys and girls could touch each other without being teased for having romantic inclinations. When a boy and girl did decide to be "together," they had to put up with a withering round of teasing that often went on for weeks.

By the time they were to change the order, with boys sitting and girls winking, Charles was mildly excited by the game and the chance grabs and embraces he had had of various girls. He was finding that girls were interesting, smelled good, felt amazingly soft and alive, and were much more exciting than any sport he had played out on the playground. As they switched positions to music played by Miss Wrigley at the piano,

141

there was little choice of partners. Charles ended with little Lula Bright standing behind him and knew he could get away if he really wanted to. First it was one of the notorious Portola sisters, Charles thought it was Fern, but it could have been Flossie. Whichever one it was, she kept blowing on his neck and tickling his ear until he was so goosepimply that he felt like a cactus. Worse than that, the fifteen-year-old girl was exciting him in a new way. He was getting an erection and was horribly embarrassed that it might be noticed, so that when Mary Mae winked at him, he made a heroic lunge, sliding out of Fern's grip and half crawling across the circle to Mary Mae's chair. It looked to everyone as though he must be desperate to get back to Mary Mae, and she got an appropriately smug look when he settled into her chair, sure, he thought, never to get away for the rest of the evening. He was called several times, once by the same Portola twin who gave him an enormously seductive wink that made him want to jump up and do something else suddenly, but he could not get away from Mary Mae's sure grip. She had a way of pinching into the skin of his shoulder that hurt and made him settle back rather than leave part of his shoulder in her fist. He had just determined almost in anger that such a grip was unfair, even for a girl, when Betty Bailey's captive got away, Paul Holton getting up slowly enough for her to stop him with one finger, and Betty not seeming to be aware of his leaving until he was in the middle of the circle. It made everyone laugh as Paul ambled over to Fern Portola's chair, sat down, and put Fern's hand on top of his head like a cap.

Betty winked at several other boys, Kick, Carl Bent, Runt, while their girls hung on like death, although Carl almost ended on the floor with the other Portola twin. And finally she winked at Charles who had been watching her so closely he felt inside her head and started out of the chair even before her two remarkably pretty eyelashes came together in the signal. But Mary Mae was ready and dug her nails into both of Charles's shoulders so he felt like he was being bitten. He struggled on, dragging away from her, feeling the nails digging in and getting desperate, pulling harder, watching Betty's smiling face and additional winks of encouragement as he struggled with the girl on his back. He pulled away from the chair with a new burst of energy, the chair slid to the floor under both of them and folded up with one of Charles's fingers in the hinged seat and Mary Mae flopping down on top of him. Charles cried out and pulled his finger free, crawling now across the circle to the screams and laughter of the other kids, the folded-up chair flat behind him and Mary Mae Martin riding his back still clinging with her arms around his neck now, choking off his breath.

And he never got there. Miss Wrigley stopped the game at that point, announcing cake and punch for everyone and the awarding of the prizes for the earlier games. Charles stayed on all fours for a moment as the game broke up and Mary Mae disengaged herself from his back. He looked up to find Betty Bailey, but she was gone in the crowd. He flopped down the floor and turned to look up at Mary Mae's flushed face. She stood with her hands on her hips looking down at him, her short mousey curls wet with sweat.

"Looks like you win," Charles said, grinning.

"Oh ha, ha, to you Charles Cahill," Mary Mae said, her face twisting with anger. To Charles's intense surprise, she began to cry. And then, shaking her head hard so the tears whipped off her cheeks, she ran toward the girls' cloak room and disappeared into that forbidden territory.

It is no longer strange that Charles can arouse in me emotions of which he is largely ignorant. For the two nights between the party at the school and the one scheduled at the Baileys' I am in an intense state of frustration that I cannot seem to overcome by any of my usual activities. Even the trickery that is usual and accepted on this holiday has not made me feel better. I have pushed over outhouses with people inside in the dark, listening to their curses as they struggle to get out, thinking it is neighborhood boys;

143

I have put gates on top of barns, and at one farm tossed the two yard dogs to the rooftree of the house where they clung like terrified fledglings unable to walk on the steep pitched roof and howling like a couple of fiends; I have frightened people almost out of their skins and made mysterious noises under windows and eaten three lambs, a dozen ducks and chickens, and a saucy cat that I still regret.

But the nights are getting colder. Soon it will be snowing, and I will be restricted in my movements, perhaps even feel like hibernating. These frustrating feelings are part of the growth process, and they will be dealt with in time. Meanwhile, I must try to get closer to Charles's life and partake more of his experiences. Perhaps in this way I can assuage the irritation that runs in my veins. I notice, in a more objective mood now, that the power to control creatures does not yet extend to people, at least not for me. I extended a feeling of attraction one night to a late walker along the highway, but it seems to have little effect other than to make him nervous. He hurries faster, but does not otherwise react. The power does work on all beasts and is a convenience and some consolation in an otherwise frustrating time.

In honor of the Baileys' party, Charles had bought a pair of black wool pants, a belt, and a white shirt and clip-on bow tie. He had to be content to put blacking on his work shoes, running out of money short of a new pair of shoes. But, looking at himself in the old-gold rimmed mirror in his bedroom, he thought he looked not half bad. At least everything fit. He had not thought that it might be cold, and that he would have to walk more than a mile to the Bailey's farm with nothing to wear over his white shirt except an old jacket he had been given by Douglas to work in. The evening was cold, but he could not bear to put the old dirty brown jacket over his clean clothes, as it smelled of sweat and manure. He decided to run most of the way there and back, trying to preserve a balance between getting all sweaty and getting frozen. Mrs. Stumway was sitting in her rocker in the parlor as she usually did, reading by lamplight with her little elliptical spectacles on. She looked over them at Charles as he sauntered through the dining room on his way out.

"Charles," she said loudly. "How old are you?"

"Twelve, I think," Charles said rather self-consciously.

"You're a big twelve, then," she said. "Fact, you look bigger than when you first came here." She looked back again. "Young kids. Never saw one grow *that* fast." And her voice subsided into an unintelligible mumble.

Charles continued to stand just outside the circle of lamplight.

"Well, go on," Mrs. Stumway said, shaking her white curls that stuck out under the aviator's helmet. "You're pretty in your new clothes."

Charles grinned. "Thank you, ma'am," he said and dashed out into the frosty night.

Although he lost his bow tie twice, he eventually arrived at the Bailey farm, panting and straightening himself out while he stood outside the white gate and looked at the big house with electric lights shining like a city hotel. He stood for a minute getting his breath and thinking about what might happen this evening, and then with a final look and a deep breath he strode up the front walk and knocked on the big white door with the window panels on both sides of it.

He stood in the glare of the porch light, feeling like an actor on a stage when the door opened and Mrs. Bailey, plump and beautiful, smiled at him in a bright and welcoming way.

"Come in, Charles," she said, putting one hand on his back and guiding him into the hallway. "May I," she said, and then noticing he had no coat, passed over it. "It is rather brisk out tonight, isn't it?"

"Yes, ma'am," Charles said, walking ahead slowly as she lightly pushed him toward the sound of conversation he heard in the living room. "It's an invigorating night for a run, I mean a walk," Charles said, grinning.

"Here is our young hero," Mrs. Bailey said to the room full of people who seemed suddenly to Charles to all be strangers. They all turned to look at him while conversation stopped for a moment.

"Happy Halloween," Charles said brightly, smiling.

And then they came unfrozen and began to take on familiar proportions and faces. Here was Betty coming forward to welcome him, her beautiful oval face more perfect than usual, her hair absolutely gleaming like polished mahogany in the electric light, her eyes darkened with something, and looking in all at least twenty years old in a party dress that was low cut to emphasize her bust. There were the Portola twins with identical scarlet mouths, semi-formal dresses with flounces around the bottom and daringly open bosoms; there was Carl, Douglas's brother, and Kick and Carol Jones, and Brenda Gustafson and Paul Holton and even the big, aloof Waldo Wickham. There were others Charles knew less well. Alfred was there in an open shirt with a silk scarf at the throat that Waldo whispered was called an Ascot, and Mr. Bailey in a dark gray pinstripe suit and a silk tie that made him look like a blue jawed gangster, and some other older people Charles did not know at all. He soon felt at home among the school friends and with the comforting ministrations of Mrs. Bailey who saw that he got a Coca-Cola with ice cubes in it and was shown where a table full of strange delicacies awaited his pleasure in the dining room. Charles held down the awe he felt at the dangling crystals of the chandelier in the dining room, the huge fireplace with brass fire dogs and a lively log fire in the living room, and at the grandeur, glimpsed through the swinging door, of a real electric refrigerator in the kitchen that kept food cold without ice and made ice cubes such as the ones in his Coke. He talked with his friends and moved with mock assurance among this glitter and opulence as if he had been born in a palace and attended school in the Taj Mahal at least. Betty was laughing at his airs, which he was exaggerating for her benefit, and he was not at all displeased to see Alfred turn away from that sight to talk with Waldo who was standing like a curly topped ornamental urn next to the fireplace.

"Now you take these, for instance," Charles said, a milk bottle lid in his eye for a monocle, "these little devils are fiendish hard to capture." He held up an hors d'oeuvre shaped like a tiny black cat arched on a cracker.

Betty Bailey laughed delightedly, putting her white, delicate hand on Charles's shoulder for support, and Charles felt that heaven was not far away.

"Betty," Alfred Kearny said, suddenly very close and tall. "Hadn't you better put on some music now? I think some of our guests would like to dance."

Charles looked narrowly at Alfred's red silk Ascot which was about at his eye level. "Now here's something you don't find every day," he began, but Alfred turned away abruptly with his hand on Betty's arm, turning her also from the scene.

Charles had not thought they would dance. It was something he had never seen done in his life except in magazine pictures, and had not the least idea how it might be done. An electric gramophone was started, a large black record put into it, and the music of Glen Gray's Casa Loma orchestra filled the living room where the rugs had been removed so people could dance if they wished. Charles sat in a large overstuffed chair with Paul Holton on one side and Carl Bent on the other watching as Betty and Alfred did graceful steps across the polished oak floor. The Portola twins were dancing, one with Waldo in a very stiff manner, the other with an older man of about twenty who might be Alfred's brother from the bigness of his ears. The dancers seemed to be enjoying themselves immensely, talking brightly, except for Waldo who walked ponderously and silently around the room while the Portola twin smiled up at his double chin as if she were receiving secretly some delightful message.

For the second record, only Alfred and Betty and Fern Portola and Alfred's brother danced. It was fast, something with a lot of drums in it that the dancers did a lot of gyrating to. Charles felt he might be able to do the slow kind, but he knew he would trample on his partner in a dance like that one.

147

Then Mrs. Bailey came sailing into the room, smiling with a frown, as Charles thought of it, looking at her expression. She stopped in front of the three boys sitting in a row and looked mock forlorn.

"Wouldn't one of you handsome men like to dance with me?"

Charles looked up at her, the glittery dress with the deep bosom open, the pearls in a triple string, the smooth rouged cheeks and hair piled up on her head, the eyes so much like Betty's, and he thought, well, this has got to be done.

"Yes, Mrs. Bailey, I would," he said, getting up and making sure his tie was still on. "But I don't know much about it."

"Nothing to it, darling," Mrs. Bailey said, taking his right hand and putting it around her waist. "I'm sure such a courageous and gallant young man as you will learn it in no time."

Charles moved stiffly at first, his left hand holding Mrs. Bailey's arm out straight while he looked down between their bodies at his feet. As they moved away into the middle of the room, he looked up and caught sight of the large breasts in front of him and realized that he might have been looking down the woman's dress as well as at his feet. He smiled into Mrs. Bailey's eyes and determined not to look down again. She guided him quite as a dance teacher would, leading him, forcing him to move more loosely, catching him gently when he got off balance, and not once getting her feet under his, so that at the end of the record, Charles felt he had done very well.

When the music stopped, Mrs. Bailey gently disengaged herself, walked back with Charles to his former seat where the two other boys were glowering at him, and thanked him for the dance. She murmured that he was really very good and certainly should ask Betty or one of the other girls to dance. Then she excused herself back to the kitchen where, she said, Millie was getting some special snacks ready.

Charles was about to ask Betty to dance the next slow record when Flossie Portola dashed over to stand

148

in front of him, looking expectant. Charles could not be less than a gentleman and asked Flossie for that dance while he heard Carl's faint "Geezus H. Crise," behind him.

Dancing with Flossie was considerably different from dancing with the older woman. Flossie was more Charles's size, supple and slender and full of bounce. Charles found himself stumbling and said apologetically, "I'm just a beginning dancer, Flossie," after mashing the end of her shoe under his foot.

"But you're learning so fast," Flossie said, moving her body in its flame red dress close up to his. "The best way to learn moving together is to get the hip-lead," she said, pressing her abdomen against Charles.

In alarm, Charles tried to back away as his face began to flush, but Flossie held on, gently but firmly.

"Now you move from the hips down," she was saying, but Charles was feeling very hot and choking as he tried to keep stumbling around the room while Flossie Portola moved her body against his trying to guide him. She moved away after a minute, laughing softly and extending her arm again in the usual style.

"You'll get it, Charles," she said. "You just need practice."

"Thanks a lot, Flossie," Charles said, feeling sweaty and suddenly as if his clothes were too tight. "But I think I'd like to try the hip-lead after my feet know what they're doing."

That record was the end of the dancing, since the "snack" was ready. Charles thanked Flossie for the dance and retired behind the slouching Carl Bent to stand in line in the dining room. They ate tiny sandwiches with some sort of fish in them, strips of carrot and celery with cheese on them, and finally each had a piece of pumpkin pie which Mrs. Bailey apologized for, remarking that her husband had insisted on something substantial in all the froth. They laughed politely and ate their pie, and then it was time for games. Charles was surprised at the changed atmosphere as they got in a circle on the floor to play spin the bottle.

Mr. and Mrs. Bailey excused themselves and the

circle of guests in the flickering light of the fire seemed to change back into school kids again. Even Alfred took on a younger look as they laughed and did the funny forfeits and penalties. Paul Holton spun the Coke bottle, and it pointed at Charles. Paul looked up, a fiendish grin on his face.

"Charles is the victim and must pay the penalty," Paul said. "And the penalty is," and he paused for effect, looking around and rubbing his hands together, "that he must kiss Betty's bare foot."

There was giggling and snorting around the circle as Betty took off her dancing slipper and the knee-length silk stocking. Charles crawled forward in the firelight until he was at Betty's foot, held out with its painted toenails to his face. He took it in his right hand, feeling it warm and a bit damp in his palm, and he looked up the smooth leg to where it disappeared beneath her white party dress, and on up to her smiling face, her head inclined to one side as if she were listening while her dark auburn hair fell in a wave to her shoulders, and he lowered his head to plant the kiss on the top of her foot as the other players leaned over to watch, and as his lips touched her instep, he quickly drew a fingernail along the sole of her bare foot. She leaped, squealing, something wet hit Charles a drop on his ear and he heard Alfred curse.

"Look at what you did, you damned idiot," Alfred was saying, backing away from the circle with his rear stuck out.

"Alfred," Betty said, shocked. "It was an accident. Don't talk like that."

But Alfred was more than a little angry. He had been leaning over Betty's shoulder, not being a game player at that point, holding a Tom Collins that Mr. Bailey had mixed for him. When Betty had leaped up from the foot tickling, her shoulder struck the Tom Collins, firing it directly back at its holder and wetting him from chest to knees. The stain was particularly embarrassing, as it was mostly concentrated on his light blue trousers at crotch level. He went on cursing and dabbing at himself until Betty insisted in stern tones that he leave

150

the room because he was spoiling the game, and he shouldn't have been drinking that stuff anyway. Alfred left, stamping up the stairs, looking back meaningfully at Charles who still sat in the middle of the circle smiling.

After the bottle game came Post Office, a game suggested by Fern Portola with much giggling and whispering to her twin. Brenda Gustafson said she thought it was silly, but she was overruled and a post office was set up in the darkened stairway alcove with the sliding doors to the parlor partly closed. Charles had never played this game either and was mystified to see Carl go back of the doors in the dark and call out, "Letter for Carol Jones."

Carol got up with much giggling and bounced out of the room to the darkened hallway. After a moment of strange sounds from that area, Carl Bent came slouching out with a wide grin on his face and sat deep in one of the overstuffed chairs where he muttered something to Paul Holton.

"Special Delivery for Frank Kearny," came Carol's voice from the darkness, and Alfred's older brother went back of the doors amid much ohhing and ahhing over Carol's courage. After that, Carol came out grinning and sat down and Charles began to get the idea. When Flossie was called back by Frank, there was a long, long pause until Betty said, "Come on, Flossie," and then some muttering from the pair in darkness until Frank came sliding out and sat down on the floor beside the door.

"Special Delivery Air Mail," came Flossie's voice from the darkness, "for Charles Cahill."

"Wow!" "Air Mail!" "Special Delivery too!" And Charles walked back of the doors where he could dimly see Flossie waiting for him in the alcove at the bottom of the stairway. He groped his way over to her and was about to ask her what he was supposed to do when he felt her arms go around his neck and her moist mouth pressing against his lips. He was surprised, tried to pull away at first, and then got the full impact of his own arousal like a shot of adrenalin

151

straight into a vein. He felt suddenly larger and more powerful, more in command, and he put his arms around Flossie's supple body, feeling her ribs and the round edge of a breast with one hand, her hips with the other, pressing her to him as he felt her mouth opening and her tongue coming past his opened lips. The dizzy sensation flowed first up into his head and then down into his loins, and it was mixed with fear and a tight longing that he had never felt before.

In that moment, I approach the surface very closely, feeling what Charles feels, not questioning or wanting to shift, just feeling what is going on in Charles's body which is at the moment like a new factory set in motion for the first time, heart pumping new blood, lungs breathing new, scented air from the girl's body and hair, glands making new and exotic products that exalt, and create new feelings for Charles and for me. All of his nerves are vibrating on the same wavelength, and his mind is lost in a non-thought realm consisting of the sensation in his mouth and hands and the mounting tension in his groin.

"Wow, Charles," Flossie said, pulling her head back and licking her lips.

He did not release his hold on her body, wanting her warmth and the pressure of her to remain where it was forever. He couldn't say anything, and after a minute she put her lips back where they had been and the kiss went on.

After what might have been a long time, a time that Charles felt as a sort of ascending spiral stairway that he and Flossie were somehow going up by pure bodily ecstasy, they heard shouts and catcalls from the living room.

"Come on, the rest want to play. Hey you guys, break it off!"

"We've got to stop," Flossie said, panting, pushing against the hold Charles still had on her. He thought momentarily of willing her to stay there, but then his mind came back, and he realized where he was.

"Yeah. I guess. Gosh, Flossie," Charles said, still dazed. He dropped his arms from their hold and

Flossie leaned over to give him one more wet peck on his lips. He raised his head, but she was gone.

He sat on the stairway for a moment, listening to the kidding that was going on in the dim living room. He had an erection, and his hands were shaking, and his eyes spun and buzzed with light spots. He wondered what he could do now. He thought, I can't call Betty in this condition, and then he thought more strongly, I can't *not* call her either.

"Special Delivery letter for Betty Bailey," he croaked.

He forgot he was sitting on the stairs, and when Betty came groping into the alcove, she at first didn't see him. "What's the matter, Charles?" And as she leaned down he began to stand up, catching her chin with his head a solid knock. It hurt his head, so he knew it must hurt her chin. She didn't cry out, but stood very straight, holding her chin and mouth.

"Oh my gosh, Betty," Charles said. "Oh, I'm so sorry about that." He felt he had just ruined the whole evening with his clumsiness.

"It's all right, Charlie," Betty said, moving back into the alcove so her back was against the wall. "It was my fault. Come over and give me the stamp, Charlie."

He moved over to her, wondering if he dared embrace her with his sweaty body and embarrassing erection, and then he forgot all about it, for she reached out to him, taking his head in her hands and kissing him on the lips, and he moved close to embrace her regardless, heedless, wanting to feel what he had felt with Flossie, but with Betty. He caught the musky odor of her skin and perspiration and the perfume in her hair, and almost automatically he opened his mouth, forcing her lips apart and pushing his tongue into her mouth.

She struggles at that moment, but he holds her tight, feeling her tense body against his, wanting her while I come to the surface so that he cannot release his hold while I am again savoring the sensations. The girl is struggling, but it seems more tantalizing to me, and so I will her to push in against Charles's body instead of trying to get away. She does, throwing her arms around

153

Charles and pushing against him so that his excitement increases. It is more pleasurable, and I am about to push further in this direction, over what seem to be some weak, conscious feelings of both Charles and the girl when suddenly the alcove is shockingly flooded with light. I retreat.

"Oh, Charles!" Betty cried out, suddenly pushing him away so that he staggered back and sat down on the bottom step. "Maybe Flossie lets you," Betty began, and then realized someone was standing on the stairs above them. They both looked up to see Alfred standing in his stained pants at the stairway landing.

Betty's face was red, her hair in disarray, and Charles's bow tie was wedged in the bosom of her dress. Alfred came down the stairs slowly, looking at Betty standing against the newel post beginning to work up anger toward him for doing what he had obviously planned. Charles sat on the step, partly because he was dazed, partly because it would be embarrassing to stand up.

"Charles," Alfred said in a low, dangerous voice, "you lost something." He picked the bow tie from Betty's bosom and tossed it into Charles's lap.

Betty stepped back startled as he did it, and turned all her anger on Alfred. "You did that on purpose, Alfred Kearny," she said, stepping up to him. "You don't want to play our games, and you don't want me to have any fun either. You're hateful, Alfred, hateful."

Betty pushed her hair out of her eyes and slipped out into the living room, said "excuse me" to her guests and disappeared into the back part of the house. The other guests were standing up now, talking in low tones, but staying out of the alcove where Charles, standing now, faced Alfred whose features looked drawn and muscular. He grabbed a handful of Charles's new white shirt and pulled the boy up close to him in tough guy fashion.

"You made Betty mad at me, you dumb little snot," he said very low, "and I'm not just giving you a warning. I'm telling you that I'm going to take you apart first chance I get." He released Charles and turned away

154

to the hall closet from which he took a light brown camels hair overcoat. He slipped into the coat and was out the front door before Charles could think of anything to say back to the threat.

The party ended at that point. The guests stood around in the living room awkwardly for a time until Mrs. Bailey came out, graciously and sadly announcing that Betty had developed a very difficult headache and was sorry she had to say goodnight. Mr. Bailey came out in his overcoat and offered to drive anyone home who needed a ride. Several of the young people accepted his offer; the Portola twins only lived at the next farm down the road, so they said they would dash home on their own. Charles said he liked to walk in the dark and really didn't want a ride, and Mr. Bailey nodded his head as if he understood. Charles put his tie in his pocket and slipped out the front door ahead of everyone. As he was leaping down the steps into the frosty darkness, he heard Flossie say something behind him that sounded like "Wait up!" but he pretended he did not hear. He wanted to run in the cool night and think about things.

It is a new experience to have the human talking to me in this way. I recall Little Robert making a deal with me once, and now Charles is angry and holding a monologue as he walks along the little dark cinder road that leads from the Bailey's lane to the highway.

"It's not fair to do that," Charles is saying, his hands in his pockets for the cold, "making me do something I shouldn't."

"We could shift and be warmer," I suggest, perhaps irrelevantly.

"I'm talking about a serious thing now," Charles says. "You helped me with the rescuing in the river, and I know I'd probably have drowned if you hadn't, but I like Betty a lot, and what you did in the hallway was really wrong."

"Did the girl object?" I ask, trying to recall what had been said after I retreated.

"She was really mad," Charles said.

"Was she angry at you?"

155

"Well sure. I mean I was pushing up against her and French kissing her and feeling her up, and, well of course she was mad."

"I thought she gave the distinct impression of enjoying it."

"You're nuts."

"Didn't you enjoy it?" I ask, knowing that he did.

"Yeah, of course I did, but girls are different. They don't like to be all sexed up like that, the nice ones like Betty I mean. If you're talking about Flossie, well she might like it. Wow," Charles concludes, his mind going back to his first Special Delivery Air Mail. "But it's still not right," he mumbled.

I am enjoying the conversation and the unique experience of speaking to the human. Neither of us is quite as alert as he should be, so that Charles is suddenly struck from behind a hard blow on the neck that stuns him and sends my awareness skittering off and down so that I feel unsure of reacting.

Charles fell to the ground and rolled to one side, trying to see what had hit him from behind. A tall dark person was slipping out of an overcoat.

"Now, you little punk," Alfred said, laying his coat carefully down on some low bushes beside the road. "You're going to get something you won't forget."

Charles got up and faced Alfred, raising his fists, wondering how he was supposed to fight someone so much taller. He tried to punch Alfred in the stomach and something hit the center of his face so hard it made pinwheels and sparkling showers go off in both eyes. He staggered back, blinded, and something else hit his right ear a ringing blow so that he was turned around and for a moment could not find Alfred.

"Here I am, shit face," Alfred said, and as Charles staggered around, a fist hit him high on the cheek. He fell into the dried weed stalks, his head ringing, eyes sparking, his mind wavering. He felt me rising back to awareness and said, his head hanging while blood or something warm dripped from his face, "No! No!" I wait, and he gropes around until he is on his hands and knees facing Alfred.

"Go ahead and beg," Alfred says, and I retreat to wait and see what Charles will do. "Won't do you any good now, you little punk, you're not with the ladies now, little Prince Charming. This is men's country."

Charles had dug his toes into the ground and now rushed Alfred's knees with his shoulders, pushing as hard as he could right at the knees, his arms wrapped around the young man's legs, and then with all his strength he raised up, keeping hold of the legs, and Alfred went down, clawing at Charles back for a hold, losing his grip as Charles's shirt came out, pulled over his back and finally ripped. Alfred hit the ground with Charles still holding his legs, and he kicked out violently, one foot hitting Charles in the mouth. Charles let go and dropped down on top of Alfred who had rolled half over so that he landed on the man's side instead of on his stomach. He got in a good overhand blow to Alfred's left ear that let the young man know he was in a fight, and then Alfred put his greater strength to use and pulled Charles to the ground beside him where he got astride of him and began punching his head and face with hard, swinging blows. Charles tried to protect his face, but he was weakening, and Alfred's much greater strength was too much for even his stubborn spirit. I am rising to the surface and whisper to Charles, "When he raises up next time, knee right there," and I indicate the spot mentally.

Charles is almost too far gone to listen, but he watches from his bleeding face, and when Alfred raises up on his knees to punch down again, Charles plunges his leg up suddenly and catches the man a bit low, just at the rectum. Alfred grunts and pitches over Charles, holding his crotch. Charles rolls out and crawls to the groaning man lying on his face. As he climbs astride the man, I feel he has a better chance and retreat.

With one big ear in each hand, Charles sat on the man's back thumping his forehead into the cinder road. Alfred was stunned. His crotch felt amputated, and cinders were being pounded into his forehead as if with a hammer. He was about to cry out when Charles felt a rock with his foot, picked it up and smacked Alfred with the softball sized thing a solid clonk on the top of his head. Alfred's body went limp, and he lay quite still.

"Oh God, I must have killed him." Charles said, panting and bleeding. He rolled the man over so that his cinder pocked face looked up at the dark, moonless sky.

"He's dead for sure," Charles said, rubbing blood off his own face. His head hurt as if hammers were hitting it in several places, and he felt a loose tooth and blood in his mouth. At that moment, Alfred moaned and moved one hand feebly. Charles, feeling like a half drowned kitten, realized that if the man regained consciousness he would probably kill him.

Charles got up, staggered down the road a few yards, realized he was going the wrong direction and had to come back past Alfred who had rolled over and was on his hands and knees mumbling. Charles staggered past him and tried to trot a little, but his head drummed with pain. Now he was afraid Alfred would catch him for sure, and his fear was keeping him from thinking straight.

I rise, feel the situation and shift.

The pain stays, and I feel the inured tissues swelling and throbbing, but it is possible to ignore because it is not mortal or crippling. I begin to run, thinking about whether I should go back and teach Alfred a lesson, but it is not a serious thought. Alfred is nothing to me. I see a car parked behind a tree ahead near the railroad crossing. There is one practical matter: I must have time to get to the highway so that Charles can cut across a field and be home. I should dislike having to hide while Alfred drives around looking for Charles. I lope over to the car, extend my senses for other things, thinking perhaps Alfred's brother is about, but there are only the usual nighttime small animals. The little Ford coupe is hidden from the road by the line of trees along the fence. Alfred had driven in through a wire gate down the road and had waited in ambush for Charles. I sniff the car. It smells deadly, like most of these machines.

I have never tried to lift one of these, but I grab one side near the bottom and raise up. It leaves the ground, but is very heavy. I put my front claws against the top of the window, brace my hind claws in the hard earth and rock it until it goes over on its side with a crunching and tinkling of metal and glass. Perhaps he would be able to set it right again, I think, so I push it on over until it rests on its top and a liquid with that deadly odor is running out of it. Now he will have some trouble chasing us this night. And I lope away in the darkness keeping low and pushing the pain out of my mind until we get to the Stumway grove of trees. Then I shift and let Charles stagger on to the house.

(4)

Charles was unaware what had transpired between Betty and Alfred or what the condition of Alfred's car might be, but he did observe that during the rest of the school year up to Christmas vacation, Alfred was not seen even once picking up Betty on Friday afternoon. The other boys told him about threats by both Kearny brothers to put Charles in the hospital if they ever caught him, and this rattled about in the back of Charles's mind for a couple of weeks until it began to seem only an idle threat. They also said that Alfred and Betty had broken up, and Flossie whispered to Brenda Gustafson who told Kick Jones who told Charles that Betty's parents were just as happy about it all the way it turned out.

Douglas Bent was morbidly interested, it seemed to Charles, in how he had "beaten up on" Alfred Kearny, which was the description given by Carl Bent after he had observed Alfred the following day in the grocery where he worked. "Geezus," Carl had said, a grin on his broad face, "he looked like he'd been kicked in the face by a mule. He had a black eye big as a tomato and patches of tape all over his forehead."

"I was just lucky, Doug," said Charles for the twentieth time. "And besides, I got hurt worse than he did, and if I hadn't rocked him he'd have really put me in the hospital."

"Did you get some guys to wreck his car?" Douglas said, pressing in again.

"I don't know nothing about his car," Charles said,

160

and then with an inspiration, "he was probably drunk and wrecked it himself. He was drinking that night, you know."

After which, it became known through gossip that Alfred had really been "stewed to the gills" and that was the explanation both for his wrecked car and his defeat at the hands of an oversized twelve-year-old kid. The reputation Alfred was building from this one incident was not entirely on the minus side, so that in the ensuing weeks, he and his brother did indeed try to forget Charles. Alfred had been on shaky ground with the Baileys for some time anyway, as his interest in the nubile Betty had been more than passing dishonorable.

Charles determined to apply himself to his studies and worked each night by lamp light in the old dark Stumway dining room until his eyes burned and he had to quit. Miss Wrigley said in a letter to Mrs. Stumway that Charles was "a brilliant boy who has never had the opportunity to show what he can do in school," a commendation that meant little to the old lady, but which did not harm Charles's position either.

One reason Charles managed to advance so quickly was that Miss Wrigley allowed him to sit in on the lessons of grades higher than the one he was working in. While he was gaining proficiency in the Third Elson Reader, he could listen and comment on the reading lessons from Book IV that the next grade was working on. This meant, of course, that he spent much more time doing homework than the other children did, but he often had the lessons for both grades three and four better than those sitting in the grade rows. If he had not been so light hearted about it all, he might have seemed obnoxious and pushy. As it was, most of the children deferred to his good sense and his sometimes strange comments on their assignments.

In mid-November, Miss Wrigley arranged for both grades three and four to read the myth and hero tale sections of their books, so that they could all join the same class discussion. Grade three read, among other tales, that of Beauty and the Beast, and grade four read a cleaned-up version of Beowulf. After they had got

161

the stories straight, and little Joe Ricci had been assured several times that Beowulf was not a werewolf like the one he had seen in the movies, Miss Wrigley called on Charles who had his hand up and a puzzled look on his face.

"It says in both stories that the monster was so unhappy it wanted to kill other people," Charles said, flipping through the pages of the Beowulf story. He found the place and read, " 'This giant hated light, and could not bear to think that anyone was happy.' And later, let's see, yeah, here, 'It made him angry to think that the men gathered there were happy.' And so he goes and kills thirty of 'em." Charles looked at Miss Wrigley genuinely puzzled. "You said they were both beast monsters, sort of, and that it took heroic deeds to get rid of them, like when Beauty gives up her home because she feels sorry for the Beast, and then Beowulf taking on the giant when everyone else is scared to death of it. But it doesn't say why the monsters are so unhappy that they have to kill people and eat 'em and things like that."

Miss Wrigley waited for comments. Sally Marshall, who was the smartest fourth grader and always held up her hand even when she didn't know the answer, held it up again. Miss Wrigley nodded.

"They, I mean the Beast and the giant Grendel, are wicked, and that's why they're unhappy," she said, very certain of her ground. "Mrs. Ottenbeck at church said that's why people are unhappy because they're wicked."

"Thank you, Sally," Miss Wrigley said. "What do you think of that answer?" The question was to the classes in general.

Kenny Grattan whispered, "It stinks," but no one paid attention.

"Well," Charles said, thinking, "maybe so, but which came first? Were they unhappy and got wicked, or were they wicked and that *made* 'em unhappy? Either way, it looks funny that they would just sit around being unhappy and wicked all the time. Looks like they were just waiting for some hero to come along and knock 'em over."

"Did you all notice," Miss Wrigley said, "that both the Beast and the giant Grendel were different from other people? And that they didn't have any friends to talk to, not a single one? Maybe they were unhappy and wicked because they weren't like other people and had no one to love them."

"That's what made the Beast turn into a handslum prince," Lula Bright said without holding up her hand. "Because Beauty started in to love him and he got handslum." She trailed off in embarrassment as some of the children started to laugh.

"Not hand-*slum*," Harry Bennet shouted. "Hand*some*. Ha! A hand*slum* prince. Oh! My Handslum Prince!" he screamed in falsetto while everyone laughed and the other grades looked up from their studies and listened.

"Harry," Miss Wrigley said calmly amid the laughter, "the next time you mispronounce a word, Lula should get a chance to laugh at you. Is that all right?"

Harry subsided and whispered to Kenny while the rest were getting their breath back. Miss Wrigley waited and then turned to Charles again. "That's an excellent question, Charles," she said with her brow furrowed. "Even if we say that the monsters are unhappy because they are different and not loved by anyone, it is puzzling because they do seem to be waiting," she paused in genuine thought and ended the sentence as if to herself, "for disaster."

Little Joe Ricci had been following the discussion but not the argument. "They're just monsters," he said, "and monsters do bad things because they're monsters, and they're monsters because they . . ." He stopped, perplexed by the circle he had created. Then his round little face broke into a grin again. "Anyway, if I was a monster I'd have lots of fun!" And everyone laughed.

The question was not solved at the end of the class time, and since no one in grades three or four really cared whether it was answered or not, Charles remained somewhat skeptical of the truth of the tales in question.

He could not imagine a being living in the way the books described. It seemed so pointless to exist in that way. It hardly helped when Miss Wrigley talked to him after school about the symbolism of good and evil. He did not grasp the idea at first, and when he did, it made the stories lose their interest to think they had been made up just to teach a lesson. The question became lost in the rush of other lessons, and he did not think of it again for some time.

By Thanksgiving vacation time, Charles had finished the third-grade level problems in mathematics, read with competence both Elson Books III and IV, and he was trying books from the library shelves marked with five and six stars on the spine. He competed with Douglas in reading proficiency if the words weren't too unfamiliar. Miss Wrigley and Charles were sitting in facing desks one afternoon after school talking about Charles's latest exploit, reading and passing a test on a fifth-grade story that that grade had read at the beginning of the year.

"I really think, Charles," Miss Wrigley said, "that we can register you in the second half of the fifth grade for the term beginning in January." She smiled and reached across to take Charles's hand that he was wiggling about to get the writer's cramp out of. "Wouldn't that be absolutely wonderful, I mean to go so fast that in one semester you travel from first grade to fifth?"

"I don't know if I can handle that Civics yet, Miss Wrigley," Charles said, frowning.

"I have the greatest confidence in you," Miss Wrigley said. And then she looked at the big octagonal clock that pointed to almost five o'clock. "I've got to be going now. I have a lot of papers to do, and I have my book club meeting in town tonight." She rose, smoothed her skirt and looked back at Charles who remained sitting, lost in thought. "Charles?"

"Yes, ma'am?"

"What are you going to be doing for Thanksgiving dinner?"

"Oh, I guess having it with Mrs. Stumway," Charles

164

said, sensing a charitable offer coming. "She's not a bad cook, you know."

"I'm sure she's not, Charles, the way you are growing. But I was just thinking that there is a family in town who are great friends of mine. I'm having dinner with them this Thursday, and I think they'd love to have a local hero and rising young scholar at their table."

Charles wanted to leap up and say yes, but he held back for a moment as if he were thinking about the impact this might have on Mrs. Stumway, an impact he estimated at about the same as her wondering whether the emperor of Afghanistan had tea or coffee for breakfast.

"Yes, Miss Wrigley, I think that would be really great, if the people wouldn't mind."

The house of Victor and Lucille Boldhuis was small, neat, and filled with interesting souvenirs from their frequent trips. In their living room a small grand piano dominated the few pieces of furniture pushed against the walls as tokens that the room was really a living room and not a piano box. Charles had never seen a grand piano and looked at the half opened lid with interest while Miss Wrigley whispered that Victor was, among other things, a piano tuner and had rebuilt the piano from a truckload of parts he had bought at an auction, and that Lucille had almost become a concert pianist when she was younger. Victor Boldhuis was a short, round, black haired man in his late thirties with a bald patch like a monk's tonsure and a face that seemed to have grown into a permanent smile. His remarks to Charles as he drove into town in the old, black Ford were mostly facetious ones that at first alarmed Charles and then made him smile and vow to remember some for future telling. Charles had decided on the ride into town that Mr. Boldhuis was harmless and a nice person, an effect that he did not realize was the man's intended attempt to put a nervous boy at ease.

Lucille Boldhuis seemed the opposite of her husband

at first, a slender, narrow faced woman with gray streaks in her hair and a mouth that turned down in sadness. Charles took her hand at the door and was amazed to see her face transform from grief into happiness when she smiled, the smile changing her whole attitude with one gesture from mourning to rejoicing. As the smile faded, she seemed again to pull back into herself and be sad. It was hard to tell how she really felt about anything, Charles thought, watching her face at the table as they ate, because she seemed to react out of a vacuum of sadness, transforming into laughter, interest, concern, or facetiousness without warning and without afterimage. Watching the opposite state of her husband's face, the permanent smile joining the round cheeks, Charles was reminded of the tragic and comic masks he had seen in the front of the eighth-grade literature book Miss Wrigley had shown him some time before.

The dinner was the most sumptuous Charles had ever seen in his life, turkey and dressing, mashed potatoes with something green shredded in them, cranberry sauce, green beans with bacon, sweet potatoes with brown sugar and marshmallows, and a plate of celery, carrots, and radishes for nibbling. There was a tall goblet of wine at each plate, red as rubies and beautiful when Mrs. Boldhuis lit the four candles in the elaborate silver candle holder that sat in the middle of the table. Charles thought it something of a shame to spoil it all by going ahead and eating, and he waited in the flickering candlelight for a signal from Miss Wrigley to make the first move. Instead, Mr. Boldhuis raised his smile to the rest of the table and sat down behind the great bulk of the uncarved turkey in front of him.

"Let us ask a blessing of the Lord," he said.

They all bowed their heads, and Charles heard him say what sounded like a standard prayer that began, "Lord, for what we are about to receive." But at the end of the prayer, as Charles started to raise his head, he heard the man go on in a different voice, "And we ask, O Lord, that you preserve for us our loved ones whom Thou hast seen it best to take unto you, that we may someday be united with them in the name of Jesus Christ. Amen."

It took a minute or two for the mood of festive eating to get back into full swing after the prayer, even though Mr. Boldhuis was being his facetious self again as he carved off bits of turkey for each person.

Charles ate, Miss Wrigley and the Boldhuises talked about books and music and poetry, about names like Hemingway and Scott Fitzgerald and e. e. cummings and Stravinsky, names Charles had never heard or seen in books he had read, and he wondered at the elevation of the learning of these people who conversed with the learned Miss Wrigley as if such knowledge and familiarity with the arts and sciences were commonplace. Not once did Charles hear cows or crops or pigs or markets mentioned, not once did he hear about relatives newly dead or ailing, babies on the way or growing up, diseases suspected or hoped for in neighbors, or the state of the weather, which was gray and threatening snow any minute. Charles sipped the wine between bites as he observed the grown-ups did, and it began to seem to him an enchanted scene, taking on the underground air of a conspiracy by brilliant criminals somewhere in a secret cave while in the upper world everyone else was desultorily eating cornmeal mush for breakfast, sardine sandwiches for lunch, and pork chops for supper and talking about each other's insides. He listened with the warm wine glowing inside him and the turkey so delicious it made his cheeks ache, and the welcome tart of the cranberry sauce, and the sweet of the sweet potatoes turning his body into a temple of delightful lust. I am enjoying it too, but with a difference, for the wine floats me to the surface of Charles's senses as it penetrates and lifts me from somnolence. Charles and I are present in a comfortable duality as he eats and drinks the bright red wine in little glad sips that please me. We listen together, not worrying whether there is conflict in our both being

167

present, and I feel that I might extend my senses just a bit to more fully savor the time, but at a warning from Charles, I realize that I have almost shifted, so comfortable and lazy has it all become.

After the main meal was pretty well demolished, Mrs. Boldhuis mentioned that there was mince and pumpkin pie with whipped cream whenever we wanted it, Mr. Boldhuis turned his grin upside down and said he was completely unable, Miss Wrigley protested that later would be better, and Charles looked about almost uncomprehending, stuffed as he was to bursting and with two glasses of wine inside him pleasantly dissolving his mind in a vague air of animal satiety. I am awash with good feeling and concerned with nothing other than the geniality of Charles's bodily workings. I retreat from Charles's side, but lie more nearly awake than I usually am as the people stagger into the living room and sit in the furniture crowded around the piano.

Outside it was almost fully dark now, and Mr. Boldhuis said he could smell snow even if he couldn't yet see it, which meant it was on its way down from Chicago by special express and would be here by six or seven. Mrs. Boldhuis came in and Mr. Boldhuis said very quietly that if she would play some Chopin while their bodies were recovering from the onslaught of the most marvelous dinner in the Midwest, then they could all attack the dishes and straighten up in jig time. The slender, sad faced woman brightened her face magically, kissed her husband on his smile and sat at the piano bench and began to play without benefit of music before her. As her hands began touching the keys, Charles felt the hair rising along the back of his neck, and as her hands moved more surely in the dimness of the living room, the evocation of the melody which fit together so beautifully, and so seamlessly pieced together poignant sounds that had never been joined before, Charles's eyes watered, and he realized he was weeping while a series of chills passed through his body, deliciously, slowly, as if he were a creature of the ocean experiencing the pull of a tide for the first time, as if,

168

indeed, he had been living in some tiny, landlocked and muddy pool in a remote solitude, but now was experiencing for the first time the true nature of his world, his proper home, the limitless ocean with its endless variety of life, its vast depths and expanses, the full width of its waters and storms and creatures, the infinite nature of its continuing creation.

I am present with Charles as the music pounds now like breakers against the shore with a heavy joy and expansive power and lightness combined that I more than just listen to, but want to live in as I live in air or water or the beauty of a cold night with a full moon as I lope along in the free air, feeling the muscles stretching smoothly, the air pulling in and out rhythmically, and the leap off a high bank into the moonlit water, the crash and spray. I am standing now with Charles and moving quietly into the shadowed hallway to stand with my back against the wall. I must feel this music as fully as only my true form will allow, I think, and buoyed by the music pouring out and filling the house, by the wine, by the exaltation of the quiet and intelligent people among whom I feel most safe, I shift and stand in the dark hallway pressed against the wallpaper in my true form, and the music suddenly floods into all my senses, making every hair on my pelt stand out, my spatial sense understanding the ripples, the reverberating harmonics like thousands of tiny winged and singing birds breaking some auditory barrier as they wing higher and higher until their circles of vibration vanish in a trans-auditory burst of rainbows and lightnings. The basses are gentle thunders overlapping in rhythm and rounded like dark cumulous massing against the horizon, as the birds winging in their ascending unison vanish and reappear in rapid arpeggios. There is darkness and color, moonlight and water, coolness and the comfort of trees in full leaf, the softness of turf underfoot and the sleekness of my pelt being smoothed by water as I race like a huge brown otter through waves that rise in green curls to smash against sand while I shoot through the greenness, a creature of water and air, life and beyond life. . . .

"Charles!"

I shift.

I am standing in the doorway. I look into the living room. Mother was playing Chopin, and Father sits in his chair listening. I want to cry out to them, "I am lost! Help me! Where are you?" But I stand in the dim hallway, shocked to be there, alive. I wish . . .

I rise, feeling smaller, wrong, tides of grief flooding into my newly conscious self. *Who?* The woman at the piano turns to look at me. Her face goes through a rapid series of transformations as it sees me. She begins to scream, scream, shattering the music. Have I shifted? I am not Charles. I hold back the smaller person whom I have become. He wants to run in to the living room. I am beginning to be afraid as the other woman looks at me and her eyes first widen, then narrow. Her expression is going through a forced change as if someone were pulling at the skin of her face, and I see the man looking at me with his smile going crooked and his mouth coming open and his face is whiter than the marshmallows as I realize there is something very wrong and turn to move back down the hallway to the bathroom door where I reach out to the door a small freckled hand that is not Charles's hand but a much smaller one. Have I shifted to Little Robert? No. It is not his hand, and in slow motion I close the bathroom door behind me and turn the lock, knowing exactly how it turns, exactly what the bathroom is like, my bathroom. I turn to the mirror on the back of the bathroom door.

I see myself, eight years old, black hair, round face, freckles and the upturned mouth that is like my father's. I wish . . .

But I must shift quickly, for I hear footsteps in the hallway. I concentrate. I shift. The mirror image startles me. I am so large, almost larger than the mirror will show, more fearsome than I realize. It is a shock to see myself. I have grown greatly and did not know. There is a knocking at the door and Miss Wrigley's voice says with a break in it, "Charles?"

I concentrate, saying the name firmly. Charles Cahill. I shift.

Charles stood, a tall, blond haired boy in the dim bathroom. He opened the door to see Miss Wrigley standing in the hallway with her hand in front of her mouth. She reached out for his hand.

"Will you come into the living room, Charles," she said. "A strange thing has happened, and we have to be very understanding. Just be very kind to these people, and I'll tell you why later. And Charles," she said as they began to walk down the dark hall, "please remember that I like these people very much."

Charles nodded. They walked back to the living room where the short round man stood by his chair, his face still white and his smile leveled out into a straight line, the gaunt woman sitting on the piano bench still half turned toward the hall doorway, both her hands touching her mouth as if the scream had in some way injured it.

Charles walked back to the chair he had been sitting in before. Miss Wrigley went to the piano and sat beside Mrs. Boldhuis on the bench, putting her arm around the slender woman's shoulders.

"I think we have all been the victim of a hallucination," Mr. Boldhuis said to the room in general. "Charles, I apologize for our strange behavior. Let me explain what I think happened here." He turned a face that had almost regained its smile to his wife and Miss Wrigley. "With your permission, Lucille?" His wife nodded, looking down at the piano keys.

"You see, Charles, we had two lovely children, Victor Junior and Danielle, who we lost in an accident when the school bus they were riding in ran off a bridge as they were returning from a Sunday school picnic. It has been several years now, but we still feel the loss very much, and I think especially on occasions like this when families are," he paused and swallowed, "together."

Charles heard the words, trying to think in several dimensions at once, to retain his social composure, to

171

understand what had happened so that it could be avoided in the future, and to piece together for his own survival the reasons for the strange shifting into an unknown form.

I am listening also, nearer to the surface than is comfortable for Charles, curious about the shift I have made in a moment of ecstasy. It is true that I have shifted into a form I had not concentrated on, a form previously unknown even in name, and it is obvious that this form has been impressed upon me by the sorrowing thoughts of these two strangers, or perhaps even by the ambience of this home. It is of interest to me that my shifting has been thus influenced by forces outside myself, but for Charles a different revelation is being made.

As supremely comfortable and happy as he had ever been in his life, Charles had suddenly been supplanted, his personality usurped in a way wholly beyond his control. He realized now that no matter how happy or how safe he felt, he was always in mortal danger. It was for him an intimation of mortality far more rigorous and distinct than the death of a loved one or the nearly fatal accident which usually shadows forth personal knowledge of the precariousness of existence. Charles knew in a flood of fear and anger that left him shaking that he might at any moment not only be put aside for a time, but annihilated forever if conditions arose that required his disappearance. Compounding this rage and fear was the knowledge that he must be unique, that he must be the only creature in the world so constituted and so threatened that the slightest accident of association or the whim of that underlying power of which he was an avatar would erase his personality as if it had never existed. In this state of sudden comprehension, he sat and tried to take in the sorrowful story of the Boldhuis children who had perished three years before in just such a causeless and purposeless act of the universe.

The incident seemed to affect his demeanor very little, Mr. Boldhuis thought, watching the blond boy's

172

face in the overhead light which he had turned on, and yet he did seem a singularly sensitive young man who could understand such a loss. But then Charles had not seen, actually *seen* a loved one appear, magically and fully alive. . . . Oh, Vic, he thought, stopped the image and closed his eyes tightly a second. He looked at the tall, solemn boy again. Mr. Boldhuis could not know the exact cause of the changed expression he now saw on Charles's features, or that these changes were prompted almost wholly by resolves being made concerning Charles's own survival rather than by sympathy with the victims of the world's causeless cruelty. Charles shook his head sadly and shut his eyes too for a moment, an action Mr. Boldhuis took to be a quite sensitive response, so that he felt a warmth and was about to put his hand on the boy's shoulder.

"No, it was real," Lucille Boldhuis's voice came sharply out of the quiet conversation she was having with Miss Wrigley. Victor Boldhuis turned, prepared for a role he had performed many times these three years. But Lucille met his eyes, and her expression told him to be silent, that this time sympathy and strength were out of place. He felt stricken as he watched her eyes, heard her voice with that painful tone of hope he had worked so long to reduce, to replace.

"Did you see how he looked at us?" Lucille said, her voice lifting. "He wanted to join us. Oh, Jessie," she went on gladly, "they *are* alive somewhere. I know they are."

Miss Wrigley looked at Mr. Boldhuis, she looking over Lucille's shoulder, he gazing back over Charles's.

"We have to admit, though . . ." Mr. Boldhuis began, but his wife cut him off.

"I know, Victor. I know. I'm not going to be ridiculous," she said, her eyes bright. "It's enough," she added mysteriously.

She rose from the bench. "I'll get the liqueur," she said, and slipped from the room while they all looked at her with varying degrees of concern.

After a long silence and the handing around of the

173

tiny liqueur glasses, they talked of school, of Charles's progress which was little less than phenomenal, and some careful filling in of his background by Charles who found he must remember what stories of his past he had told Miss Wrigley so as not to contradict himself. He found Mrs. Boldhuis watching him from beneath half lidded eyes as she sipped the green liqueur and was flattered by her attention until he realized that she must be seeing that vision in the dim hallway again and wondering what connection he could have with it.

"Jessie tells us you will be in the last half of fifth grade after Christmas," Mr. Boldhuis said. "At the rate you are progressing, you may well be in high school in a year or so. Have you thought about whether you might want to pursue a college oriented curriculum?"

Charles looked blank. "A college what?"

The adults laughed suddenly, and Mr. Boldhuis said kindly, "We aren't laughing at you, Charles. It's just that you are such a literate young man that I forgot I was not talking to someone of seventeen or eighteen, and my vocabulary got away from me." He smiled his smile at Charles in such a friendly way that Charles laughed.

"I guess I forget how old I am myself sometimes," Charles said. "I started out this fall reading about Happy and Sally, and now I'm trying to figure out the difference between legislative and judicial branches of government."

"How remarkable," Mrs. Boldhuis said, looking straight at Charles over the rim of the tiny liqueur glass. "How old are you, Charles?"

"Thirteen, I guess," Charles said, feeling uncomfortable at all the attention to what he felt was an oversized and overly awkward body.

"And not only that," Miss Wrigley said, getting up and smoothing her gray wool skirt, "you would hardly believe how Charles has grown physically since he began school." She walked to Charles's chair and took his hand. "Stand up, Charles. I want to show them how much you've grown."

174

Charles stood, felt awkward and bent over, and Miss Wrigley put a hand firmly in the small of his back, making him stand straight.

"Look at this," she said, placing Charles on the floor like a potted plant and standing so that her back was against his. "He's almost as tall as I am, and when he signed up this fall I distinctly remember that I could look at the top of his head."

Mr. Boldhuis stood up to look at the two and murmured that if Jessie were to take off her heels, Charles might be just a bit taller than she. Miss Wrigley slipped off her low heels and stood in stocking feet.

"Yes," Mr. Boldhuis said, placing one soft hand on the woman's head and bumping the boy's head with his fingers. "Charles has an edge of about half an inch. Isn't that remarkable."

Miss Wrigley turned around and swung Charles about with her hand as if he were a museum exhibit. Charles felt like a prize ox and was more than a little flushed at Miss Wrigley's bumping her buttocks against his during the height comparison. He was finding with some surprise that it was more than Miss Wrigley's learning and kindly ways that was attractive to him. Charles swallowed and looked at his teacher solemnly, pushing all other thoughts out of his mind and wondering if he was in danger of becoming a sex maniac.

"Charles," Miss Wrigley said, looking slightly up into the boy's serious eyes, "how can you have grown so fast?"

"I don't know, ma'am," Charles said, "but it's something all right."

"Three inches in three months?" Mr. Boldhuis said, laughing. "Why at that rate, one might sit around on dull days and simply watch Charles grow!"

They all laughed at that, and the topic went on to colleges and degrees and questions to Miss Wrigley about when she was returning to Champaign to take her four-year degree from Normal, a conversation that Charles found so opaque that he lost the thread of sense entirely at many points and contented himself with examining the bookshelves beside his chair. Many of the titles Charles had trouble with, and he realized that all of these authors whose names appeared on the spines of the books like cabalistic symbols must be famous and well known to the three adults who had attended college and now moved above the earth in their minds instead of mundanely upon it as did the farmers Charles lived among. Some of the titles were in what must be a foreign language, for even sounding them out, he could make no sense of them. There were two that he supposed must be some sort of humorous books because they had a word like comedy in their titles, but when he opened them, he could see at once they were in languages he didn't understand. One was called *Divina Commedia* by a person named Dante something, and the other was *La Comédie Humaine* by somebody Balzac, and although they were not in English, they were not in the same language either. Charles felt stunned at the erudition necessary to read three languages as these people must do when he was making such slow progress, as it seemed to him, in mastering one. He felt as he had felt on that day when, having suddenly understood the intricacies of division, he knew the elation of having mastered the four processes of mathematics at last, only to have Miss Wrigley say, "Yes, but there is so much more. Algebra, geometry, calculus, trigonometry." So that he was stunned again by the endless vistas of the mental world.

Later, in the dining room after they had eaten pie and whipped cream until Charles felt once more sweetly stuffed and a bit sleepy, Mr. Boldhuis read poetry from some thin books, some clever ones by Edna St. Vincent Millay, some brusque ones by Ezra Pound, some silly ones by e. e. cummings, and finally a sad one by the classic Tennyson, some of whose poems Charles had read in his school texts.

Riding back along the highway toward the widow Stumway's house, Charles sat in the back seat of the old Ford listening to the muted conversation of Mr. Boldhuis and Miss Wrigley in the front seat while the snow whipped at the windshield like storms of arrows, and the cold crept into his shoes. He thought about how large the world really was, and how much there was that he wanted to learn about it. And he resolved to hold on to his piece of the world, to never let it disappear from him at any cost.

(5)

Mrs. Stumway's house had a coal furnace down the basement, but she liked to economize on all but the coldest winter days by using the tall, ornate iron and nickel stove in the dining room. That and the cooking heat from the kitchen kept the two rooms comfortable, and the big parlor had been curtained off with a double thickness of patchwork quilts and bedspreads hung in the archway from hooks that her late husband had installed many years ago. This kept the upstairs bedrooms in a condition of arctic frigidity relieved minutely by opening the floor registers an hour before bed time. Consequently, Charles and the old lady in her aviator's helmet sat in the dining room each night after supper like some oddly assorted characters out of a fairy tale, the tall, blond boy hunched over the table at his homework, the old gaunt woman in her rocking chair, head tilted to one side as she read in her dusty books or leafed through magazines neighbors would sometimes send over as a kindness. She never read newspapers and had little interest in what the rest of the world was doing, so that Charles depended on school and Miss Wrigley for his contact with life, thinking of his home with Mrs. Stumway as a sort of deep freeze in which he was preserved between the times when he could escape to live in the real world.

It came as a shock, then, when Mrs. Stumway said casually one evening, "Christmas is coming, Charles, and we're to have some company."

"Oh?" Charles said, preoccupied with the history of the Civil War and hardly hearing what had been said.

"My daughter Claire will be staying a few days."

Charles stopped reading and looked up, the words sinking in. "Your daughter?" he said stupidly, looking at the old lady.

"Oh, I have family, young man," she said, putting down a piece of sewing she had been working on. "I don't often see them anymore. No, not even when there's trouble," she said in a thoughtful voice. "But they write, and I think about them. Claire's my youngest, though she's not so young anymore either, and she's had her share of trouble."

Charles sat attentive and dutiful, listening to the old lady's voice that he seldom heard unless it was giving him directions or assigning tasks about the house. There was something in the back of his mind about the name of Mrs. Stumway's daughter that bothered him. He could not possibly know her, but he thought of a picture of a young girl in a long black bathing suit. He listened.

"I know you'll be on your best behavior, Charles, for you are a thoughtful boy. She's a widow like I am. Poor Bernard, her husband, taken in the prime of his life by that terrible World War and no reason nor rhyme to it."

She paused and removed her little elliptical glasses and wiped her eyes. "Oh the men in our family, what happens to them? And I said, Claire, you must marry again, for you can still have children—she was only twenty-seven and a lovely girl, but she wouldn't have any of those men came courting her. Said they were all after Bernard's estate money or they were mean, or they drank too much, or were restless. None of them good enough, and I guess she knows. She's been over most of the world on ships and airplanes now. She's done well with the money and the land he left, hardly lost a cent in the crash. Well, and here she is going on forty-four, no, forty-five next February, middle aged, though she don't look it."

Charles sat and wondered why the old woman was

179

saying all these things until he realized she was in a reverie and hardly remembered he was there. Her voice trailed off into a mumbling and then silence, so that the boy was startled by the sudden reemergence of it.

"Oh, but she's a good girl, a fine person. And Catherine, oh my Catherine, whatever will become of *you* now? All of us left alone, lonely old women. It's so hard, so hard to be alone, and my poor dear Catherine with her tragedy so fresh and her wild letters full of nonsense." Mrs. Stumway stopped rocking and bent double to lever herself up out of the chair, pausing on her way to the kitchen to look at Charles as if he had suddenly materialized at the dining room table.

"And you, an orphan, alone like all of us. Do you know what she sent me?"

"No, ma'am."

"Here now, Charles, I shouldn't be talking to you about my family, giving out all our private matters, but you're not one of us, and sometimes I talk on like you can't understand, like you was a dog or something for an old lady to talk to. There now, Charles, I'm sorry, and I do feel you need to be in a family, for you're a lone one too, after all." She leaned over and patted his head, making Charles feel even more like a dumb animal.

Mrs. Stumway moved over to the old secretary with its tall bookshelf encased in curved glass and pulled down the desk part. She rummaged in the papers, looked in the little drawers and found something heavy that she brought back and plunked down on the table. It was a carved piece of stone about four or five inches high that might have been the figure of a bear with a hole bored through the neck for a thong or light chain. It was smooth as if it had been handled by many generations. Charles looked at it for a moment without interest, but something about the shape of the figure was compelling. He reached to pick it up, and as his fingers touched it he felt a tingling as if a static discharge were tickling his skin. He drew back and looked at it again. It had some lightly incised figures or letters all down both sides.

"It's all right, you can handle it," the old lady said, pushing it toward him so that it toppled face down with a clunk. "Piece of junk some medicine show fake sold my poor Catherine. Poor woman." The old lady hobbled out to the kitchen for a drink of water, muttering that the talk about relatives had made her arthritis worse.

Charles reached out to the stone figure again. There was the tingling again, not painful, but as if the stone were in rapid and invisible vibration so that it shook his flesh and bones like waves of sound. He picked it up, holding it tightly. It was cool, a stone, gray and smooth with white lines, and it looked like a standing bear with its muzzle lifted as if howling. The paws seemed held to the sides by a band or belt pulled tight around the whole figure. In all, it looked like any primitive carving, blurred with age and handling, but Charles held it near the lamp and saw a line of very fine markings on the band around the paws, and he felt increasingly uncomfortable. He was aware that Mrs. Stumway did not feel the tingling that he felt, and that there was more to the stone than she imagined. The markings along the sides of the figure resembled crude drawings of clouds, lightning, birds, and stick men; but the intricately curled and flowing figures on the band were of a different sort, like the graceful letters of some unknown language.

He put the stone down on the table. The tingling stopped. He picked it up and held it to his ear, but could hear no sound. On his cheek it was cool, and it made the skin tingle with a buzzing like the dry ice they had played with that night at the PTA party. He put it down, puzzled and a bit afraid. It made him unable to think clearly. What was he doing holding it to his cheek? Why was he picking it up and laying it down so many times? The old woman would think it strange. He picked it up again, unable not to. It tingled.

Mrs. Stumway was standing in the kitchen door looking at him. "You like it?" she said, sipping at the jelly

181

glass of water. "I'd say that you could have it, but just suppose poor Catherine comes for a visit and wants to know where her, what did she call it? her 'Mawky Stone,' is. Something like that. Some such trash. Suppose she does, I have to have it here to show her." She reached down and picked it up.

Charles watched her face to see if she noticed anything. He felt stunned, as if he had been struck on the head with something hard, and for a moment while Mrs. Stumway put the stone figure back in the desk, he could not think. He felt after a moment that for the past few minutes he had been *alone* for the first time in his life, and it was not for some time that he was able to grasp the implication of that feeling.

In the final week before Christmas, Charles outdid himself and passed some exams Miss Wrigley had prepared for the fifth grade in the next semester, so that she kept Charles after school on the last day and looked at him with a barely perceptible smile. He was standing before her desk at the front of the room which was getting cold now that the fire had been allowed to die down in the stoves, and he was wondering what had happened with the exam. He had tried as hard as he possibly could, pushing himself every night to study so that the other kids in the school hardly talked to him, or he to them, in those last weeks.

Miss Wrigley looked up at him with her hands folded in front of her as she did when she had something good to tell the kids. She smiled with such affection that it made Charles's stomach suddenly drop away.

"Charles, I have a Christmas present for you," she said.

"But you already . . ."

"No, I don't mean the presents I give all the children, I mean something less tangible, but more important."

"The exam?"

"You did nearly perfectly, Charles. I'm going to

register you in grade six for the beginning of school in January."

"My gosh," was all that Charles could think to say. The same grade as Paul Holton and Runt Borsold, a grade of Doug Bent. He felt as if he had been left stranded on a height.

"Gosh," he said again as Miss Wrigley got up and came around the desk and took both his hands in hers.

"You are a truly remarkable young man, Charles," she said, looking up now into his flushed face. "Oh, Charles, you are going to be a great scholar someday, a brilliant person." And she threw her arms around him, hugging him hard.

Charles put his arms around Miss Wrigley very delicately, lightly touching her wool jacket. He smelled her hair and felt intensely happy as she pulled back and held him by the shoulders. "I'm so proud of you, Charles," she said, her eyes looking as if she would cry. "Do you know that teaching in a school like this . . ." she began, but then she stopped and turned back to the desk, catching her breath.

When she turned back to Charles, she had become his teacher again, and he realized with amazement that there was not really all that much difference in their feelings, even though he was immeasurably beneath Miss Wrigley in learning and experience. He felt that in that moment he had grown toward adult understanding almost enough to match his rapid physical growth in the past few months.

Then she told him goodbye. She was leaving for the Christmas vacation to be with her family in Joliet and would not be back until the fourth of January when school began again. Charles walked out of the schoolhouse and down the steps in the twilight, feeling the cold hit his teeth, and realized he was still grinning widely. He began a long legged dash through the drifts along the side of the highway, headed for Douglas Bent's house to tell him the news.

The exciting winter vacation days before Christmas were a round of snowy games, sledding, chases, rabbit hunting with the older men, the cutting of Christmas

183

trees on the Peaussier farm for just about everyone in the farm community, riding the Bents' horses when they could get permission, jumping from the highway bridge into the snow drifts on the creek bottom. Bashful Kenny Grattan took a dare and grabbed the back bumper of a milk truck and went zipping along on his sled until he hit a patch of bare cinders near the highway turn and came off the sled on his face. Rudy Bent fell through the river ice and had to be rescued with a ladder and was in danger of pneumonia for a few days they said, but he got over it. And Charles got two Christmas presents stuffed in the old widow's mailbox: a jackknife from a secret admirer (Douglas said it was Brenda Gustafson) and a handkerchief from Flossie Portola with his initials embroidered on it. And he was hard at work making presents too: a carved wooden pistol that was an exact replica of an Army .45 automatic for Douglas, a butterfly carved out of a piece of walnut and a wooden pin to go through the carved hole so it would hold a girl's hair, and that was for Betty Bailey who would not get it until after Christmas since she was away with her parents visiting relatives in Chicago. And a hand-drawn calendar for 1936 with all the holidays marked with red designs and pictures for Mrs. Stumway was almost finished, since she had said she was always forgetting what week it was. He had already given Miss Wrigley her present, a handsome gilt brooch with a setting of petrified wood which was the only store bought present he had money for and which she had received with much delight.

And then the day before Christmas, Claire Stumway Lanphier arrived, pulling off the highway into the short drive that Charles had shoveled the snow out of and roaring the engine of her new cream-colored Auburn convertible before turning it off. Douglas Bent spotted the car as he and Charles were coming back from the sledding hill across from the schoolhouse. He let out a cry and dropped his sled rope to go hopping in his ungainly, stiff-legged run until he stood panting beside the car. It was different, Charles saw, from the cars he had seen. It had a pointed rear and large shining tubes coming out of the sides of the hood and disappearing under the fenders. In front was a single V-shaped front bumper and a stylized naked woman hood ornament with her head thrown back and her chromium breasts thrust forward to cut the wind.

"Wow, it's an Auburn Speedster," Douglas said, touching the cream-colored metal as if it were living skin. "I've never seen a real one. I bet it's the only one in this part of the country."

Charles watched the smaller boy move minutely around the car, touching it gingerly here and there. He laid a hand on one of the shiny pipes, found it warm and decided the visitor had arrived only a few minutes before.

"I guess it belongs to Mrs. Stumway's daughter," Charles said, not overly interested. He could not understand Douglas's infatuation with machinery and found his patience tried on many occasions when Douglas would have to stop and examine some entirely uninteresting piece of industrial craftsmanship.

"Guaranteed to go one hundred miles an hour," Douglas was saying. "She must be really rich."

"I guess she is," Charles said. "Mrs. Stumway said—" but he stopped rather than talk about what the old lady had rambled on about the other evening. "She's going to visit for a couple days." He watched Douglas kneeling in the snow to look under the car, peeking into the interior, and finally became irritated. His feet were freezing. "I got to go in and meet her, Doug." And then he recalled he had not given Doug his present, and he made that his pretext. He ran into the house, dashed up the stairs to his bedroom without taking off his boots, and rushed back out with the present wrapped in brown paper with Douglas's name on the home-made tag. He sailed off the top step into the snow, finding Doug still admiring the car.

"Here, Doug. I made it myself, and it's really authentic." He laid the package in Doug's outstretched hands. "What's the matter?" Charles said, noticing the other boy's face turning sad or angry.

"I ain't got anything for you." Douglas stood

185

straight with his braced leg at an angle. "Pa said we didn't need to get things for people outside the family, 'cause . . ." He stopped, looking down at the package.

"Geeze, Doug, you've already given me so much I can't ever pay it all back," Charles said, putting his arm over the other boy's shoulders. "Merry Christmas, Doug," he said, patting the boy's shoulder.

"Merry Christmas, Charles," Douglas said. He looked up with a smile. "I got something for you after all, and you're really going to like it. Okay if I bring it down tomorrow?"

"Sure, but you don't have to if your Pa said not to."

"Oh, this is okay. It's already mine, I mean mine to give."

With that, Douglas hobbled off to the highway, gathered up the sled rope and headed for home with a backward wave. Charles felt sorry for Douglas for a minute, and then he thought, who was he to feel sorry for a guy with all that family and probably a really great Christmas coming up tomorrow. Charles was not overly concerned about presents for himself, as he expected very little, but he did want to give things to people he liked, and he felt that he had pretty well covered the field. Not until this moment did it occur to him that he would have a very slender holiday himself. He thought of it for the time it took to pull his boots off in the porch and then shrugged it away. It just didn't seem important.

Standing next to the stove in the kitchen, Charles became aware of the new presence in the house by several subtle aromas that he began to perceive as a difference in the environment. There was perfume, of course. Every woman just about had some sort of stuff she put on to smell good, and this perfume was beautifully delicate, not the usual lavender or lilac or rose oil stuff, but something warm, like putting a clean fur up to your nose, a scent that might have been a very exotic flower, perhaps a night flower; and there was an overlay of acrid scent like burned wood. Charles wondered what that could be, since it was new to the house, not like the smell of wood or coal burning in the stove.

"Charles, boy, will you come in the living room?" Mrs. Stumway's voice came, high and strained, from the newly opened living room.

Charles ran his hand through his hair, but it was sticking up in all directions from wearing his stocking cap. He shrugged again and walked somewhat self-consciously through the dining room and stood in the wide doorway of the living room.

"Charles, this is my youngest daughter, Claire Lanphier," the old lady said.

A woman in dark green with some sort of fur around her neck rose from the sofa and offered Charles her hand. As he shook it, he noticed she was holding a glass of light brown liquid in the other hand, and knew it was from her drink that the odor of burned wood came. He looked into Mrs. Lanphier's eyes, seeing her for the first time as she smiled at him and settled herself back on the sofa. Standing, she had been a bit taller than Charles, her hair pulled back from her face and done in some soft kind of roll behind her neck, around which was a white silk scarf knotted like an ascot, and tucked into the front of the dark green dress which Charles thought must be expensive by the heavy, smooth look of the material. Mrs. Lanphier had a familiar look, he thought, sitting down in the other living room chair and smiling. Her mouth was wide with a full underlip and it turned up at the corners, making a rather pretty and complex curve, even though there were fine wrinkles in her throat and around her eyes. Her nose was long and straight and a shade too large for prettiness, but her eyes made up for that by being wide and blue and very expressive. He noticed that as she talked they acted an accompaniment to her words. Actress's eyes, Charles thought, taken with the woman's face as he tried to recall who she looked like.

"So you are the local hero and prodigy, Charles," Mrs. Lanphier said, and her eyes twinkled to assure the boy she was lightly teasing.

"Now Charles, don't let her embarrass you," Mrs. Stumway said. "She's just a terrible tease."

Charles could see the old lady was pleased with her daughter, that there was nothing the daughter could do or perhaps had ever done that would not please the mother. He smiled again.

"That hero stuff came in pretty handy for buying clothes and things. I thought about going into the rescuing business, but I guess the Elks wouldn't pay regular for that sort of thing."

"He got twenty-five dollars in prize money from the B.P.O.E. in Beecher," Mrs. Stumway said. "He rescued one of his playmates from the river," she went on, imitating the newspaper account without thinking.

Charles could see that old Mrs. Stumway's mind was almost paralyzed with the pleasure of her daughter's visit. He watched Mrs. Lanphier's eyes, taking more enjoyment from their changing expressions than from the conversation they accompanied. The talk was of school and local news for a few moments, Charles working up some social enthusiasm as he seemed able to do on any occasion, talking from the top of his mind while he studied the interesting new person in his world. Mrs. Lanphier sipped at the drink in her hand until it was almost gone, and then she opened a flat cigarette case and took out a thin, long cigarette.

"Do you mind, Mother? Charles?"

"I don't like it, but I guess everyone's doing it now, even the women," Mrs. Stumway said, but she didn't really mind, Charles could tell.

"Charles, would you help a lady trapped in the wilds of the Corn Belt to another Scotch and water?" Mrs. Lanphier held up her almost empty glass plaintively.

"Sure," Charles said, almost leaping from his chair. "Uh, well, I don't know how to do it though." He laughed, holding the glass in his hand as if it were an obscure artifact.

"Two fingers of Scotch," Mrs. Lanphier said, one eye squinted over the illustrative two fingers, "and the same of water, and some ice." She looked sad momentarily. "Oh, you have no ice, and with all this winter around too."

"I'll get you some," Charles said. He leaped out of

the room, set the glass on the sink and slipped out the
back door, reached high up to the right and broke off
a long icicle from the porch roof. He looked through it
to make sure it was clean, but this time of the year it
would be, since the roof had been ice covered for
weeks. At the sink again, he unstoppered the bottle of
brown fluid, poured two fingers and almost dropped
the bottle with the strength of the odor rising from the
whiskey. He put water from the pitcher pump into the
glass and stirred it with the icicle, broke off a length
of the ice that stood up in the glass, took it out and
broke it again, getting some of the drink on his fingers.
He licked them and shuddered. How could people
drink that stuff? He rushed back into the living room
with the drink.

"Charles, you are a sweetheart," Mrs. Lanphier said,
taking the drink and admiring the icicle. She said
"sweetheart" as if it had capital EE's in it, making
Charles squirm with pleasure. "Will you be my official
Scotch and Water and Icicle maker for the term of my
visit? Say you will?"

"It'll be my pleasure, ma'am." Charles felt as if he
had just been knighted. He watched as she took the
first sip, waiting for her eyes to approve. She looked up
at him over the edge of the glass, and her eyes twinkled again while he felt his heart thump a couple of
times.

"Chivalry in the most unusual places," she murmured. She took a delicate sip from the cigarette, tap-
ping its edge on the saucer that served as an ashtray.
"Won't you have a drink, Mother?" she said. "It is
Christmas Eve, after all, and we are together for the
first time in, how many years?"

"Oh, Claire, I don't know. I think it must be five or
six. I don't like to drink that stuff, but I will have some
of that wine you sent last year."

"You still have that wine?" Claire began to laugh
and leaned back on the sofa. "Oh, Mother, that was
last year's present."

"I know, I know, but I don't drink it very often.
Charles, will you go down cellar and get that bottle,

the one with the dent in the bottom. It's layin' on the ledge to the right of the stairway. Now be careful you don't drop it."

"Yes, please," Claire said in a very low voice that Charles was sure her mother couldn't hear.

And so it turned into a very pleasant evening, although Charles had not had anything to eat since noon. He had a glass of the wine with the old woman, and then he made Claire another drink as it became quite dark in the house and Mrs. Stumway lit lamps and made some little sandwiches with bread and some gray paste out of a can that Claire had brought with her. The wine was beautiful deep red with a soft, smooth tang that made Charles feel that he could taste it in several places rather than just with his palate, and the sandwiches were sharply spiced and liverish tasting, but delicious with the wine. They sat in the dim living room speaking quietly of Christmases past, looking at the little tree Charles had got from the Peaussiers as a gift for doing all the cutting, and the presents under the tree which looked like quite a respectable pile when Claire added the half dozen she had brought.

"Oh, yes, Charles," she said. "Some for you too," as he looked puzzled at all the packages.

It got later, and Charles noted it was snowing again as he fixed Claire another Scotch and Icicle. He had drunk two glasses of the wine and wondered if he should pour himself another one. The old lady had fallen asleep in her chair as she sometimes did, so that he and Claire were alone. He poured himself another sip, feeling very manly and tall. In the dim living room, Claire and Charles toasted Christmas and sang "Silent Night" very softly, Claire leading, although Charles knew the words from singing at school. When they finished, it was silent. They could hear the fire muttering to itself in the stove.

I feel the wine as Charles becomes more comfortable and sleepy, but I am waiting in these times, for he takes the powerful stone with him when he leaves the house. It is in his coat pocket now, and when it is in the house I find it difficult to rise to consciousness, as if I were in hibernation. The voices I hear and the dim senses that come to me are lost in a dream, soft, yielding, unimportant. I feel that it would take much to wake me now. It is not important. I sleep again.

Together they helped the old lady up to her musty smelling bedroom, and Charles staggered off to bed while Clair helped her mother. There were soft goodnights, Merry Christmases whispered, and he got into bed not minding the cold, even admiring the foggy clouds of his own breath in the candlelight before he pinched it out and fell into a deep sleep almost at the same moment.

It was a wonderful Christmas, Charles thought, remembering with a sense of strangeness that it was also his *first* Christmas. Presents were unexpected and perfect, the way they always should be, and even though he had not been able to get Claire a present, how gracious she was and how knowing of what he might want. The soft wool sweater in dark blue cable stitch was the most sumptuous thing he had ever seen, and it fit. She had brought her mother half a dozen beautiful long candles to go in a crystal candle holder that she whisked out of a soft felt bag like a magician producing a glass bird of paradise. It stood on the dining table of the old farmhouse gleaming like a huge irregular diamond, its facets throwing rainbow glints that made Charles long to see the big cities and far countries that Mrs. Lanphier must know. There were tiny bottles of what she called cordials for sipping on winter nights, and a long shawl in delicate green and gold that Claire said was Cashmere wool, and a tooled leather belt for Charles, and an ivory comb for Mrs. Stumway, and it did seem that the miraculous flood of gifts would never stop. The last package Charles opened proved to be a flashlight, with batteries included and a clip on it to hook to his belt. It was all so great that he went in the kitchen on a pretext of making a pot of coffee and wept with his head against the wall while he felt the figures in the belt that he had put on over his pajamas.

The afternoon was colder than it had been any time

that winter, with the windows Jack Frosted solid so that it seemed the house had sunk beneath a glacier, and they were all closed in for the winter. Charles had to keep the small furnace full of coal and the upstairs stove full too, and still a cold draft would sneak in under a door or around a window, stretching a white finger of frost along floor or window casing as if the winter were pointing with derision at the poor beings trying to keep warm. Douglas came over with a box wrapped in tissue for Charles and said Merry Christmas to everyone and admired Mrs. Lanphier's car again, although it was almost unrecognizable under the new cover of snow. Charles opened the box while Douglas had some hot tea to warm up in the kitchen. Inside the flat box were several rows of white and gray stones, flat and chipped looking. He looked at Douglas with a smile but not really understanding.

"Indian arrowheads," Douglas said, grinning. "It's an arrowhead collection I got from my uncle in Wisconsin. They're all genuine too."

Charles was at a loss, but he recognized Doug's need and exclaimed over the collection until the smaller boy glowed with pleasure. Doug pulled the carved Army .45 from the pocket of his coat.

"Look, Mrs. Stumway, what Charles made for me." He waved it around and the old lady ducked involuntarily. "It's really swell, exactly like a real one. You can really carve, Charles."

And after Doug had left again into the blue white cold and the door was slammed against the winter, Claire asked for a drink, and they retired to the living room again. The afternoon got darker and later somehow without Charles knowing that time had passed, that they had eaten again, the turkey sliced for sandwiches with dressing on the side and milk, and now it was late again, and he was in the kitchen fixing another drink for Claire. He poured the last drop of wine into his glass. He seemed to wake up at that moment, looked around him at the dim kitchen, the lamp on the table, the two empty bottles in front of him. He wouldn't be able to make her another drink, the bottles were empty, and who had drunk the rest of the wine? Surely not Mrs. Stumway, for she had been sitting smiling with her shawl around her shoulders and was now asleep again. He had drunk it. How had that happened? He walked back into the living room holding two empty glasses.

"Looks like the end of Christmas," he said, holding up the glasses.

"Oh, dear boy, not at *this* point," Claire said. She looked genuinely pained. "Where is that other bottle I bought?" She sat back thinking, and Charles watched her face get old for a moment, her expressive eyes falling shut. "I left it," she said sadly. "I left it on the hall table, and I'd told myself I was going to leave it if I didn't put it in the whiskey box of the car, and I left it." She looked so sad that for a moment Charles thought she was going to cry. He felt helpless and awkward.

"Well," she said, brightening, "there's always more whiskey in the world, at least this year there is. The year before last was a horse of a different shade." She stood up, raised her arms over her head and stretched like a cat, yawning and patting her lips with one hand. "Are you game, old fellow?"

Charles was not sure what she meant, but he nodded, grinning.

Claire staggered slightly as she stepped forward, and Charles caught her elbow. "Quite all right, old fellow," she said, putting her arm on his shoulder for support. "Short dash to the Caledonian Isles and the Scottish succession is assured."

They dressed warmly, Claire making obscure jokes that Charles laughed at the whole time. As she opened the door and looked out into the blue black and whirl of snow, Charles felt the reassuring weight of the carved stone in his mackinaw pocket, pulled his stocking cap down over his ears and dashed out first into the snow. They dropped off the porch into snow up to their knees, Charles getting the powdery stuff up both sleeves and into his shoes as he worked to clear the car windshield and headlights. He realized he had forgotten his boots but let it go. They would be in the warm car.

"This thing is guaranteed to go a hundred per," Claire said as the starter whined, groaned and then turned the engine over with a horrible grunting sound. "If you can get it going." But at that moment the engine caught and roared. "Ah, the marvels of the Indiana natives," she said, spinning the wheels as they slewed back out of the driveway and bounced backwards onto the half cleared highway. Charles felt warm inside with the wine and the excitement of going away like this with a beautiful woman, even if the woman was old enough to be his mother. That didn't seem to matter.

The car roared in first gear, its rear end skidding across the highway until Claire realized the road was packed hard with snow and slippery as glass. "There now, sweetie," she said, apparently to the car. "Mama will take care of you, you big brute. Jus' control yourself." And when they started again, it was with less fishtailing until eventually they were straight on the roadway, headed for Beecher. In the dark interior of the coupe, the wind spitting tiny needles at them through invisible cracks, the dashboard dials glowing across in front of them, the speedometer needle wavering and holding at fifty as they raced into the turn at the city limits, Charles felt exalted and rare with the potent thrill. The car began to slide as it lost hold on the curve, but Claire pulled it expertly back into line, although it was lucky the road was deserted, since the maneuver took up the whole highway. They passed the first tavern at the railroad bridge because its lights were out, and then the big Beecher Saloon beside the DX Diner was also closed and a horrible feeling began to dawn that maybe all the liquor stores and taverns were closed. Charles said as much, and Claire pulled to the curb in front of the Diner.

She put her arm on the back of the seat. "Charles, I used to live in this dogforsaken place, and the liquor people do not close except on Sunday, and it is," she paused, "ah, Wednesday."

"It's Christmas Day," Charles said, feeling that he was responsible for it.

"Ach, the Prince of Peace," she said. She struck

her forehead with the heel of her hand and tipped back the little green hat with its perky feather so that she looked like Maid Marian in Sherwood Forest, Charles thought.

"All right, Scrooge," Claire said, snapping the car into gear and roaring in a wide fishtailing turn into the middle of the street, across the old streetcar tracks and back again, straightening out for the turn at the bridge. Somehow the slewing of the car and the roar of the engine made Charles feel better, and he laughed.

"You don't really mind anyway, do you?" He held on to the dash as they took the corner at the end of the bridge where cinders had fortunately been sprinkled for just such drivers.

"It's not my mind, old fellow," Claire said, shifting into high at the city limits again. "It's the old spirit that needs the support of fellow spirits. Scotch ones, to be precise."

"But everything's closed."

"Now you're a smart lad," Claire said as they roared into a turn at the route 17 junction and headed east. "What does water do when it gets too hot to be water?"

"What?" said Charles, confused by the sudden change. "Oh, I guess it turns to steam."

"Precisely, Dr. Einstein. And what is that clever move on the part of our friendly H_2O called?"

"Gee, I don't know what you mean," Charles said. He was trying to follow the woman's joke and not succeeding.

"For shame, old fellow. It's called what we are doing right now, a change of state!" And Claire laughed briefly.

"Oh, I see," Charles said. "You mean that across the state line in Indiana?"

"The State Line Tavern. There's always a state line tavern. There's one in Texas, across from blue nose Oklahoma, and one in California across from blue nose Arizona."

"Blue Nose?"

"My boy, there are two kinds of people in the world, disregarding the unimportant details of sex, race, age, and place on the Social Register. There are Blue Noses and there are Red Noses, and that's the world for you."

Charles began to laugh, finding the woman's tone irresistible. He looked past the laboring windshield wipers at the long white road that raced beneath their wheels, the streaks of snow that lanced at them, curving curiously downward to fly directly at them in the headlights that punched a broad bright swath in the darkness. This was the whole world, right here in this racing automobile that now went faster even though he heard the engine roaring less loudly. They seemed not to be touching the road at all now, whispering over the snowy surface and the black lines of tar that he would glimpse where the snowplows had scraped the concrete bare, the black lines whipping past under them, and the snow bursting its arrows impotently against the small hard panes of the windshield as they raced toward the line.

"Oh, Sweet Charles," Claire said, reaching over and squeezing his knee just behind the joint so that it almost hurt. "You are so gloriously young and innocent and perfectly at home in the world." Then she stopped and concentrated as an approaching car beamed intensely bright lights into their eyes. "The bastard," she muttered. "You know, young man," and she glanced at his eager face, "I might well get into trouble with the law for taking you to another state for immoral purposes." She paused as if considering that for a minute, making Charles almost think she was serious.

"I thought I was too young to be immoral," he said, not knowing quite what she meant and not caring.

"Dear old fellow, you must have heard of White Slavery and the Mann Act? In a sense that some of my lawyer friends could prove in court, I am transporting a minor interstate for the purpose of violating the law," she said, but in a lower voice as if she were thinking of something else. "The hell with that," she muttered. "What we need is a breath of the Auld Orkneys, and I believe they are not far ahead."

Charles barely saw the sign announcing their entry

196

to Indiana before he felt the car slowing and saw the red and green blinking lights of a tavern far ahead on the left. It was terribly cold, he realized as they got out of the car's heated interior and ran for the tavern door, and his feet were colder than they should be already. He felt the carved stone in his pocket. He had forgotten his gloves too.

All might have been well if Mrs. Lanphier had not decided to see if there were any old buddies in the bar section. Once she had installed herself on a stool and ordered a double Scotch and a glass of red wine for Charles, time began to pass behind their backs as they drank and laughed at the drunk next to Charles who kept dipping nose in his beer, and talking to the bartender whom, it seemed, Claire had known a long time ago in some different context. There were more doubles, more wine, which the bartender said he shouldn't serve to Charles, but that he thought it was okay since he was with his mother. And that stopped Claire's glass as it was rising with smooth precision to her lovely curved lips once more.

"His *mother!*" she said in mock horror.

"He was kidding," Charles began, but he saw that he was not really in the conversation at all and sat back somewhat hurt as the banter went on.

"Larry, you mean to say," Claire began, grabbing up the bartender's hand, wet with wash water. "And I was going to take him to Crown Point and marry him."

"Claire, you're the same as ever," the bartender said, slipping his wet hand back into the wash water.

"Well you're not, you old muskrat," she said, finishing her drink. "You're getting bald and experienced looking. And if you don't chase that one with a new one," she said, sliding the glass off the bar so that he caught it as it fell, "I'll burn the hide from this lad's innocence by telling him about your own youth."

The bartender was indeed bald and fat, and not at all handsome, Charles thought, but he glowed under Claire's jokes and allusions to his lurid past. So there was that drink and another one, and Charles didn't know if he'd had one glass of wine or three because

197

he couldn't keep track of his own thoughts, and he kept feeling the stone in his pocket because it was his one charm in an unsafe world, and he didn't even notice when he could no longer feel the buzzing in the stone, or rather the buzzing seemed to have taken over his whole body while the stone fell still and cold. And then he was being pulled off the stool, and he cracked his eyes open to see a shape in a green hat with a feather like an Indian maiden, or was it Maid Marian with an arrow in her head, taking him by the sleeve and lunging toward the door while confused noises burst around him like multicolored thunder and lights swung double and back to single and then double again, and so did the bartender's face, and then the cold hit him like a hard slap.

"C'mon Charlie old fellow, got to get back to the old fireside," Claire was stuffing him into the car. She left his right leg hanging out in the snow and staggered over to her own side. "H've to do the rest yourself, old feller. I can't bloody well lift yer leg fer ye."

He stared down at his leg resting its shoe in the snow and thought of Douglas. How Doug would like to ride in this car, but it mattered so little to Charles, if it was Charles who was mattering at the moment. The car engine roared and something grabbed his neck and pulled on him.

"Get it in here, now."

He pulled the leg up and put it in the car, reaching out over a precarious abyss to get the door handle and pull it shut. The car was lurching backwards and forwards strangely. Charles made a great effort to come awake and saw the red and green sign blinking "State Line Tavern" going to the right and left wildly. At his side, Claire was cursing steadily while she shifted back and forth, and then with a final lunge and spinning and fishtailing, the car shot out and away to the left, leaving the sign flashing red and green on the snow behind them. The motor roared for awhile, Claire shifted down with another curse, and they saw the straight highway stretching away in front of them again.

It seemed a long time that he was asleep, no sight,

no sound, just gone, and then he awoke to a lurch of the car that threw his shoulder against the door.

"Would you believe what demon rum has made me do, old fellow," Claire was saying thickly. "We're heading wrong, going to New York, b'God." She began singing a song about Broadway and muttering between verses that there was no goddam place to turn around without getting stuck, and then the engine roared as she downshifted and the back end of the car seemed to leave the road, and Charles's breath went out of him as he saw the lights picking up trees, road, trees, bridge, trees, and realized they were spinning around and around in the road, and now not on the road at all but down, too steep a place, down too fast through drifts, the engine roaring and then suddenly stopping in a terrible silence as the lights seemed to be making the world turn over, and something hit his head so hard he began to see sparks and stars, and then saw nothing at all.

"Charles! Charles!"

Someone calling his name. What voice was that? It was too cold to wake up. Go back to sleep. I hurt my head, Mommy.

"Charles!"

"Shut up," Charles said savagely. He tried to raise up and couldn't move. His body was all folded up with knees by his head, neck bent over so he could hardly breathe, and only his right arm free. There was a great weight on his neck and head. How was that possible? He was upside down!

"Charles!" The voice was not audible. It was in his mind. It was coming from inside of him. Was he dead?

"You will be in a short time, Charles, unless you let me help. We will both be frozen to death."

"Where's Claire?" Charles tried to feel around, but his left arm was pinned tightly under something, and his neck was beginning to hurt like hell along with the side of his head. He could not even move his feet or feel them, and he thought with sudden fear that they might be frozen.

199

"Not yet, Charles, but they will soon be gone," the voice said, softly, coolly, as if commenting on someone else's death. "The woman is alive, I believe, but she is also helpless. She is wedged against your left side."

He tried to turn his head and could not. He struggled again, trying to move one leg, but he could only move his right knee slightly up and down, or down and up, since he was on his head and apparently the car was on top of them. He moved his right arm experimentally.

"It's in your pocket, Charles, and I believe you can reach it," the voice said.

Charles found the pocket with its burden still there, almost against his right cheek. He could touch the stone through the cloth, but he was having trouble finding the entrance to the pocket. If he could just get some room, he thought desperately. To give up the stone now meant he might not get it back. He would be without its protection, subject to the whims of . . . His body slumped downward slightly, putting its whole weight on his bent neck, and an excruciating agony lanced from his shoulder blade through his neck and up into his already throbbing head.

"Don't be a dead hero," the voice said quietly.

His eyes spurted tears in the cold silent darkness. "Can't you help?" he said finally aloud, his whole body beginning to feel far away and numb except for the arrow of pain in his neck and head.

"Not while you have the stone. You must simply remove it from your person. It need not be far, just out of your possession, I believe."

He touched the stone. That was the way in. He grappled with the pocket until it came inside out, and the stone fell into his face, bounced off his chin and was gone somewhere above, or rather below, his head.

Now I rise and shift.

It is the most difficult position I have ever been in to use strength. There is no leverage, but the difference in body configuration makes it possible for me to push up hard with my hind feet while I hold the weight on my shoulders instead of neck. The woman's body is delicate, and I must try not to break any of her bones. I push hard, taking the whole weight on my hind legs and shoulders. The car begins to move with a creaking, tearing noise of metal and ice. I push harder, straining with all my strength, and the weight lifts slowly. I put one forepaw under the side nearest me and try moving the weight sideways as I push up. It is moving up more easily now, more tearing sounds, and I hope some of them are not part of the woman's body, but we must get out of this, and the only way is to lift it straight off. At last I heave with hind legs and right arm as hard as I can, and the car slides away to the left as something rips apart across my shoulders. The car goes onto its side with a groan and crash of glass, and I hope the woman's arm or perhaps her head is not beneath the left side. The cloth top of the car is ripped, and I finish the job with my claws, tearing wide strips until I can see the stars and feel the icy wind.

The top torn away, I wriggle out and feel around for the woman's arms and head. They are all right so far. I pull her out of the car carefully. It is like sliding some creature from its shell. She is long and soft like a creature taken from its shell. There is blood on her face, but I sniff her and feel about with my senses, and she seems not seriously injured. Her shoes have come off, but strangely, her hat is still on, the feather sticking up defiantly. It is amusing, and in spite of the cold and my own throbbing head, I laugh, standing in the flat of a frozen pond, the car on its side, the woman in my arms, and that feather sticking up on her head. I laugh as I carry her through the deep snow. It is funny because of the wine. I am still drunk, and that is funny too, so that I am a strange sight on this Christmas night, as I trudge up the snowy bank to the road, a huge, laughing, furry creature carrying a woman with a feather on her head. In the cold wind that does not yet bother me much, I think about walking away with this woman, digging a burrow for her and myself, making her a mate for me. But it is all the wine in my head, and I hear somewhere far back the voice of the boy Charles crying, crying for something. The stone, Charles? I cannot bring it now, Charles. It is nothing to me, but you must see to that. I carry the woman to the road, looking about for a house, but can see none in the whirling snow that is more fierce on the highway than it was down in the ditch. I extend my senses through the bitter cold dark feeling for life, for a house, for warmth. Nothing. I must walk, and now I must keep the woman warm, for she is lightly clothed and already very cold. With nothing to cover her, I can only try to keep her warm with my own body as I trot up the road in the direction from which the car came. What if a car comes along and sees me? I care little enough for that now, having been broken out of my enforced sleep by the whims of this drunken woman. Let them see me. I trot on into the dark, my senses feeling out ahead of us for some house or sign of life, but it is as if the planet has been swept clean of humans. The few bits of life I sense are the wild creatures dying of the cold or curled so deep in sleep that they are almost inorganic. Then I feel a small building ahead and speed up my pace.

But there is no life there. It is only an abandoned shed, empty but for some wooden flats for fruit and some old sacks in one corner. I lay the woman on the sacks inside and step back into the wind. Feeling to the limit of my senses, I can find no human life or other shelter. I wonder if I should run as far as I can, but no, the woman is very cold already, and she will surely freeze. I must warm her first. I go back into the shed where she is lying as I left her. I close the door and wedge it shut against the wind with some of the boxes. I lie down and take the woman in my arms, wrapping her body in my fur. I put her feet between my hind legs, her hands under my arms, willing more heat from my body. As I feel her icy feet and hands begin to warm, she stirs in my arms, moves her face against the fur of my shoulder. I feel that she is almost conscious, but her mind is not awake, and what she says makes no sense.

"Roger, you mus'n now, sweetie. What will the hostess think?"

I find myself rocking the woman in my arms as if she were a young one. Can I feel such emotions for a human being, a woman? I feel very gentle toward this aging woman. It is pleasant to hold her body with mine, and for a time I drift into sleep, erecting my fur to keep the cold away, pulling some of the sacks across our bodies as I drift into a light dream and the wind outside moans in the dark snow.

When the light begins, I hear Charles crying again, far back where I have pushed him. The woman is warm and breathes easily but is not awake. I allow Charles to come closer.

"That's not fair, now," he says. "You can't step in like that. I am glad you saved us, I'm really grateful, but it's my life."

"Our life, Charles."

"You can't stay here. There's going to be people out and find the car, and there's your tracks coming here."

"The wind has blurred them."

"Get up now, and let me out!"

"I am comfortable. I like the woman's body. She is comfortable. You cannot keep her warm."

"If she wakes up and sees you, she'll die of fright."

I enjoy talking with Charles, and while he talks I am holding the woman and feeling how pleasant is her warm body against me. "What of the story, Charles?"

"What are you talking about?"

"Beauty and the Beast."

"You're crazy. That's just a fairy tale. That never happened."

"Perhaps it did. But then the woman was the hero in that story."

"She's not your friend. She's mine. She doesn't even know you exist."

"I could be her Beast, and she could learn to love me." I gently slide one paw against the front of her dress below the waist, feeling her sleeping body respond.

"Stop that," Charles screams. "That's awful. Stop it!"

The woman grunts a tiny little sound of pleasure and puts one arm around my neck.

"You see, she could like me."

"She's asleep! You're rotten, doing things to her when she's asleep."

The boy is in a frothing rage. I stop stroking the woman and put my arm back around her. She snuggles closer against me, breathing more quickly.

"Maybe we are not so different, Charles."

"We are," he says. "You're not . . ." Then he screams again, "You're just keeping me talking while you lie there hugging her."

"Now, Charles, I saved your life—again."

Silence.

"I like talking with you, Charles."

Silence.

But unfortunately the boy is right. I am sensing movement outside. There is car noise now, and it stops down the road. Humans get out, three of them. I can almost hear them talking. Well, it has been nice, Mrs. Lanphier, I murmur in her ear. But now we must part. I give you Charles Cahill, boy hero.

I concentrate and shift.

Charles sat up, took Claire's head in his lap and shook her, patting her cheeks and watching her eyelids. "Claire, Claire, wake up. There's people out there. I've got to go out and holler to them." She hunched her body up with the cold. He shook her again and then rushed to the door where he had some difficulty getting the boxes away and the door open. The cold wind hit his face, and he realized as it made his eyes feel stiff that they would indeed have frozen to death. It must be twenty degrees below zero. He stepped out into the knee-deep snow, noticing the tracks were blurred as the Beast had said. The Beast? He pushed the strange idea out of his mind. His feet and hands already prickled with cold as he took a few steps out into the snow, hearing it snap and creak under his shoes. Down the road a pickup truck had stopped where the Auburn had gone over the embankment. Men were moving up and down the ditch and around the pickup. One of them suddenly noticed the tracks and pointed to Charles. He waved wildly and motioned them to come to the shed. Behind him he heard Claire stirring, and then she appeared in the doorway of the shed, hugging herself with cold.

"Oh, Charles, my head," she said thickly. "What did you do with your fur coat?"

In the middle of January, Charles received a small cardboard package with a letter enclosed:

My Dearest Young Hero,

I'm sure I saw you carrying this stone amulet on the night I was so very foolish and endangered both our lives. The repairmen who worked on my poor car found it and kindly returned it. If it is not yours, then we have perhaps discovered an ancient archeological site of pre-Columbian relics, and I should make a career of running my car into ditches in hopes of finding more. A friend of mine here in Chicago says it is certainly a rare piece, and he offered me an interesting sum of money for it, so if you would like to sell it sometime in exchange for a year of college, let me know.

You will be gratified, dearest Charles, to know that I have thought carefully over our last words together at the train station, and I have turned over a new leaf. I have not once visited the Caledonian Isle since leaving your side, and it is my intention to become a complete Blue Nose. Thanks to you, Charles, I have not only had my life saved, I have had it renovated. I do remember you with much affection, and please remember that my invitation to visit or stay with me in Chicago or wherever I might find myself living is heartfelt

and genuine. Keep well and stay as high minded
and courageous as I remember you.

Love,
Claire Lanphier

Charles felt that last admonition keenly, for he had
been increasingly aware of the burgeoning of some
power within him that obsessed his waking moments
and took over his dreams with an endless movie of rape
and seduction. In school he was for the first time having trouble concentrating on studies, his mind seeming
no more than a skittering steam bubble on a burning
hot surface. In attempting to memorize the exports
of Great Britain's colonies, he would find his eyes fixed
on the pleasing lines of Betty Bailey's calf, or the
fascinating mystery of Flossie Portola's bosom, or even
the swing of Miss Wrigley's skirt as she walked briskly
up the aisle between the desks. His face would burn
hotly, and he would curse what he felt was the Beast
power inside him that turned his mind and his dreams
into a bawdy house of lust. But it was still January,
colder that year than many old residents could remember, and there was at least the distraction of cold out-
door sports and long tramps through the snow rabbit
hunting with the Bent boys.

After he received the amulet from Mrs. Lanphier, he
seemed miraculously cured. There were still times of
daydreaming in the overheated schoolroom as he would
catch sight of Brenda Gustafson's secret smile when
she looked at him, or as he touched Betty Bailey's
hand when taking a paper from her and saw her flirta-
tious look at him, but possession of the stone inter-
posed a barrier between Charles and the unbearable
fires of lust he had begun to suffer. In dreams he still
found himself doing the most hideously wonderful
things, having sexual adventures that would have worn
out a Casanova, but these were dreams. Reality had
now, at least, taken on a sane appearance again, and
he could once again concentrate on school work so that
Miss Wrigley smiled more often now and encouraged

him again after what she called his "slump" at the beginning of the semester. There was no longer the urge to get up and go out in the middle of the night so that power inside him could romp in the snow and kill things in people's barns. Charles did not often think of what he might remember from those nights right after Christmas. It was another sort of dream, and if some of the boys at school mentioned wolves coming down from the north and terrible depredations on local livestock, Charles resolutely shut away any sort of memories he might have of those nocturnal massacres, resisting the impulse to say, "That's a lie, Harry. It wasn't four sheep. It was only two."

In February came the big snow. At the end of the first week in February, with a foot of snow lying old and hard on the ground, it began to come down heavily one afternoon. Charles and the other children sat in the schoolroom gazing as if hypnotized out the tall windows at the thickness of the snowfall. They could not see the cottonwood trees in the middle of the school yard, and then the fox-and-geese track nearer to the building could not be seen, and then it was as if the whole world had sunk beneath a whirling sea of snow, and there was nothing beyond the windows but the crash and tumult of flakes. Charles imagined he could feel the building foundering in the ocean of snow as his balance became disoriented by the sight of all the windows of the schoolroom filled with the same endless looming and whirling whiteness. Gradually the classes stopped. The students stood at their desks or walked as if in sleep to the blank white windows. Miss Wrigley laid down her big history book and stood, one hand on her hip, the other touching her cheek, looking at the windows where nothing could be seen but snow.

They went home early that day, farmers and their wives meeting some of the children on the road to help them home in the blinding storm. No vehicles moved on the highway, so that it became merely a flatter stretch in the arctic whiteness, a guide to the filled in lanes and driveways that led to the invisible houses looming suddenly out of the white darkness as people fought with heads down through snow that was at first pleasantly exciting, then a tiresome nuisance, and finally became a menacing and impersonal danger that even the children began to feel uneasy about. Once inside again, the farm families would stand by the windows as the afternoon darkened and look blindly out into the storm as the children at school had, mesmerized by the sudden emergence of nature's possibilities for destruction and bland horror.

No one in the local community died that night, though many gained a new respect for what was called in Charles's geography book "the temperate zone." In nearby places where the great storm covered the earth and filled the atmosphere for more than eight hours, there were deaths among all warm blooded creatures who found themselves lost in it. Cows and sheep died standing helplessly mired in snow deeper than they could walk in, people in cars and buses would start out for help and get lost in the white darkness, go in circles, and finally stop to rest, to be found days later mere humps in the level sea of snow. Two sisters in Wisconsin started home from an afternoon party, became separated in the early darkness and both died less than two hundred feet from their own back door, coming toward their house from different directions. A middle-aged man left his wife in their car with the engine running and the heater on while he went for help. He floundered off into a deep, snow filled ditch, wore himself out, stopped to rest and froze to death. His wife died before he did, of carbon monoxide poisoning while the car engine idled on until it ran out of gas, and then it got very cold so that they could not tell, three days later when the car was found, if she had frozen or died of gas poisoning. Out of a bus load of children who were returning from a skating trip to a local lake, the driver and four children died trying to reach help after the bus missed the road at a turn and ran off into snow so deep it came up over the bus windows. The rest of the children remained with an eighteen-year-old counselor who built fires out of the bus seats and saved everyone by huddling them like chickens that night for warmth until they were found next afternoon by a contingent of skiers. And worse than the snow itself was the insidious cold that came shortly after, dropping temperatures as much as thirty-five degrees in three hours. Trains moved more slowly, following the rail plows, cities began to run short on supplies of milk and eggs, the road plows began to break down after thirty-six hours of steady use, and three days after the big storm, another arctic mass of air moved in from the Northwest, dumping another foot of snow on top of the already devastated Midwest.

After the first big snow on Friday, there was a day's shoveling to do, a few wandering stock to be found, brought home and fed, supplies of food to be checked over, and wood and coal to be piled for the coming weeks. And by Sunday afternoon it was play time for the farm boys who found the snow too deep to hunt in and too heavy on the lanes for sleds, so they resorted to digging caves in drifts that were in some places fifteen feet high. Charles, Douglas, and his brothers built a labyrinth of tunnels in the long drift that ran like a delta from the corner of the highway bridge near the Bent farm across the creek bed and far along the drainage ditch. In a solidified wave of blinding white the drift covered over the wing of the bridge, filled completely the twelve-foot-deep creek bed and lifted to a graceful curl beyond the corner of a long low implement shed. Charles had been the first to see the possibilities and had begun a small tunnel along the hard blue ice of the creek where the edge of the drift stopped at the bridge. Soon they had tunnels going in half a dozen locations, a large room big enough for Douglas to stand up in and were installing elaborations like shelves and ventilation shafts.

Charles sat, panting, his hands numb from digging, his white breath clouding the whiteness of the tunnel. The light filtered in at the top of the big room, a frosted whiteness like a heavy cover of cirrus clouds on a bright day, and further down the sides the whiteness shaded to blue gray, and back in the tunnels it was a darker gray, but near any source of light the tunnel walls and ceiling were a sheer sugar white, whiter than salt, whiter than clouds, Charles thought, with a dark line near the floor that showed the stratum of the old snow.

A scream from outside frightened him, a scream of rage. It sounded like Rudy. Then there was a whoomp sound like a huge fist plunging into a giant pillow. Some snow sifted down his neck. He looked up at the lightest part, the ceiling of the big room, as the whoomp came again. More snow fell, and he crawled out along the tunnel that ended at the creek bed. It was brighter outside the tunnel, so that he blinked while listening to the cries and curses from the Bent boys. They were up on the highway bridge. He looked up in time to see a bundled form come sailing off the bridge rail and smack down into the snow caves, causing the tunnel Charles had just come out of to cave in with a cloud of bursting snow. Charles cried out. They were jumping down off the bridge wrecking everything. He climbed into the drift trying to get at the boy who was trying just as hard to get out and away. It was Paul Holton, covered with snow and laughing.

"Hey, sucker, you're busting up our tunnels," Charles cried, trying to get at the floundering boy.

Another form came leaping off the rail to smack into the area of the big room, and it went down like the crystal palace with a cloud of snow shooting out of the tunnels. Charles was crying out with anger now, and he almost had Paul.

"Now cut it out, Paul," Charles said, grabbing at the boy and getting his cap. But Paul got away up onto the highway, and Charles turned to see Kick Jones emerging from the drift. "Hey, we been working a long time," Charles began, but then he saw another figure on the bridge rail, the tall figure of Carl Bent, dark against the sky. With a whoop he leaped and landed spread eagled on the area Charles had just left. It collapsed.

Charles was silent, climbing up to the highway where

Douglas was standing watching the other boys leap off the bridge rail to demolish the tunnels and rooms they had spent the whole morning building. Charles felt angry, but he was thinking about jumping too when he saw Doug had tears in his eyes and stood awkwardly watching as Rudy climbed up on the rail. When Douglas shouted out from beside him, he flinched in surprise.

"Fat ass Rudy! Fat ass Rudy!" Douglas said, his tears overflowing.

Rudy turned from his height on the bridge and snarled at his brother, "Shut your mouth, you cripple." And he turned to leap off the rail.

Douglas took three quick steps, his stiff leg slicing two wide arcs on his right side, and as Rudy left the rail, Douglas grabbed one pants leg tripping him up. Rudy squealed and fell face down into the drift. Douglas leaned over the rail watching as Rudy crawled backward out of the hole he had dived into. The older boy's face was packed with snow in eyes, nose, mouth so that he looked as if he was wearing a plaster cast on his head.

Rudy cleaned his face as he climbed back to the bridge, murder in his eyes. Charles moved next to Douglas, hoping the brothers wouldn't fight if it meant involving him.

But Rudy never stopped to talk or consider. He climbed up the drifted bank, got to the road and came straight for Douglas. Charles instinctively stepped aside, but then grabbed at Rudy's coat as he began pounding on his brother with both fists, snorting and panting curses. Douglas tried to fend off the blows, covering his head with his arms, and before Charles could figure what to do, Rudy had swung a fist under Doug's arm hitting him squarely in the nose. Douglas screamed and turned away.

Charles pulled Rudy away, pushed him hard a couple of times until Rudy got the idea he would have to fight Charles if he kept on.

"It ain't your fight, big hero," said Rudy panting. "He ain't your brother."

"Leave him alone," Charles said.

"You ain't nobody," Rudy said, his face red. "You're only an orphan, and you ain't really nobody." He stepped back and a cool smile came on his face. "You ain't really smart. You're just gettin' in Miss Wrigley's pants."

Charles did not for a moment know what he meant, having some vague image of a pair of pants hanging on a hook while he went through the pockets, but in the next instant he heard Kick Jones and Carl Bent laughing as they leaned against the bridge rail, and his face flamed red.

"Everybody knows he's teacher's pet," Kick said.

"He stays after school and gets some free feelies," Carl said, grinning.

Charles stood astounded as their meaning broke over him. At first he could not believe what they meant, and then he could not believe that they had so quickly turned against him. Like most people, Charles had the inborn notion that everyone loved him, at least those who had nothing against him. Now he was finding out that all of these boys harbored a secret grudge because he had advanced in school so quickly. It was too much to take in all at once, and he stood there with his mouth open stupidly while they taunted and laughed. Behind him Douglas snuffled while his nose dripped bright red drops into the snow.

"He's a big lover all right," Paul Holton said, sauntering back from the spot he had run to when Charles was after him. "Flossie says he's hot stuff. She says he tried to do it to her."

"That's a lie," Charles said, feeling guilty for his daydreams. "And if you're stupid, it's not Miss Wrigley's fault." He felt confused facing the four boys who leaned in a row against the bridge rail and grinned at him. There seemed nothing to say to them that would make an impression. They stood relaxed, a jury that had made up its mind. Charles felt convicted. There was nothing he could do, short of attacking all four of them and getting the tar beaten out of him.

"Charles is going to be a great man," Douglas said

213

suddenly, sounding as if he had a bad cold because his nose was still full of blood. "He's smarter than all of you stupid farmers put together."

The four boys along the rail laughed and pointed at Charles and Doug. Charles knew it was hopeless and turned to pull Doug away, but the younger boy was enraged. His face was smeared with blood as if he had been painted with a brush, and a large red drop welled from each nostril. He looked like a war casualty, Charles thought.

"You're just jealous about him because he's going to pass you all up this year, and it took you all this time to get in the grade you're in, and Paul can't even do his multiplication tables past six, and Carl can't read big words, and . . ."

Charles had him by the neck of the coat, dragging him away. He would get them both bloodied, and he might feel like getting beat up, but Charles knew how it felt and was not eager to feel it again.

"That don't matter," Rudy said, grinning. "You'll always be a cripple." And when Douglas wrenched away from Charles, Rudy added, "And I seen you jerkin' off last night in the outhouse."

Then Douglas went insane with rage, tearing part of his coat collar off as he pulled away from Charles's grasp and tried to get at his brother. Rudy easily stepped in and hit Douglas twice more, once in the face, once on the top of the head, until Carl told him to stop.

Douglas was staggering, his eyes glazed. "Tattle tale, tattle tale, hanging on the bull's tail; when the bull takes a pee, you'll have a cup of tea," he screamed in a high baby voice, chanting it over and over until Charles took him by the arm and began walking him to the house. The boys at the bridge rail were still laughing and making obscene signs when Charles got Douglas to the Bent house and put him in the care of his mother. Inside the warm house he heard the screaming of the youngest Bent, another boy, born early in December, and he listened to it with sudden clarity. It was a child, and it would grow up to be a boy, then

214

a young man, go to school, get a job, get married, have children, maybe become famous. He could do that, the baby. And as Charles mumbled something to the angry Mrs. Bent and backed out of the house to start the walk home, he kept thinking about the baby's cry, how it was born, how it would live. He walked back up the lane ignoring the boys still standing on the bridge. It wasn't really important, what they said. But what mattered could not be changed. He might beat them up one at a time, maybe even Rudy and Paul at the same time, but it wouldn't make him be any different. He felt the cold, buzzing stone in his pocket, the leather thong he had put through the hole and pinned into his jacket so he would not lose it. If he did not have this, what would happen?

Was he, Charles Cahill, the only creature of his kind in the world? Or was it like Doug when he jerked off in the darkness thinking his was the only guilt in the world? Was everybody like him? But they didn't ever show it. Maybe the whole world is like me, Charles thought with a sudden burst of illumination. But the next moment he knew it wasn't true. The notorious gangsters in Chicago like Machine Gun Jack McGurn who had just got killed battling police, they were murderers, but most people weren't. Animals were animals, people were people. But what was he? As he approached the dark stand of woods and the hidden house of the widow Stumway, Charles felt again the uncertainty, the empty feeling of fear in his guts that he always felt thinking back about what had happened at Thanksgiving. For a time then, he had simply not existed. He had no memory, no feeling of being when the Beast had shifted into someone else by mistake. He recalled the thing that stood in the dim bathroom of the Boldhuis house, looking at its giant bulk of power and terror, and feeling that it was part of him. But then he knew that wasn't right, because of the strange shift that the Beast remembered but he did not. And he knew he had it all turned around. It was not part of him, even if it did save him from death and try to keep him from getting hurt. It was only trying to survive. He was part of it, and he would exist only as long as that power needed him for its own ends, whatever they were. Unless he could always have the stone, what Mrs. Lanphier called his "amulet." If he always had that with him or in the house he was in, couldn't he be like other people?

He stood on the widow Stumway's back walk that he had shoveled off yesterday and watched blankly as snow started to drift down again. Looking into the dark trees back of the house as the snow began to fall harder, he could see the image of that powerful creature he remembered from the mirror. It was fearful, horrible, teeth like knives, small mean ears set close to the back of the long muzzled head, the heavy rounded shoulders that could lift a ton of automobile. He thought of Beauty and the Beast, the light-hating figure of Grendel, the wicked ones, the unhappy ones. Was he waiting for a hero to come along and rub him out?

Charles grew wary of his conduct, always giving some excuse when Miss Wrigley wanted him to stay after school to do extra work or to talk further about the lessons, talks that Charles had loved before and missed so that he gritted his teeth thinking about them. He hated the thought of giving in to the suspicions and gibes of the other boys, but what if all the kids thought things like that? His manner grew noticeably cool toward the girls, noticeably more reserved and deferential toward the older boys. Miss Wrigley recognized the signs and thought he was having growing pains, seeking entrance into the secrets of manhood. She felt a warmth at her own understanding.

By the end of March, it seemed winter had been forever. Snow had become a way of life, as it is to Eskimos, and then almost overnight in the first week of April, it was gone. Rain began in the night, rain and a warm southwest wind that carried with it odors of growing things and warm wet earth that the farmers and their families had not smelled for an eon of cold. Charles woke in the night to hear the rain like low

216

voices on the roof. He slipped out of bed, surprised at how warm it suddenly was, so warm he could not see his breath. He lifted the window and opened the little wooden vent on the storm window. The breeze that came through that little slot melted something, like the icy crystals that had prevented the little boy from seeing truly in the Snow Queen story. Something around Charles's heart fell loose, and he prickled all over with a new excitement. Spring!

The warm weather might not last, and there might be more snow, they said, but the odors in the air, the birds returning, the cows going crazy, running with their tails in the air, the dogs dancing in the school yard, the horses rolling in the fields, all said spring was near, spring was coming, coming at last, and like a frozen river thawing, Charles felt the cold bands of winter snap and his heart leap forth. He wanted to be strong, to show off for the girls, to do dangerous and idiotic feats so they might watch and see he was bravest, strongest, most handsome of all. But of course, the other boys felt the same way, so his own behavior appeared perfectly natural to Miss Wrigley who stood at the tall windows during lunch hour watching the boys swarming up those dangerous old cottonwood trees to see who was brave enough to get into the dead fork at the top, who was enough of a fool to leap from the third branch and grab the lower branch, swing out and drop. And the girls would stand along the edge of the building or sit in the new grass around the south side of the old tool shed and pretend not to look, giggling in the way girls do when they are being performed for by boys in the spring.

Two more months, she was thinking as she watched the primitive rites going on in the school yard. Two more months of living with those dreary people in their dreary round of labor and silence, of trying so hard to make a mark on these children, to give them something more to think about in their lives than bringing crops in and whether a cow was going to freshen or not. Miss Wrigley was still young enough to be idealistic, hardly into her mid twenties yet, but her two

217

years in this country school had taught her that in the pursuit of ideals one might very well lose one's own life. She had determined to return to the university, to get past this isolation, the wearing away of her soul against the many uncaring faces that had to be taught the same things again and again. But at that thought she felt ashamed. There were rewards, children like Sally and Douglas, and of course Charles.

What a puzzling person Charles was, she thought, watching him now in his distinctive red shirt. He waved at the other children from the top of the cottonwood, standing on one foot in that dead fork that might break. Well, she thought, they must do that. But he has grown up in less than one school year, grown almost into a man from a boy not much bigger than Douglas to a man as tall as Waldo. And how old was he, really? A mystery, but surely destined to be a great success in the world. If he didn't kill himself, she thought, watching him swing down like Tarzan from the cottonwood. Now he was running after Kick Jones who waved a jacket around his head. They had so much energy, these boys, like young horses. She stiffened as she saw Charles tackle Kick Jones and a fight begin in earnest. They were hitting each other in the face now. She raised the window and screamed, but it did no good. As she was about to turn away and run into the yard to stop them, she saw the Jones boy suddenly break away, still holding the other boy's jacket. Now Carl Bent had tackled Charles and was holding him down. Miss Wrigley ran for the door as the screams from outside began to take on a serious tone. She arrived to find Carl Bent on the ground doubled up like a snake that has been stepped on, Charles running to the far corner of the yard where Kick Jones was in the act of throwing something into the flooded creek.

"Charles's gone crazy," Mary Mae Martin said, her eyes wide with fear. "He hit Carl so hard, and he said he'd kill Kick for taking his jacket."

The other girls were moving toward the schoolhouse, the noon hour being about over and the boys having got too rough again. Miss Wrigley stopped a moment to see if Carl was all right, but he only groaned and would not speak except to motion her away. She turned to scream at Charles who seemed indeed to have gone crazy, for he had leaped the barbed wire fence and was sliding down the creek bank in the mud and high water of the spring rains. She ran to the corner of the yard as Kick Jones came limping past with blood running out of his mouth. She looked at him with concern, but he only shook his head.

"Charles!" Miss Wrigley screamed at the tall boy who was waist deep in the flooded creek. "What is it? Charles?" But he would pay no attention, only groped around harder to find what the Jones boy had thrown. He would not answer any of her questions and ignored her command to come in, that the noon hour was over. She finally turned away, more hurt than angry that he would ignore her so for anything, a jackknife or some piece of foolish wealth, even a love token from a girl. She felt a childish sense of rejection and became angry at herself for that. She marched back into the schoolhouse, ignored all questions about Charles, sent Kick and Carl home to be repaired, and began the afternoon lessons with a firm and unfaltering voice.

At a quarter to four, Miss Wrigley decided it was enough and dismissed the children. Charles had never returned, and she assumed he had gone home, since he was probably a mess from being in the creek. She walked down the back stairs to the basement landing to make sure the back door was locked and glanced out past the school yard at the brimming creek. As she turned away, she caught a movement, a head appeared in the coils of muddy water. Good Heavens, Charles! She wrenched at the back door, tried to find her keys to unlock it, fumbled with the right key that would not go into the lock, finally got the door open and dropped the whole ring of keys as she rushed out across the yard screaming.

"Charles! Charles, get out of there. You'll die. Oh, Charles." She had a time getting through the old sagging barbed wire, catching her skirt in several places. And the muddy field was over her shoe tops. Charles's head appeared again downstream from where he had been before. He stood up in the chest deep water, leaning against the swift muddy current and looked at Miss Wrigley as if he had just heard his death sentence. She was frightened by the lost look on his face as much as by the fact that he might have been in that freezing water for more than three hours, unless he had gone home and come back. She stopped, ankle deep in the mud of the bank and held her hand out.

"Come out now, Charles," she said softly, urging him by stretching farther over the creek bank and waving her hand at him.

He looked at her, his face streaked with mud, his hair muddy and stuck to his skull. His eyes were dull, and his whole body shivered in spasms which he ignored. He ducked under again in a whirl of water.

She waited, slipping down the bank a bit more, digging in the heels of her ruined shoes. Five dollars, she thought irrelevantly, gone in the mud for this crazy boy. Charles's face reappeared, sputtering in the same place he had been.

"Charles, if you don't come out of the water now, I'm coming in to get you. I've already ruined my best pair of shoes, and this wool skirt is the last good one I've got, but I'm going to come right in there after you if you don't come out."

To her intense amazement, Charles stood in the chest deep water and began to weep, his face crumpling up like a baby's while the tears rolled out and mixed with the creek mud, and his body shuddered in great spasms. Miss Wrigley muttered something, stepped out of her shoes, leaving them standing fixed in the heavy mud as if she had been plucked out of them and carried off to heaven, and walked unsteadily down into the icy water. It was unbelievably cold as it rushed around her legs, then up to her waist, and then she stepped on a slanting stone and fell forward so that she went in over her head and came up gasping and spitting. She walked forward resolutely until she had the boy's arm in both her hands. She pulled him with all her strength, feeling the heavy drag of

220

the creek water urging them both downstream. Charles came along, docile enough now, weeping and shuddering, his skin ice cold to her touch. She got him out, through the fence and into the schoolhouse where she began poking up the fire in the back stove that had almost gone out. When it was going again, she threw her cloth coat around Charles's shoulders and told him to take off his clothes. She dried his muddy hair with her scarf and went back to the girls' cloak room to find something she could change into. There was nothing but her own raincoat that she had left there a week ago when it had rained in the morning and turned beautiful in the afternoon. She peeled away her wet clothes and put the raincoat on, holding it tight around her shivering body. When she came back, Charles was hunched down beside the stove, the coat pulled around him, his wet clothes scattered on the schoolroom floor.

Miss Wrigley put her arms around the boy's shoulders. His body shuddered in regular waves now, and when he looked at her, she saw his skin was blue.

"Oh, Charles," she said, hugging him and rubbing his back vigorously. "What was so important? What could he have thrown in the creek that you would risk getting pneumonia for?"

"My amulet," he said, but his eyes looked dull, as if he hardly realized she was there, as if he might be simply repeating something he had been saying to himself for hours.

She continued rubbing him, feeling shivery herself. "Were you in that creek the whole time?"

But he would not answer except to repeat the same phrase. She wondered how she was going to get him home, and what she was going to do herself, wearing only a raincoat and her hair all draggled and wet. It was not far to the widow Stumway's house, just across the road and a couple of hundred yards down the highway. She was just thinking about going back to the creek bank for her shoes when she heard the front door slam shut. She half turned, her arm still around Charles's shoulders. Paul Holton stood in the hall door looking at her strangely, his little round mouth hanging open. She felt the direction of his gaze and realized he was looking at her bare legs where the raincoat had pulled away when she kneeled down. She pulled the coat down over her leg and said with as much authority as she could, "Paul, Charles has been in the cold creek for just hours, and he's going to be very sick unless we can get him home and into a warm bed right away. Now you run down the road to the Peaussiers and tell them I'm in trouble and must have help. See if there's someone there that can drive the car so we can get this boy home fast." She looked hard at Paul who simply stood there as if he had not heard what she said.

"Paul!" she screamed viciously. "Will you do that?"

"Yes, ma'am. Go to Peaussiers and get a car. Yes ma'am." He turned and bumped into the door jamb, as he went out running.

He was in his bed, but it kept changing to the snow storm. It was so cold, and then he was burning, burning in a forest that was on fire, the trees all like huge candles burning all the way down, and he had to slip between them. And then he was holding the amulet, but it was big, bigger than he could carry, and it kept wanting to fall on him, it was so big, and he had to keep pushing against it to keep it from falling on him. The dream went on so long that he forgot there was any other world, that he was a person living in a world that did not change momentarily from cold to hot. There were only the dreams, and now it was getting hotter all the time, and it never got cold, just hotter and harder to breathe so that it seemed the air was like smoke or like soup that he had to try hard to breathe in and breathe out, and then he was under water and was breathing the water, and at first he was frightened to death that he would drown, but then he realized he was breathing the water, and it was not hurting him.

"I can't say, Mrs. Stumway," the short, bald man in the tweed coat said. "It's not like the movies where the doctor comes out and says everything's all right.

The fever's not going any higher, I don't believe, but I can't promise he'll pull out of it right away." He shook his head, putting his stethoscope back in the little bag. "There's not much more to do now. Not really a case for the hospital, since his condition appears stable and his breathing has cleared some."

Mrs. Stumway stood in the door of Charles's bedroom, pale and narrow in her old brown dress, looking down at the quiet face of the orphan boy. "He's really not my kin, Doctor Mervin," she said, her hands together in front of her. "But he's such a good boy, and my daughter says he saved her life when she wrecked her car at Christmas. I hate to see the poor thing sick. He's so active. Such a good, strong lad." She followed the doctor downstairs to the door.

"I'm not saying he's out of the woods," the doctor said, pulling his coat around his shoulders, "but he's young and he's getting good care. If his breathing gets to sounding stopped up and rattly again, you call me, no matter what time of the day or night. All right?"

Something was in the water with him. He tried to see it, but it was always behind him, like his shadow when the light was in his eyes, he couldn't ever get a good look at it. He could hear what it was saying, and he wondered how anybody could talk under water.

"It's your body, Charles," the voice was saying softly. "You're in charge of it, and I must let you get well. I can't do that for you, Charles. You do make some foolish mistakes sometimes."

Charles felt anger, but somehow the water, which was warm like a hot bath, made the anger less strong. He couldn't really be mad, so he just listened and felt the water pull at him and lull him until he stopped dreaming altogether and went really to sleep where there were no dreams at all.

Miss Wrigley had visited him, he saw when he opened his eyes, and there must have been a doctor there, because there was a doctor smell in the room. She had left his jackknife and the old husking gloves he used when he played softball. And the jonquils in the tall vase were probably her idea. He took a deep breath, but his chest still hurt considerably. It felt as though something had hit his chest many small blows, for it ached all over like a big bruise, but it was easier to breathe, and his eyes felt less burning hot and sandy the way they had. It was dark except for the lamp out in the hall that threw a long dim bar of light across his floor. He tried to sit up and his head throbbed so that he dropped back in pain. Well, he was not dead, anyway. And then he thought about what he had lost.

It was nearly two weeks later when Charles wobbled out the door into the sunlight of late April. Leaves were speckling the woods like a flock of butterflies, and the birds were singing, dipping between the branches. Flowers were poking up everywhere around the house, and the squirrels that had been so hungry they tried to eat the roof off of the house during the bad snowstorm were racing up and down the trees, chattering as if they had never almost died in the cold, as if the world was always going to be warm and wonderful now and winter was gone forever. He walked to school with Douglas who had come for him, trying to be happy and pleasant, although he felt in his heart the stone-heavy weight of his loss, the new insecurity that he knew he must endure now. Douglas seemed more than usually quiet.

It was not the same, Charles felt, sitting in the third row from the windows, the sixth grade row with Runt Borsold, Mary Mae Martin, Paul Holton, and Brenda Gustafson. The lessons were all dull, and it hardly seemed worth the effort to read the books anymore when just by moving his eyes slightly to the left he could watch Flossie Portola trying to flirt with him, or just by leaning back and whispering over his shoulder could ask Brenda to scratch his shoulder, which she would softly giggle and do with one sharp fingernail so it made his hair prickle. And he couldn't get his mind on the homework that Miss Wrigley gave, coming to school more often than not without ever looking at it after a night of running wild in the fields. It wasn't that he was tired. That sort of thing did not tire him.

It was just that the books seemed irrelevant. He did not meet Miss Wrigley's eyes anymore, did not speak up in class much, and seemed more interested in the outside of the school than the inside now. Miss Wrigley looked a bit sad and stern at him occasionally, but she did not get angry or curt with him. She did not ask him to stay after school anymore, either, Charles noticed with some relief.

The last PTA meeting and party of the year was held on a warm night in May. Charles hardly entered the schoolhouse, but stayed outside with the other boys, smoking cigarettes and swapping dirty stories. They came in to be recognized once and stood around awkwardly while Miss Wrigley announced the attendance awards and grade awards for the year. And Charles had to come to the front of the room once to receive a special award, a walnut plaque with a little brass plate on it with his name and the date and his grade level achieved engraved on it. He suffered with a red face while Miss Wrigley stood very formally and handed him the plaque while the kids and the farmers and their wives all clapped. Then she held out her hand for him to shake, and as he took her hand he looked up and saw the disappointment in her eyes, and he held her hand a second too long and blushed. Then he sped out into the dark again and had to go through the snide comments and jokes of the other boys. He had learned to take it now, feeling they were only doing what they needed to do, confronted with Charles as the teacher's favorite, as he admitted now that he had been. But they didn't pursue it. There was something else going on.

"C'mon out to the old tool shed," Runt said in a hoarse whisper. "Carl's got an eight-page-bible."

Charles had heard of these wonders, but had never seen one. Inside the tool shed that held the mower and hay rake that were used on the school yard in summer, a crowd of boys was humped in one corner, a flashlight gleaming intermittently as they shifted around, watching something on the dirt floor.

"Geezus!"

"Wow, look at that!"

"Quit shovin'."

"He ain't shovin'," another voice said. "He's cream-in'," and there was a low snicker from the group as if it were a single organism responding.

Charles worked his way forward and looked over shoulders at what the flashlight was pointing to on the floor. He saw a small opened book with black and white drawings on it, and for a moment he could not make out what the drawings were of, but then someone turned a page and a clearer set came into view. Buck Rogers and Wilma Deering, naked except for their helmets, were engaged in a fantastic orgy, using some sort of ray to enlarge their organs, until on the last page there was a huge phallus spouting enormous amounts of sperm while the woman flew off into a corner. Charles found himself panting as someone turned back to the first page and began it again.

"God, Carl, where'd you get it?"

"Oh, I bought it off a high school guy for half a buck."

The tool shed got hotter and mustier by the minute, and the heap of boys writhed and cursed and said obscenities as the pages were turned. Charles felt tense as a slingshot pulled tight, looking at the crude pictures and knowing it was all ridiculous, but wanting to see them more, wanting to feel this tension more, wanting it to be greater and greater, until someone knocked the light down and Carl grabbed his book and the whole group burst out of the tool shed whooping and hollering and chasing each other around the dark yard.

When they had worn themselves out, they went to sit on the dark outside stairs, listening to the gabble of adults inside as the refreshments were served. Charles said he was going to get something to eat, and some of the boys went with him while some stayed in the dark, grumbling they didn't want any old cardboard pie and Koolaid. Inside the school again, the light was blinding for a moment, and then Charles found the refreshment table, took a plate full and looked around for a chair. Flossie waved at him and patted a desk beside her own. He went over and slouched down in the desk grinning at her.

"I always thought you were going to be different, Charles," Flossie said, licking pie crumbs off her lips. "But there you are, out in the dark with the rest of the dumb boys."

"I got tired of being a gentleman," Charles said. He took a great gobble of the cherry pie.

"I'll bet you haven't," she said archly "You're just being careful so the other boys won't kid you so much." She put her hand on his arm. "What made you stay in that creek until you caught pneumonia?"

"Lookin' for something."

"Looking for what? Honestly, Charles, I never heard of such a crazy thing."

"Something of mine."

"Well, you must have really wanted it to just about die for it. Honestly, Fern and I were so worried. Did you know we came to visit when you were so sick, but Mrs. Stumway wouldn't let us come up?"

"No. Thanks, Flossie." Charles looked up, straight into her eyes so that she laughed. "You're a really good friend." He finished his pie, noticed her hand was still on his arm and felt a warmth rising in him again. "Hey, why don't we walk home, to your house, I mean? It's a nice night."

When they were out of sight of the school and had left behind the two younger boys Charles had had to threaten with a beating, they reached out and held hands until they were almost to the railroad tracks. Charles recognized the area. Over there, across the tracks and under that tree, was where he had pushed over Alfred's car, or rather, the Beast had pushed it over. He felt disoriented for a moment and stopped. Flossie misunderstood as they stood there in the dark moonless night with the bright stars in a clear black sky, and she turned to him, taking his other hand, and she kissed him on the mouth with soft lips, just touching his lower lip with her tongue. In an instant, Charles felt as though he were on fire, all memories and thoughts lost from his mind. He closed his arms around

227

Flossie's slender body, cupping her head with his left hand, and they kissed long and earnestly until they were both breathless.

"Wow, Charles," Flossie said. "You haven't changed. Or maybe you've got better." She rubbed his back, arching her body up to his so that his pulses pounded in a dozen separate places in his body. "Yes," she said, moving her abdomen against him, "lots better."

They broke apart and walked to the grass under the tree where the car had been turned over back in October, and in spite of the grass being wet, they lay down together.

I am rising to be with Charles now with such pleasant sensations available to us both. The blood carries us both to an ascending tenseness that I recognize now. Charles knows I am here, but he feels I will not interfere, as it is for our mutual pleasure. I help him exert some will as the young woman seems not to object to our going on, to doing more things with her body as she wriggles and caresses Charles's head and neck. The sensations are becoming exquisite, almost unbearable for us both now as the caresses become more intimate and the young people begin to tear at each others' clothing. A great need is building up, and I must exert all my will not to shift and break this moment. I must be content to go with the boy here, for it will not be possible for me with the woman. She would be terrified, and the sensations would not continue. I hold to the body of Charles while I feel his mind slipping back as I push forward and apply more force to make the woman go on with this act.

Now we are near, the boy's body quivering with excitement as he searches for the way to do this thing we have never done. I am loosing my hold so as to feel it all more fully. But what is happening? The woman is crying out and trying to get away. I regain my hold and she stops, lies quiet for a moment but is no longer trying to make it pleasurable. Again we approach the consummation of this act, and I must let go again as the flood of pleasure bears me away from the scene, but again she is struggling.

"No, Charles, no! Please, Charles, not all the way. Oh please, Charles, I don't know why I let you go this far." She was crying uncontrollably now, trying to get out of the boy's grip that was like steel on her body. But then he stopped. "Oh please, please," she cried, her eyes filled with tears, but still holding to Charles's body with her arms.

Charles came to himself, found himself so near the goal of his lustful fantasies that for a second or so he believed he was in a dream again, and then he saw Flossie's terrified eyes, knew where his hands were and what he was about to do, and he drew back, wrenching himself off the girl's body with a painful cry. He lay rigid on the ground, his groin in pain with the agony of unsatisfied lust.

I am coming back into Charles's sensations again, and I cannot understand why the boy and girl have stopped. It is a terrible frustration that we feel, a bad sensation that I can savor but do not particularly enjoy. They are not going to continue. I feel rage beginning, but it is not a time for me to appear, and I must ride my own disappointment for the moment. This should not happen. It is not a good feeling.

"Flossie," Charles said, his teeth gritted. "I'm sorry, I don't know. I got too excited. I'm sorry."

The slender girl, only a shadow in the dark, pulled her skirt down and lay down beside Charles, putting her arm over him, saying next to his ear, "It's all right, all right. I know, Charles. I want to, but we can't, but oh, Charles, I really want to." And she began to cry harder now while Charles lay on his back looking up at the star filled sky and felt the blood calming gradually to a bearable level again. He was thinking that he could not allow this to happen again, that these situations must be avoided, since the power would sometime force the act to a conclusion, and he would be guilty of violating some poor girl who could not resist him. He felt tears in his eyes at the utter frustration of it, the inability to control his own life, the constant lust he felt, and the terrible and immediate sickness that made his stomach churn and ache and his leg muscles knot and release.

When they could walk steadily, they went on across the field in a short cut so as not to meet anyone else. At the Portolas' gate, Charles and Flossie held each other in a long kiss, but just as the sensations began to build up again, the girl broke away and ran for the house. Charles heard her cry back to him a good night, and she was gone. He ran for awhile, cutting back through fields, avoiding the roads and lanes, hating the Beast, the monster that he felt so close to him now that he could almost feel the hot, predatory breath in his ear, seeming so real and present beside him that when it spoke in his mind he jumped.

"Charles, I believe that what you call the monster and the hero are the same thing."

"They're not," Charles said aloud into the spring darkness. "You're strong and clever, like a bear or a weasel, but you don't care about being good and honorable because you aren't human."

"We are the same creature, Charles. We stand in the same space, breathe the same air, eat the same food."

The boy stopped, his smooth face wrinkled into a frown of disgust. "I don't eat raw meat," he said. "I don't make dogs howl at night and people run away scared of my shadow, and I'm not a monster that will go around taking advantage of a poor girl just because she's all hot and bothered."

"I take what I need. It is right to do this."

"You'd do it to anybody. You wanted to do it to Mrs. Lanphier that night in the blizzard." He stopped, ashamed of the memory.

"These females wanted to do the sexual act with you—and with me," it said from inside him, although the voice seemed at his ear, almost a breath he could feel, warmer than the warm night air. He began walking again, hearing the real rush of night breeze in his ears.

"You don't know what it is to be human," Charles said at last. "You could never be courageous or heroic or be really in love because you're not human."

230

"I recognize that you are trying to insult me, Charles," the voice said softly. "But I do not wish to be human any more than you want to be me—but it is necessary. We are together, and we share the same emotions. You are making us uncomfortable for no reason."

"It's my own reason," Charles said. He could see the light in the schoolhouse far across the fields seeming to blink on and off as distant trees came between him and the light. "It's a human reason," he said, almost saying "heroic" for "human," knowing that he felt larger and more manly when he pulled away from what he wanted, denied himself that ultimate pleasure that the Beast was talking about.

"But you can't just make me disappear, Charles," the Beast said, softly, insistently. "We are together, one creature."

Charles had walked into the open now, seeing the schoolhouse lights like a beacon across the clear, dark fields. He felt the uprush of hopelessness that always came over him like a chill when he realized that. The Beast was right. There was only one creature. He would never stand beside that huge, fearsome thing, look at it except in a mirror as he had that one time, run from it in fear or leave it behind. It was himself. No, he corrected, feeling a weakness in his arms and legs, he was part of It. As he went forward across the plowed furrows he saw the schoolhouse lights go out, the outline of the six tall windows disappearing into the background of night as if they had never been. She had closed up, then, and would be walking out now, up the cinder lane to her little room at the Peaussier farm.

He almost swerved off to the right to walk through the stand of trees and get home when he realized he had left the plaque. Miss Wrigley would be terribly disappointed if he didn't think enough of it to even take it home. He broke into a trot and made for the school, running harder now, thinking that if he caught her just going out the gate he could apologize and get the plaque. But he could not make good time across

231

the freshly plowed fields, and he glimpsed a walking figure heading out the school gate and down the cinder road toward the farm a quarter of a mile farther on. He slowed to a walk, panting and keeping up a good pace, but not sure why he was still going on. She would be home in a few minutes, and it would be too late, and he certainly didn't want to be jumping out of the dark and scaring her. But he walked on, some obscure reason making itself in his mind, or perhaps he was not thinking at all, but did not want to go home.

Strangely, as he followed the dimly seen form of Miss Wrigley, she in the center of the cinder road, he behind her and on the field side of the fence, he felt no particular motive. Rather, he felt it was play. He was a detective, and she was a suspect he had to shadow, because . . . But that was silly, he thought, picking his way carefully so as to keep one of the roadside trees between him and the woman in case she turned around. I don't want to scare her, he thought. She was almost to the Peaussier farm lane, and Charles could hear some animal in or near the barn grunting in a painful way. It was a long, heaving grunt with a little squeak at the end. He stopped, puzzled at what it could be, and then remembered Runt talking about Mrs. Peaussier's little Jersey being, as he called it "hot for the bull," but that they would not breed the Jersey to their Holstein bull, so the bull was wearing himself out with the smell of hot cow in his nose day and night. Charles had a moment of deep and inarticulate sympathy for the old bull out there grunting in the dark.

When he looked again, Miss Wrigley had disappeared into the Peaussier farmhouse. Charles felt itchy, his stomach felt separated into four tight parts, and his groin felt as though it had been kneaded in a cement mixer. For a minute he stopped, turned about and almost started across the field for home. But he did not take the first step. Instead he turned again and continued on, crossing the last fence that took him into the Peaussier's garden plot and brought the two

232

dogs out silently to see who he was. He got down on his knees and talked to them so they recognized him and wagged their tails. He had been at the farm many times, walking home with Miss Wrigley and talking right up to the back door, sometimes standing in the cold until both their feet were numb, talking about faraway cities and mathematics and poetry.

She had never invited him in, of course, for she was a maiden school teacher, and he was a growing young man, and the Peaussiers were silent but watchful. She boarded with them, living in their upstairs room over the back porch as her predecessor had done before her. The Peaussiers were a stoical bunch who worked the soil like peasants, kept their family at home as long as they could, and had all the virtues of thrift and economy their ancestors had practiced in the Old Country. Charles had seen Mr. Peaussier and his youngest son, who was out of high school and living at home, but he had never exchanged a word with them. He had on occasion seen Miss Wrigley bundled into their old touring car, going into town on a Saturday morning. She with her lively smile and waving hand, packed among the straight and silent Peaussiers like a living woman among a load of hickory fence posts.

The dogs knew him. He walked through the garden plot in the dark, hoping he wouldn't step into some newly dug pit or on some boards with nails in them. It was that dark. He watched the outline of the buildings that surrounded the backyard and saw the sudden soft illumination when a lamp was lighted in an upstairs back window. Miss Wrigley was in her bedroom. Charles moved through the barnyard as if he had a purpose, slid past the crib and the milk house as if he knew what he was doing, but he was not actually thinking at all. He moved as if in a movie of himself that he could not remember, as if it was all planned out beforehand and needed no thought. Now he could see the window, the swept back lace curtains and the shade pulled almost to the sill. He

233

watched the illuminated shade and was rewarded by a shadow that moved across it.

There was a trellis at one end of the porch, but it was made of little half inch strips that would not have held a monkey. The porch pillar at the other end, he thought, slipping off his shoes, and the drain-pipe, if it didn't come loose, would make one big step to the roof of the porch. He pulled his socks off, stepped up on the porch and onto the railing, going very carefully in case some of the wood might be rotten. But no part of the Peaussier place was allowed to be rotten. All was strong, newly painted, firmly nailed, as was the iron strap that held the down spout. The roof was gritty, but not too slanting, and now the narrow slot of light at the bottom of the shade was just ahead of him. He crawled on his stomach up to the window sill and peered through that slot. At first he didn't see her, and his heart gave a great jump. What if he had made a noise and old man Peaussier was coming out with his shotgun? But just as he was about to back down away from the window, she came back from somewhere, perhaps the toilet, since the Peaussiers had an indoor bathroom. She was dressed in the dark, shiny dress she had worn at the PTA meeting. He watched as she put some things away in a desk and then stood at a closet unbuttoning the dress down the front.

Charles was so absorbed in watching this entirely new aspect of Miss Wrigley's life that he was almost unaware that his body was beginning to react in two distinct ways: fear and lust. His heart thumped against the porch roof so hard that someone standing under him might have heard it, and sweat ran down into his ears even though the night was turning cool, and his hands on the gritty roofing quivered as if in palsy. Miss Wrigley had hung the dress in the closet and taken a long white nightgown out and laid it across the bed. Then she disappeared again for a moment, came back with a book, threw it on the bed, moved the lamp to the night stand, and finished undressing. Charles had never seen an adult naked woman except in certain ragged, smuggled pictures Carl had loaned to Douglas. He was suddenly galvanized with emotions pulling him in two directions. He could not tear his eyes away from the woman as she bent to remove her underwear, and as she straightened up, tossing the underthings into a hamper, he felt an intense shame wash over him. He looked at her body, the naked, helpless woman's body, the round breasts and belly and the black vee of pubic hair and the rounded hips, and then he looked at the calm face as she rubbed the red mark on her belly where something had been too tight, scratched the outsides of her thighs where there were more red marks, and as naturally as if she were always in a nude state, reached for the nightgown and slipped it over her head so that it slithered down like a white cotton curtain falling on the night's performance. And the calm face was Miss Wrigley's face, a loved face that had nurtured him in learning, that had cared about him as much as any person on earth had cared for him, a loved person whom he had just betrayed in a hideous way by sneaking to her window to watch her undress. The shaking was all over his body now, and he could not imagine moving, trying to get down off the wretched height to which he had climbed for such a purpose. His guts ached, and he hated the throbbing in his groin and the painful erection that had come back again. He moved one foot to try to turn away and, still looking at the woman's face through the lace curtain, saw her flinch, her eyes widen as she looked toward the window. She had heard him. He dared not move.

His breathing labored in his chest so that he felt strangled as he tried to control it, and now he could feel that hated presence again, the powerful urge coming over him as it rose inside him, and he whispered inside his mind, "NO! NO!" But it came on, flooding him with tension and a presence, as it had with Flossie. Now if he were found here. No. Anything, but don't make a noise now. He clung to the sandpaper-feeling roof as if it were tilting him over an abyss while the idiotically happy Beast rose in him, coursing in his blood, and he feeling its awful joy in his agony of shame and frustration, actually to feel it luxuriating in his flooded nervous system as he shook with fear and lust and shame, and all he could do, his eyes still boring through the curtain as he was afraid to make any movement at all, was to hold himself still as that thing inside him crawled about its loathsome business of savoring his painful state. Miss Wrigley had gotten into bed and was reading her book, glancing in the general direction of the window once and then again. Finally, she put the book down and blew out the lamp. At the moment she turned her head to blow out the flame, Charles lowered his head, feeling dizzy and almost demented with agony and shame. His defenses were low, so concentrated was his attention on not disturbing one single particle of that roof. And his mind was saying, what if old man Peaussier is down there, watching me, waiting, has been watching me all the time, so that his body shivers and quakes as he tries to move.

I rise in the boy, feel his disturbed state and am growing angry at this constant irritation and frustration he seems determined to put himself and me through. I must do something. I rise and shift.

With one spring I leave the roof silently and hit the ground next to the two dogs. They would cry out, but I have no time for them, so I grip each one with a claw and hold their throats until they are almost dead. Now they will not bother me for a time. I feel the surroundings with my full senses, the yard becomes bright as a lighted field. I sense two cats getting ready to fight over near the crib, the rabbits on the other side of the garden plot in the weeds sitting like warm stones in their darkness, the barn full of life radiating its vibrations, its joy, into the darkness where I feel my full power again. An odor catches me as I drop the dogs. Tantalizing, musky, exciting, almost as if there were something waiting especially for me in that barn. Yes, the Jersey. It is her odor. My excitement is high as I stalk the odor, letting it guide me precisely, feeling as it wavers to one side of my path or the other, like a beacon. I move silently across the barn-yard, the cats scatter like snowflakes from my path. Beyond the barn I hear the poor bull in his agony. That will not be my fate again. I have entered the broad door. To the right, the box stall. I hear her stirring now and smell the sweet alfalfa odor of the cow like a setting for a jewel, the jewel of mating scent that fills me with desire now and blocks out all but the most peripheral of warning senses. I look into the stall, grasping the form with my spatial sense, closing on the odor, I snap the latch on the door, swing it wide, press my face into the scent that is so delectable, pressing my face to the cow, feeling all the liquids in my body turning hot and heavy, pressing along her side, her smooth flank, whispering to her, "I could be your bull, my dear. I could be your lover, but you must stand me as I am, sweetheart, for I have suffered. How I have suffered."

The cow, the lovely ginger and velvet black Jersey flicks her ears like signals, stamps her feet, begins to bawl a little. I mount her and begin.

I try to remember not to hurt her with my claws, but it is so hard, as the movements make themselves astoundingly without my volition, and I float upward on an ascending rise of beating blood to which I keep time. There is music, I hear and feel music as in that dark hallway, piano, drums now, there were no drums, but yes, drums, ascending. I hear outside my reddened universe of pleasure the cow moaning and crying now, but nothing can stop me now as the blood inside me begins to explode, explode, and goes farther and explodes more, and I am crying out with much pleasure, raking the cow with my claws and crying out. And I feel all my life and energy and blood lust and power spurting out, shooting in a great trajectory into pitch blackness, and I fall forward across the cow's back, my hind feet wedged in the sides of the stall, still engaged with this animal, my mind completely gone as the dark almost closes around me.

Lights go on suddenly, brilliant, blinding lights. I cry out, but there are people coming from outside. I am confused and weak, must not try. I use my last concentration and shift.

There is a medley of screams, some of them coming from the young man, Charles, who has found himself compromised by the perfidy of that power which he now knows he must serve or be destroyed. Some of them come from the gathering of usually silent Peaussiers who have rushed to their barn to safeguard their most valuable cow from what sounded like an attack by the bull that must impossibly have broken in to get her. And the most piercing of all comes from Miss Jessie Wrigley, twenty-four-old local teacher who had been roused earlier by some noise and was the one who woke the family. Miss Wrigley witnesses a sight that may to the end of her life remain stamped in her memory, if she does not resolutely deny its reality in a moment or two, or if she does not faint, which she is not in the habit of doing. She sees in the sudden illumination of the electric barn lights which have only this month been installed, her favorite and star pupil, Charles Cahill, obviously in a painful state of post-coital remorse, lying over the back of the Peaussier's favorite milker and valuable cream cow, Sherry, who seems less the worse for wear than her student who appears to have died in the act.

The details of Mr. Peaussier, a man not to be non-plussed by any natural or unnatural act of man or beast short of doom's blast, withdrawing Charles from his love object are not lost on the stunned onlookers, so that there is no doubt in the minds of any present what has been happening. The young man stands as if he were a puppet whose strings had been cut, sagging and obscene until Mr. Peaussier steps forward and says his first and last words to the boy.

"Get yourself decent."

And with suddenly maddened eyes, Charles Cahill leaps at the aging farmer, knocks him to the floor of the barn and speeds out into the darkness where he vanishes in every sense of the word. Twenty feet from the bright lighted rectangle of the open barn door where three standing people and one recumbent one watch, along with a rather scratched-up Jersey cow, something else appears and disappears, something very large and very fast, so that the watchers can only individually assume they have seen a trick of the light, an optical illusion that none of them will ever mention to anyone. The incident itself has been quite enough.

If this hill has a name, I have not heard it. Hills are so rare in this country they are not even named, called perhaps just "The Hill," but it is a good vantage point from which to survey the little river valley. Now in the first cool silence of dawn when even the birds have not thrown off the dimness of night, I exult in my newly discovered sensations and wonder at Charles and his human foolishness. All this night he has been only a burning rage inside of me, like a sour stomach, I think, grinning. I sit on my haunches at the edge of the steep side of the hill, the east side, looking down at the brown pathway of the Iroquois River half a mile away. If I turned back the other way I could see most of the county where my last nine months have been spent. How much I have learned here, I think, yawning suddenly, surprised by fatigue. The river is not yet struck by the rising sun that is just up and tangled in the trees and farms along the horizon. The river is as brown as a road, an unpaved road leading northeast.

"Charles," I call again, having called him many times in the night, receiving for answer only the slow burning of his absent rage.

"This is no way for a hero to act."

Silence.

"We can leave here, go to the woman, Claire Lanphier, in Chicago. She loves you, Charles, would be your mother, help you. You might go on to high school, the university." I cannot continue against his resolute absence.

"If I had not shifted," I say, "they might have killed us both."

"Charles? It's not that bad. People forget."

239

But there is no answer and my fatigue reduces my patience with the boy. I have always liked Charles, even with his ridiculous ideals, as if he were a Midwestern Sir Galahad. I turn back and look over the low, level farmlands to the west, the Peaussier farm laid out like a checkerboard of new grain and corn, a line of tiny cows being drawn out to pasture along the almost invisible string of their path. Nearby, along the little black cinder road, the oblong schoolhouse sits in its yard with the two cottonwood trees and the outhouses like tiny toadstools, the copse of solid foliage in which Mrs. Stumway hides from the world, the double siloed and immaculate farm beside the highway bridge where Douglas Bent is perhaps strapping on his brace to begin another day, the far off town with its low haze of smoke.

One last try. "So Beast wins the Beauty?"

I listen, but even the hot fuming of his rage has disappeared now.

"Well, Charles, my dear hero, farewell. Who knows, perhaps this monster will yet become a prince."

And I set off down the hillside for the river, heading north-east.

The End of
The First Book of the Beast